Challenged By You

Steph Nuss

Copyright 2016 by Steph Nuss

All rights reserved.

This book is a work of fiction. Any references to historical events, real people, or real locales are used fictitiously. Other names, characters, places, and incidents are the product of the author's imagination, and any resemblance to actual events or locales or persons, living or dead, is entirely coincidental.

Prologue

June 2003

Positive.

Two lines meant positive, but one of the lines looked a little more faded than the other. What the hell did that mean?

Standing in the bathroom, I shut my eyes tightly and shook the test like it was a damn Etch A Sketch, hoping the more faded line would disappear altogether. Another fearful glance at it told me the shaking only made the line appear more clearly.

The knot thickened in my throat and tears pooled in my baby blues as I stared back at my seventeen-year-old self in the mirror. In my opinion, I didn't look the same as I did yesterday. Maybe it was my imagination, but my boobs already felt heavier. My long blond ponytail, pulled in its usual sleek style, felt almost too tight, like it was giving me a headache. The minimal makeup I wore did nothing to hide the fatigue etched into my ivory skin.

With trembling hands, I laid the test back down on the vanity.

This cannot be happening. I'm seventeen years old; I can't be having a child! Especially when its father just graduated high school yesterday and plans to move across the country to play college football on a full-ride scholarship.

I sighed and looked away from the mirror, talking to myself aloud. "I *cannot* be pregnant right now."

A knock on the bathroom door resonated, giving the first tear permission to drop onto my left cheek.

"Paige?" Mom asked in a worried tone. "Everything okay?"

"Uh-umm," I stuttered nervously, taking a few deep, shuddered breaths to try to calm down. How would she respond to this news? Her baby girl—the head cheerleader and president of her class—getting knocked up by the star quarterback. What a fucking cliché. "Not really, Mom."

The knob turned and she peeked her head in. "May I come in?"

Turning my back to the mirror, I nodded. Rachel Abram joined me in the bathroom, closing the door behind her. She wore perfectly pressed jeans and a pink cardigan. Her hair, the same blond shade as mine, was tied back in a poofy ponytail with a scrunchie instead of a hairband.

My mom and I were close. She was more like a friend than a parent most of the time. Both of my parents were more friendly than authoritative. They grew up during that hippie era, where it was all, "Make peace, not war," so they were laid-back but intuitive.

She took one look at me and immediately knew something was wrong. "Why the tears, baby girl?"

Her comforting voice alone was enough to push me over the edge. I covered my face with my hands and uttered, "I'm pregnant."

"Oh, sweetie," she soothed with a sigh, wrapping her arms around me in a hug. She kissed the top of my head and squeezed me tightly. "It's going to be okay."

Holding onto her, I buried my head into her shoulder and cried harder. "I never missed taking a pill, I swear, and Drake always wore a condom."

She ran her hand down my ponytail. "Things can still happen even when you use protection, Paige. You know that."

"I know, but I-I-I didn't expect this to happen."

"Nobody ever does," she replied calmly, dragging her thumbs over my cheeks. "It's all going to be okay. Just take some deep breaths and—"

"Gah!" I cursed, pulling away from her. "Could you please try to be a little bit angry about this? This. Can. Not. Happen. Drake leaves for California in a few weeks to start football practice! The last thing he wants is a high school girlfriend with a baby on the other side of the country. This is going to ruin his life."

"Paige . . ." Her brows furrowed as she took a step back. "Drake loves you. Maybe that's why I'm not upset about this, because I know you love him, too. I knew you guys were serious a long time ago, when he was all you could talk about. You both used protection, but by some miracle, you still managed to get pregnant. This wasn't just some stupid mistake you guys made, a baby is never a mistake. And I promise, it is not going to ruin either of your lives. Your father and I are here for you, and I know Drake's parents will support you guys, too. It's not the end of the world, it's the start of a life. A life some women never get the opportunity to create."

"None of that changes how scared I am about this." I knew she was right, but at the moment, I could only think about the future. I stared back at her and told her what scared me more than anything. "I'm scared to tell him. I'm scared I'm going to tell him and he's going to do something drastic, like forget all about his full ride to USC and football so he can stay here and be supportive of us. You know that's something he would do because he's one of the good ones." More tears threatened as I looked down at my flat stomach and fingered the hem of my shirt. "I can't let him give up on his dreams for us, Mom. I love him too much to do that to him."

Mom sat down on the edge of the tub and reached for my hand, pulling me down beside her. For the first time, I saw tears glistening in her eyes as she held both my hands in hers and smiled weakly. "You can't make that decision for him."

"YOUR MOTHER'S RIGHT!" Dad shouted through the closed door. "YOU HAVE TO TELL HIM!"

"Dad," I whined, leaning into Mom as a wave of embarrassment washed over me. The door opened and he joined my confessional. He squatted down in front of us, shot Mom a wink, and placed a hand over ours as he smiled at me. "Could you at least look mad, like you might kill Drake for knocking me up?"

He chuckled to himself, shaking his head. "No way, because I'm going to be the best goddamn grandpa you've ever seen, and my grandchild is going to have the best throwing arm in the nation."

"It could be a girl, Cal," Mom quipped playfully.

"And she'll still be able to out-throw all the boys if she inherits her dad's arm."

"This is true," she laughed. "But either way, it'll inherit our baby girl's beauty."

Their excitement caused an honest smile to spread across my face, a smile that wasn't weighed down with worry, and for the first time today, I thought, *I can do this.*

"Okay, I'm going to tell him."

***

I jumped in my Jeep and headed west toward Drake's house. I nervously tapped on the steering wheel as I drove by the same handful of estates I always did on my way over to his place. Drake and I grew up in Bedford, New York. His mom inherited a dairy farm, and my dad's writing career had landed us a home almost as big as theirs. Bedford was known for its estates and rural appeal. It was close enough to the city but still far enough away from the rush of it all that we could see the stars at night when we laid in the back of Drake's old Chevy truck. Bedford was home for us, but as I drove by the old, abandoned Massey Estate, the one I dreamed of remodeling and calling my own someday, I thought about where we'd call home if it were just the three of us. Drake and I frequented the place for alone time, but a couple of teenagers with a baby couldn't afford to remodel an estate that had been left to rot.

Pulling into the Wilkins' driveway, I took a deep breath and threw the car into park. Their home was just as beautiful on the outside as it was inside. It didn't look like a farm from the front, but behind the home sat a tennis court and a pool surrounded by barns and acres of farmland that catered to the cattle.

Lilian, Drake's mom, stood at the door, expecting my arrival.

I shot her a knowing grin as she opened the door for me. This had become our routine. She'd greet me at the door and tell me where I could locate my boyfriend.

"He's up in his room," she said with a smile.

"Thanks, Lilian!" I said as I started up the winding staircase.

On the upper level, I turned left and headed down the hall to his room. When I came to his closed door, I knocked softly and turned the knob. On the other side, I found the most beautiful guy stretched out on his bed, tossing his beloved football up in the air. Drake Lyle Wilkins had the best set of muscles a girl could find, buried underneath his creamy pale skin that made my body tingle just looking at him. His short, wavy black hair was pushed back out of his face and his bright blue eyes smiled when they caught mine.

He leaned up and pulled me down on the bed beside him, eliciting a loud giggle out of me as he curled an arm around my waist to snuggle and kissed me on the neck. "Hey there, P.J."

"Hey," I replied, before relishing in the softness of his lips as I ran my hands through his silky dark strands. He'd given me the nickname P.J. after learning that my middle name was Jane. "How are you feeling today? Do you feel like a high school graduate?"

He laughed, laying my head on his shoulder as his fingers skimmed up and down my back. "A very *hungover* high school graduate, but it was well worth it."

"Good." The longer I stared at him and the more my hands roamed, the less I wanted to tell him what I needed to say. He'd given me all of my firsts. My first dance. My first kiss. My first relationship. My first sexual experience. My first love. Now, my first child. I couldn't wrap my head around how I wanted this to play out. One part of me wanted him to be elated, but the other part still didn't want him to know. He had a heart so big, he'd give up anything for me, and I wasn't sure if I could live with knowing he gave up chasing his dreams to be here for us.

Lying together, the silence grew between us, and I could tell he was thinking about something as his eyes searched every inch of my face. Those bright irises grew darker, which told me he was worried; it was the same look he got when he was worried about landing his scholarship.

"Have you thought about how this year is going to play out?" he asked in a nervous tone. "My parents have drilled it into my head that I need to stay focused on school and football, but all I can think about right now is us." His fingers entwined with mine. "What happens when I leave?"

I swallowed around the same knot that was still lodged in my throat. "I don't know, Drake."

"Well," he started, "what do you want? This past year has been all about me, and all I can think about right now is how you're not coming with me when I leave for California. Do you still want to go to USC next year after you graduate like we'd planned?"

Of course, I wanted to go wherever he went because I loved him, but things had changed now that I was pregnant. I'd have a baby next year, and I couldn't imagine trying to raise a baby and attend college full-time, especially on the other side of the country away from my parents.

"I don't know," I repeated, turning to stare up at his ceiling, unable to watch the devastation take root in his eyes. "I haven't really thought about what I want to do."

"That's what I mean," he stated, turning my attention back toward him. "I have no idea what you want to do with your life because we've been too busy trying to make sure I got into USC to play ball. We've only been focused on *my* dreams, on *my* football career, but I don't want to take away your chance for you to chase after your own dreams. If yours don't include me, I'll understand. I just feel like I need to give you the opportunity to figure out what you want to do, especially after all the love and support you've given me, Paige."

Tears reappeared and I struggled to keep it together in front of him after already breaking down earlier at home. This was it. This was our good-bye. He was letting me go, and I couldn't even try to fight him. But I'd be lying if I said this was what I really wanted. "My dreams will always include you, even if you're not physically here with me."

It was a feat that his pillow wasn't drenched in my tears.

"I know Barrett and Zoey are off to college too come fall, but you should spend your last year of high school living it up with your friends and making sure USC is really what you want."

I nodded, unable to speak as the regret trailed down my face.

His thumbs caught the tears, wiping each one away after it fell, and then he pressed a soft, sweet kiss to my lips and rested his forehead against mine. "I love you. You know I will always love you."

"I know," I whispered as a sob rattled through my chest. Tightening my arms around him, I tried to memorize everything about him. The way he always smelled of freshly chopped firewood and musk. How he always kept a stick of spearmint gum on hand so his kisses tasted delicious. How his dimples popped out with his infectious smile. His baby blues that appeared brighter than mine. The cute cleft in his chin that caught my attention the first time I met him. The dark, smooth strands of his hair that felt like silk between my fingers. The hard planes of muscle that corded through each extremity and beyond, creating a man of steel that looked magnificent without any clothes. The sound of his laughter and the fact that he couldn't carry a tune when he sang while driving. But most importantly, the way he'd touched every part of me, even the parts he physically couldn't reach. "I love you, too."

He continued stroking my skin as if he never wanted to stop. "Make this year all about your dreams."

His comment was like a swift kick in the ass from reality. My dreams were no longer my own. He had his, and I'd be damned if I was going to ruin them. I pulled out of his embrace and scooted to the edge of his bed, where I gathered myself, drying my cheeks with the backs of my hands. I cleared my throat and stood, righting the twists out of my clothes, and then shot him a weak smile over my shoulder. Tears glistened in his eyes. His lips pursed as he grimaced, and a hard swallow crawled down his throat, revealing the feat it took to not come after me. "Good luck with football, Drake. I know you'll be great."

In that instant, I'd made my decision: I'd tell him about the baby after it was born, so he could see that I could do this on my own.

I walked out of his room without looking back, and when I walked by his mom on the way out, I smiled politely and said, "Good-bye, Mrs. Wilkins."

On the drive back home, I focused on coming up with a plan instead of crying my eyes out like I really wanted. My whole high school life so far had been about Drake and me. My friends were his friends, and we did everything together. I didn't know how it was going to be without him, or even Barrett and Zoey, but I wasn't alone even now. I had a baby to raise. A human life that was my sole responsibility. By the time I rounded the corner and pulled into the garage, I had a plan set in mind, but when I walked through the door and my parents greeted me, I completely lost it again.

"What happened?" Mom asked, leading me over to the couch. "How did he take it?"

"We broke up."

"You told him you were pregnant with his child and he broke up with you?" Dad asked loudly in disbelief.

"No," I cried, shaking my head. "He let me go, and I let him."

Mom and Dad shared a secretive look with each other, had a whole unspoken conversation right there in front of me, and then leveled their attention on me.

"You didn't tell him," Mom inferred.

For the first time today, Dad appeared genuinely concerned. "Dammit, Paige, you should have told him."

Drying my eyes, I pushed up from the couch and gazed back at them. "He wanted me to focus on my dreams and what I wanted to do after high school. Well, this is what I want. I want him to play football because that's all he's ever dreamed of. That's why I didn't tell him. If I take classes this summer, I can graduate early and prepare for the baby. I figure I'll have it before he's back for spring break, and I will tell him then, when he can see that we can do this without him, that he can still play ball and know the baby and I are doing fine on our own."

"Sweetie . . ." Mom said, shaking her head. "He needs to decide if he—"

"Mom, you said you guys would support me," I interjected, throwing her words from earlier back in her face. "Please just help me keep this a secret until he's back for spring break."

Mom shared another apprehensive look with Dad and then pursed her lips together and nodded.

"Thank you," I said, rushing over to give her a hug.

"On one condition . . ." Dad stated.

Turning around, I saw the smile widen on his face. "Name it, although I'm not naming him or her after you."

He laughed lightly and threw his arm over my shoulder. "I get to document every moment so Drake doesn't miss a thing. That means pictures and videos, and I'm probably going to make you keep a journal, and you don't get an ounce of say over it. You know how I get about the details, being a writer and all. If I'd missed one second of your mom being pregnant with you, it would have crushed me. From one father to another, let me do this for Drake."

I had the best parents in the world. "You got it, Dad."

Chapter One

January 2015

Paige

It was the first day back after the new year, and this morning Sabre & Edelmen would name the one lucky individual from our staff who was being promoted to a new senior account manager position at the PR firm. I'd spent the past six months working my ass off for this promotion—dealing with clients nonstop, catering to all of their ridiculous needs and picking up all the pieces when they screwed everything up. So, I was determined to dress like a boss today. I wanted to prove to the rest of the office that the position was rightfully mine.

Slipping black hosiery up my legs, I stood from my bed and wiggled into the gray pencil skirt I'd chosen for today. Pairing it with its matching gray blazer and a white blouse, I felt completely put together as I took in my appearance in my full-size mirror. My makeup was light. My blue eyes accentuated with black mascara and shadowed with a dusting of gray for a smoky eye look. Cheeks powdered with a light pink blush that matched the barely noticeable shade of lipstick that lined my lips. Bangs straightened and brushed to the side, the rest of my gold bob hanging in natural waves around my round face. The complete look came off as stylish and strong, as I always did. I gave one last tug on the hem of my blazer and shot myself a small smile, reminding myself that today I wanted to make a subtle impression and let everyone at S&E know they made the right decision by choosing me for the manager position.

After a couple of spritzes of my signature scent, Euphoria by Calvin Klein, I stepped into my beloved pair of black Louboutins, the ones with the pointed toe and four-inch heel, and tied my peacoat around my waist. Grabbing my purse, I headed out the door into the blustering cold of the city. With a loud whistle and a wave of my hand, I quickly hailed a cab and rattled off the office's address as I slid into the backseat.

My apartment was a fifteen-minute drive to work, so in the meantime, I pulled out my phone and checked my messages. I had tons of emails from clients or people wanting something from my clients. I quickly read through those messages, shooting off emails to the necessary people, but I also had a text message sitting in my inbox from my assistant, Skye.

Skye: Bad news. I'll tell you once you get here.

Fucking great, I thought, rolling my eyes. I'd learned in the six years I'd been at the firm, and the five that I'd been working with Skye, to never enjoy a text message from your assistant.

I paid the driver as he pulled up to the Sabre & Edelmen building, and then got out of the car. With precise steps and my head held high, phone in hand, shoulders pushed back and my resting bitch face perfectly in place, I walked into work like I always did—like I owned the damn place.

The coffee boys rushed up to me, badgering me for a cup, which I turned down. Every. Single. Day.

Normally, I ignored them and kept walking, but today my ferocious bitch from within wasn't tolerating it. I stopped in my tracks and glared at the both of them. "I have never ordered a damn thing from either of you, so I would appreciate it if you would stop bugging me with your incessant questions on whether or not I want to caffeinate myself every morning. The answer is no. The answer will always be no. But if for some reason I ever do desire a cup of that nasty shit, I will have my assistant hunt one of you bastards down. Got it?"

The skinny one looked back at me like he was about to piss his pants, and the other's hands shook as he nodded in understanding.

"Now, get the hell out of my way and quit antagonizing everyone when they walk through the door." I started toward the set of elevators, but continued my ranting as I went, "If they want a cup, they'll let you know! I'm sure I'm not the only one who thinks you're a bunch of pains in the asses who only got hired because you're the boss's grandsons."

The elevator opened and I walked in with a bunch of other suits trailing in behind me. I pushed the button to my floor, ignored those around me who told me what floor they needed, and exhaled a satisfied breath as the doors in front of me started to close. But before they could, an arm shoved between them, and they quickly slid open again.

I wanted to groan but held it back when the doors revealed my coworker, Owen, standing there in his wrinkled dress shirt, suit jacket thrown over his arm, dirty blond hair a total mess, and a coffee cup—courtesy of the two dipshits—in hand. The guy was a great publicist and coworker, but he always looked like he'd just woken up, hit the snooze button about ten times and then realized he needed to get to work. Surprisingly, he was never late, but he never took the time to put himself together either. Hence: the wrinkled shirt and uncombed hair.

"Owen," I stated, smiling at him as he took a spot next to me. I ran my eyes up and down him, taking in his appearance, and smirked. "What? You don't think you're going to get the promotion?"

He laughed, shaking his head at my remark. "We *were* all up for the promotion, Paige. Now that it doesn't matter, I decided to not give a damn anymore about impressing Sabre & Edelmen." He leaned in closer to me, checked our surrounding audience to make sure nobody from the office was nearby, and whispered, "They can take their promotion and go fuck themselves."

Brows furrowed, I glanced at him and noticed the irritated tick in his jaw, and my stomach instantly dropped. "What are you talking about? They haven't announced who they're giving it to yet."

The doors opened and everyone around us immediately rushed out. Owen grabbed my hand and pulled me out and then started walking with me toward our offices.

"I heard they hired somebody outside the company to take the position," Owen stated, bracing himself for my reaction.

I pinned him with my glare. "You've got to be fucking kidding me. They said they were going to give it to a seasoned executive. We've been working our asses off for this."

Owen and I had started at S&E at the same time and had almost the same number of clients. I dealt with more artists, while he had most of the athletes. "I know. My assistant heard about it from one of the assistants to the higher ups."

Of course. The assistants in this place were better than most private detectives.

"Skye texted me this morning and said she had bad news, but she didn't state what it was," I said with a frustrated sigh. "I swear I will lose it if these rumors are true."

He stopped at his office door and shrugged before opening the door. "I think it's a pretty done deal, Paige. There's nothing we can do now."

Like hell there wasn't.

I continued making my way to my office and found Skye sitting at her desk when I stepped inside. Determined to get to the bottom of this, I stepped inside my personal office, tossed my bag on the desk, and threw my coat over the back of the chair. Skye leaned against the doorjamb, arms folded over her chest.

I narrowed my eyes at her. "Please tell me the rumor isn't true."

Pushing her purple hair out of her face in annoyance, she sighed. "It's true."

"Dammit!" I said as I started to pace the length of my office. "What was the point of telling us there was the possibility of a promotion when they planned on hiring someone new anyway?"

"Uh, if you haven't realized yet, Paige, we work for assholes," she retorted.

"I know, I know." I pushed her comment to the back of my mind, even though it was true. Our bosses were assholes. Sabre & Edelmen used to be run by a couple of old guys who actually had respect for their employees. Gary Sabre and Henry Edelmen had hired me on as an intern, and after getting my master's degree, they offered me a full-time position as a publicist. They were like a second set of grandfathers to me. They groomed me into the position I had now, teaching me all the ways of the PR industry. How to smell the bullshit and how to handle the chaos. How to put up with the hot-headed celebrities and how to care for the normal, sane clients. I had a ton of respect for them and had really enjoyed working under them. Until they retired.

Now their daughters ran the company, and spent most of their time spending their daddies' money and toying with employees any chance they could get. A no-fraternization policy was instituted. No one had been granted a raise. But we were all still expected to kiss their asses and make sure our clients looked good because they made S&E look good.

I tried to stay clear of the bitches because God knew I had it out for them, but today they'd just scraped the edge of my iceberg.

"There's a mandatory meeting in the conference room in five so they can introduce the new guy," Skye added.

"Perfect." I usually came up with an excuse to miss their "mandatory" staff meetings, usually pinning it on a client or a more important meeting of some sort, but there was no way in hell I was missing this one. "Let's go."

"Oh, we're actually attending this one?" Skye quipped, wearing an evil grin as she began texting all the other assistants on staff. "This ought to be good."

Leading the way out of my office, the loud clicking sound of my heels digging into the marble flooring sounded throughout the hall. The conference room was on the other side of the building, so Skye peppered me with questions as we passed other staff members on the way.

"What are you going to do?" Skye asked, eager to get the first scoop. "Are you going to tell those fat cows off? You know they hired a male, right? Some guy who is probably super hot with a huge penis that they can admire whenever they're in the office."

I rolled my eyes at my feminist assistant's comment. "And you're surprised?"

"I can't have purple hair, but they can hire some cabana boy to salivate over all day," she remarked in a disgusted tone. "Equal opportunity employer, my ass. You don't move up in this place unless you have a penis, and even then, if it's not a good-looking penis, you're fucked."

Poor Owen, I thought for a second, even though I didn't know what his penis looked like. Skye made a good point; the Banger Sisters loved their men. "Stop talking about penises. It's inappropriate."

"You know I'm right though," she continued. "For two women, they are very discriminatory towards their female employees."

"I know," I said with a soft snicker. "I've worked for them just as long as you have. It's only because we're their competition."

As we got closer to the conference room, the buzz coming through the doorway was audible. Most of the staff was eager to meet the new guy, or opted to talk about work in general, but for a handful of us—the ones who'd been fighting for the promotion—we were pissed. As I walked into the room, I could see the anger in the eyes of my fellow executives, but when my eyes landed on Trish Sabre and Mercedes Edelmen at the head of the table, I trudged over to the opposite end and glared at them until the room quieted with my presence.

"What the hell is wrong with you two?" I snapped. "You bring in a new guy after telling the rest of us there was a possibility for a promotion?"

"Miss Abram,"—They routinely called their employees "Miss" or "Mister" as a tactic to make the rest of us feel beneath them—"I'm surprised you even knew where the conference room was," Mercedes quipped.

Trish put down her nail file and sighed. "His qualifications—"

"No," I interjected. "Don't give me some song and dance about how we didn't meet your qualifications. Nobody could meet your qualifications if they tried. Your fathers hired us because we are qualified and we're good at our jobs. The only reason S&E has any clients today is because of us. We're the reason this PR firm is afloat. Now, if you want us to change that, then certainly keep feeding us your pile of shit every chance you get, but I suggest you don't. I can get every single client out of their contracts faster than I got them out of their previous ones."

"Are you threatening us, Miss Abram?" Mercedes asked, crossing her legs. "You know, you're easily replaceable."

Blood boiling in my veins, I placed my hands on the table and replied, "You want to fire me? Go right ahead. But I guarantee the moment your daddies hear about it, your asses will be the ones packing up your shit and leaving. You want to know why? Because I'm damn good at my job."

"Oh, please," Trish scoffed, rolling her eyes. "You're not—"

A throat cleared behind me and everyone turned. I immediately straightened my posture, running my hands down the front of my blazer, and then looked up and came face-to-face with my past.

No.

"Everyone," Trish said excitedly, standing from her seat. "I'd like you to meet our new senior account manager, Mr. Drake Wilkins."

An eruption of clapping ensued around me, but I stood there motionless, unable to breathe at the sight of him taking in the room. He caught my stare and held me captive as a smile stretched across his face, carefully masking his surprise in seeing me again. He looked like a god in the black suit that was perfectly tailored to his solid frame. His features had aged, but in a deliciously, rugged way that every girl imagines her high school sweetheart to age. His jaw was covered in dark scruff that had recently been trimmed. His eyes were the same oceanic blue, and his black hair was the same short-but-wavy-on-top style he sported back when we dated. His smile emulated that boyish charm I remembered so well, but the man standing in front of me was no longer a boy.

He was all man now.

As I eyed him, Trish continued rambling on about Drake's background and qualifications—things I already knew about him. Where he grew up. How he was our high school's beloved football star with the golden arm. The fact that he went to USC to play ball, only to have his dreams of going pro crushed a few years later when he was injured during a game. How after the injury, he focused on his studies and graduated with a master's degree in communications and currently managed his little sister's rising music career.

I already knew it all because we were from Bedford, where everyone knew everything about everyone, even when you no longer lived there. My parents had kept tabs on the son they never had—the boy they dreamed would marry their daughter someday. But I hadn't seen him face-to-face in over a decade, and seeing him now was like a tight, tantalizing squeeze to my heart. Gripping and painful, bringing back memories that had been locked away for too long; the hot-blooded misery a woman was supposed to feel when she saw the man she pushed away so many years ago.

The love of her life who had no idea what had happened. To her. To them. To their child.

Focus, Paige.

Mentally shaking away thoughts of the past, I reminded myself to keep that door shut. For now. Taking a deep breath, I signaled for Skye to follow me, and then I forced a smile and nodded graciously as I walked by him on my way out. "It's nice to meet you, Mr. Wilkins."

Once we were out of the conference room, I caught my breath and rushed back toward my office before I had a full-blown panic attack and started hyperventilating in front of my co-workers. Relief came when I closed the door to my office and could finally breathe again knowing I was closed away from everyone.

"Are you okay?" Skye asked through the door. "I know Mr. What's-His-Name was hot, but he wasn't *that* hot."

"I need a minute, okay?" I answered. "Please don't let anyone through my door. Alright?"

"You got it, boss." I heard her combat boots trail away from the door and then the squeak of her chair as she sat down at her desk.

Breathe, Paige. Just breathe. Like actual real breaths that are beneficial to staying conscious. It's going to be okay. You can do this. He's just a guy. Just. A. Guy.

A guy who has seen you naked. A lot.

A guy who gave you the greatest gift a person could give someone. A guy who knows nothing about said gift because you haven't told him about him.

Squeezing my eyes shut, I commanded the tears to stay away as the painful memory of our son crept into my mind. He looked just like Drake when he was born; all eight pounds, seven ounces and twenty-one inches of him was from his dad. The dark, beautiful head of hair. His pale, smooth skin. He even shared the same facial features as Drake, like the curve of his lips, the adorable little chin-butt, the shape of his nose and the almond-shaped blue eyes I imagined turning just as bright as his dad's with age. He was all Drake, and it killed me knowing that neither of them knew that.

I hated myself for it.

A knock sounded on the other side of my door, pulling me out of my thoughts as Skye answered her door.

"Paige is busy right now," she said in her assistant tone. "Can I take a message for you, or have her contact you whenever she gets a—Hey, what do you think you're doing? I told you she was busy."

Banging ensued on my door and I jumped away from it in fear. *I am not ready for this. I am not ready to talk to him. I can barely look at him.*

"Paige," he said, uttering my name in that same tone of voice that still made my skin tingle. "Can we please talk?"

"Mr. Wilkins, with all due respect, I know you're the new guy and technically you're our superior, but I already told you that Paige is busy. I'd appreciate it if you came back at a later time."

"And I'd appreciate it if you'd stop lying to me," he said, calling her out. I could hear the smirk in his tone and knew without even seeing him that he was a second away from laying on the charm. "You're cute when you're protective. I like your purple hair."

"Thanks, but I like women," Skye retorted.

I held back a smile at Skye's response as a chuckle fell from Drake. "I like women, too."

Skye stuttered. "I-I mean, you're hot, and you have the bluest eyes I've ever seen, but penises really don't do it for me."

"Me either," Drake replied.

A few seconds went by, and I knew, from knowing how Drake operated, that he was just waiting her out, biding his time until she crumbled.

"What's your name?" he asked.

"Skye."

"It's nice to meet you, Skye. I'm Drake," he continued. "Call me that from now on. None of that mister crap."

"Okay."

"So, will you let me in to speak to Paige?"

Hold your ground, girl.

"How do you know her name?"

"We went to high school together," he answered, nostalgically. "I haven't seen her in years, and I'd really like an opportunity to catch up with her. You think that'd be okay?"

When she didn't immediately shut him down, I grew worrisome. She was crumbling.

"I don't know why not."

Shit.

I backed away and nonchalantly leaned against my desk as Skye opened the door to my office. My past walked on in with a victorious smile lingering on his lips. I turned my gaze to Skye and excused myself.

"I need to speak with Skye for a minute."

I led her out of my office by the arm and glared at her. "What the hell was that?"

"I know, I know," she groaned, with a dreamy smile plastered on her face. "I'm sorry, but have you seen his eyes? They're so blue! I might be gay, but I'm pretty sure those blue eyes could make any woman's South Pole thaw."

"You're pathetic," I teased.

"Get back in there, and you'll see what I mean," she whispered. "When was the last time a guy visited your South Pole anyway?"

I smacked her in the arm. "That is none of your business."

"Whatever," she said, rolling her eyes.

"Hold any calls or messages until I'm done with him, okay? You think you can do that?"

"Yeah, yeah," she said with a flip of her middle finger in my direction.

Turning on my heel, I sauntered back into my office and slammed the door shut. Drake was admiring the minimal decor on the walls, but directed his attention at me as I walked over to the floor-to-ceiling windows that overlooked the city. His savory, woodsy scent filled the room and challenged me to stay strong. The one thing I'd mastered after our breakup was masking my emotions. So regardless of how he made me feel on the inside—wretched yet aroused—I wore steel-cold armor on the outside.

"What are you doing here, Drake?" I asked curtly.

He sighed. "You cut your hair, P.J."

The utterance of my nickname generated the first chink. Only Drake had referred to me by my first and middle initials, and I hadn't heard it in years. Staring off into the distance wistfully, I shook my head and corrected him. "I'm not P.J. anymore. Just Paige now."

He moved across the office closer to me and leaned against the desk. "Look, I know you're upset about not getting the—"

"Did you know I worked here when you applied for the job?" I interjected, folding my arms over my chest.

"No," he started. "I didn't know. How would I? You stopped answering my calls. You stopped replying to my emails and texts. I was just as surprised to see you as you were me. But like I was saying, I know you're upset, but—"

"You're damn right I'm mad." I faced him and narrowed my glare in his direction. "Do you know how many opportunities we get to move up here? None. This was a chance for one of us to maybe get a raise, but they hired you instead. And you don't even need the job! Lennox signed with a label now and she's on her way to becoming the next Taylor Swift, and I'm sure you've got a stake in her music. Like your family needs any more money."

He quickly pushed away from my desk as he snapped back. "How the hell would you know what I need now, huh? *You* pushed *me* away, Paige. So don't act like I did you wrong."

"Working together will ruin us."

"There is no us! You ruined us all on your own."

I know I did. Clenching my jaw, I turned my back to him again and sighed in annoyance. "I don't think we should have this conversation at work. In fact, I would really appreciate it if we kept this between you and me. Nobody here needs to know about our past."

Shaking his head, he stepped away from me. The silence between us set in. We never used to snap at each other. We had arguments like any other couple, challenged one another from time to time, but we talked it out like adults even when we were just kids. We never had snide comments drawn on the tips of our tongues ready to lash out. We never punished each other with the silent treatment. It was as if we'd regressed back to our teen years, when acting this way and fighting about two different things was perfectly normal. But even then, we didn't act like teenagers.

We acted like two people whole-heartedly devoted to each other, so much so that whenever we fought, we were still there for one another.

The silence grew, but I could still feel his eyes on me as he paced in a small circle behind me, probably trying to figure out the woman he no longer knew. The woman standing before him in designer clothes and heels wasn't the girl in ripped jeans and tennis shoes he dated back then. That girl didn't mask a thing. Her smiles and laughs came easy. That girl didn't have any regrets because the boy she loved taught her to live that way. Where the girl was the warm embodiment of everything that was young and carefree, the woman was cold and hurt in more ways than she'd ever described to anyone and it was all her fault. Her smiles were forced and she hardly ever laughed. That's what life could do to a person. It could take every colorful, carefree characteristic and turn them black in a second.

But he was quickly bringing the color back into my life by making me feel everything I thought I couldn't anymore.

Even the pain.

Drake stopped short in front of me and leaned against the window with his hands in his pockets. Those beautiful eyes staring into mine, studying me with precision. "I didn't come in here to fight with you. I just wanted to talk."

"I know," I whispered.

"Paige," he stated softly. Reaching out, he waved his imaginary white flag by cupping my left cheek in his hand and brushing his thumb across my pale skin. "Please just talk to me."

The sweet gesture created the second chink, nearly breaking me as I turned away from his warm touch and shook my head. "I'm not discussing this right now."

"You're right." He nodded and slipped his hand back into his pocket. "This isn't the time or place, but would you be willing to talk to me?"

I eventually have to talk to him; I have to tell him.

"It's been a long time. Give me the time, and I'll even let you pick the place."

I know exactly how long it's been. "I'll think about it."

"Okay." His demeanor immediately relaxed with my words, and he shot me a smart grin. "You let me know when you're ready."

I nodded silently, thankful for the disintegrating tension, and then I watched as he made his way to the door, admiring the swagger he still carried along with that glorious ass.

Grabbing the doorknob, he glanced back at me and his smile widened. "I like the shorter hair, P.J."

I scoffed aloud, which only caused him to laugh harder as he threw open the door and left. "Old habits die hard. You'll always be P.J. to me!"

And you'll always be D-Dub, I thought as I stood alone, feeling both tortured by and fascinated with his reappearance in my life. Skye's voice sounding over the intercom brought me back to work as she rattled off all the people I needed to call back.

***

At noon, I walked into Elly Jennings' psych clinic to join her and her assistant, Tessa Wilder, for lunch. I was excited for a chance to get away from work and the drama of my morning. Two of my best friends sat at the table chatting, eagerly waiting for my arrival. Elly had already torn into her sub since she was eating for two. Her big, adorable baby bump was something I tried to ignore. Our group of friends thought I had a phobia of being pregnant, but if they knew the truth, they'd know I felt the exact opposite; I loved pregnancy. I loved the feel of those tiny legs kicking from within. The glow pregnancy bestowed upon an expecting mother was absolutely divine. My hair had been long and thick, my skin became smooth and nearly blemish-free, and my nails grew stronger. I'd been there, and I'd felt healthy and beautiful and needed, all because I was growing a tiny human inside of me. I'd never felt better in my entire life.

So, I wasn't sure if I was envious, sad or a mixture of the two, but when I saw an expecting mother, even if it was a friend, I missed it. I missed *him*. But the last thing Elly and her husband, Carter, needed to deal with as their impending parenthood approached was a jealous friend. It was easier to let them think the whole situation scared the shit out of me than to let them know that I'd already been through it all.

"Paige!" Tessa exclaimed, patting the seat next to her. "I have to show you the place Justin found this morning."

I sat down and placed my purse on the table. "So, you have him house hunting while he's stuck at home?"

Last month, another one of our friends, Justin Jameson, was injured during a shooting at NYU, where he and Carter taught. Justin took a bullet to his shoulder. The whole situation was hard for all of us, but especially for Justin and Tessa, since they'd just started dating shortly before that. But it wasn't long after he was released from the hospital that he proposed.

"Here. Check out the pictures." Tessa handed her phone over to me, and continued talking about Justin as I scrolled through them. "Justin's eager to get back to work. In the meantime, he's looking for a place for us while I plan our wedding. I think he's actually enjoying the house hunting."

"That's great, and I love this place he's found. Great location and lots of space." I went through the pictures one more time as I ripped open the packaging on the granola bar I'd brought for lunch. I usually picked up a sandwich or a salad on my way here, but I wasn't in the mood to eat today given the morning I had.

"Please tell me you're eating more than just that," Elly begged with her mouth full of food.

I shrugged and gave her a weak smile. "I'm not really that hungry."

She patted her mouth with a napkin and sat back. "Since you're barely eating anything, I take it they haven't announced who received the promotion yet?"

Of course, she remembered today was the day. She knew me well enough to know that I didn't have an appetite when I was nervous.

"They'd be stupid not to give it to you," Tessa stated confidently.

Taking a deep breath, I gulped down some water and then stated with what little pride I had left, "They actually decided to hire somebody new for the position. So, none of us got the promotion, which I guess is fair, but it still sucks."

Tessa's smile fell sympathetically. "I'm so sorry, Paige."

"That is bullshit," Elly said, rolling her eyes, "especially when they told all of you they were promoting someone. You should just open up your own PR firm. I don't know how you work for those two witches."

Me either, I thought.

"So, did you at least get to meet the new person?" Tessa asked.

My mind immediately went to Drake in his suit, and a small smile broke across my face.

"Oh, she definitely met *him*," Elly laughed, pointing her finger at me. "Details!"

Tessa giggled and clapped her hands together. "Yes, details, please!"

Rolling my eyes, I shook my head. "No. It doesn't matter because he's my superior, and at S&E there's a strict no-fraternization policy. So, even if I was attracted to him, there would be no acting upon said attraction."

"You are a total buzzkill, Paige!" Tessa proclaimed as she uncapped her water bottle. "You know, for once, I just want you to think naughty, rule-breaking thoughts instead of the prudish thoughts you normally think. Having sex with your boss would be totally hot."

"Oh, really?" I asked, amused. "So, you'd have sex with Elly, because she's your boss?"

"No!" Elly shouted playfully, setting her sandwich down as uncontrollable laughter shook through her.

Tessa actually thought about it for a second and then answered. "If I was into women, I totally would, but I'm not. The whole eating pussy part makes me uncomfortable. Like, it's okay for guys to do that to us because we give them blow jobs, it evens the oral playing field. But I have a vagina, so I don't want to eat one. And I imagine if I had a dick that I wouldn't want to suck one."

Elly stopped laughing for a second, and we stared at Tessa in complete shock before the three of us broke into a fit of laughter.

"That's probably the sickest, best lunch topic we've ever discussed!" Elly exclaimed, wiping tears from her eyes.

"I know!" Tessa stated proudly. "It's such a shame that Carter and Justin weren't here to witness it."

I smiled at the two of them and chugged some more water, thankful for friends who could easily brighten my day. Then a discarded, balled-up napkin hit me on the side of the face, and I glared over at Tessa. "What was that for?"

"For trying to change the subject," she smirked. "Now, back to your hot boss. Are you attracted to him? What's he look like?"

If I were honest with them, I'd tell them I'd never stopped being attracted to Drake Wilkins. Seeing him again for the first time in a very long time just confirmed how much I still loved him. Especially the arousal that set in at just the sight of him, and then the way it heightened at the sound of his voice and my name rolling off his tongue. The touch of his hand against my face, like he'd done so many times before, felt like being wrapped up in my favorite blanket again. But I couldn't tell the girls any of that. They'd want to know about our past, and that was a subject my friends didn't need to know about yet.

"Every woman in the office is attracted to him," I stated in an irritated tone. "Even Skye thinks he's hot."

"Why are you letting some stupid policy get in your way? I think you owe it to your lady box, which hasn't seen any male action since I've known you, to break the damn rules for once. You need to stand up for her and get some."

I looked over at Elly, and she shrugged in agreement as she took another bite. "Sorry, but I'm with Tessa on this one."

"Well, it's not happening," I said sternly. "I'm not going to get fired for something that could possibly hurt my chances of getting any other job in the future."

"I wasn't suggesting you hook up with him while at work," Tessa commented.

Elly nodded. "Yeah, your bosses shouldn't dictate what you do outside of the office. You should be free to do whatever or whomever you want."

"I know." But that was easier said than done when the guy was an old flame.

"Look," Elly started, putting her hand over mine. "We just want you to be happy, like you've always wanted for the rest of us. Life isn't just about work, Paige. I'm sorry you didn't get your promotion, but maybe that's a good thing. You already work so much. I think it's time you tried to have a little fun for yourself instead of worrying so much about your career. You're always encouraging us to give love a chance, but I think it's time you take some of your own advice and do the same."

But I'd already given love a chance, and it blessed me with two guys that I will love until the end of time.

My son and his father.

Chapter Two

Drake

That night, after my first day of work at Sabre & Edelmen, I came home to my two-bedroom apartment and changed into a pair of sweats before heating up leftovers for dinner. My apartment wasn't incredibly over-the-top but it was spacious, something I required in a home since I grew up with acres of land surrounding me. It was an adjustment to say the least. I was used to the homes in Bedford and the condos in California where you could see for miles in every direction, and you could drive wherever you wanted. But home would always be in New York. So after college, I moved back to Bedford and helped my little sister, Lennox, launch her music career. I reluctantly followed her to Manhattan and found my own place a few months ago. If I wanted to have any sort of career in communications in New York, the city was where it was at, even if I wasn't a fan of the concrete jungle.

Just as the microwave finished renewing my two-day old lasagna, I received a text message from my buddy, Barrett Gallagher.

Barrett: How'd your first day go?
Thoughts of Paige instantly flooded me.
Me: I work with PJ.

A few minutes passed before my phone started ringing, and I decided to make him wait while I grabbed a beer and my food and made myself comfortable on the couch. I turned the TV on, lowered the volume and punched in the channel for ESPN. When the second-to-last ring chimed, I finally picked up my phone and mocked him.

"Hey, Barrett, so nice of you to call."

"Shut up, asshole," he stated firmly. "How in the hell did you manage to land a job at the same PR firm that your ex works at?"

I sighed. "I don't know, man, but I did."

His end went quiet and I could tell he was fuming over the news. He used to be a fan of Paige back when we were all in high school. His wife, Zoey, and Paige used to be best friends then, and the four of us had been inseparable. But then Paige and I broke up, and the three of us went to college without her. I wasn't sure how it all happened or why, but eventually Paige cut herself off from all of us.

"Well," Barrett started, his tone filled with annoyance. "Did you see her? Talk to her? How'd she react to seeing you again?"

I replayed the morning over in my head. "She was surprised to see me, but we talked a bit."

"Please tell me she got fat and looks like shit now, or that she's unhappily married to some lazy bastard with a shitload of bratty kids."

I laughed lightly but then exhaled a long, audible sigh.

"Dammit, Drake!" he said curtly. "I know that sigh. That sigh is not good, my friend. You cannot go through this with her again. I won't let you. The last time you guys broke up, Zoey and I nearly broke up, and we're married now. I can't afford a divorce."

"She cut her hair," I commented, smiling. "It looks good on her, but it took me by surprise at first. She's all woman now, if that makes any sense. I know we're older and not the kids we were back in high school, but she doesn't look like she did back then. Maybe it's because I haven't seen her in a long time, but she just looked so . . . good. More beautiful than I've ever seen her look before and that's saying something."

"Yeah, it is," he muttered. "You thought the sun shined out of her ass back in high school."

"But she's not the same person she was then. At least she doesn't seem to be. She could barely look at me. I mean, I finally got her to smile and agree to meet up with me so we could catch up, but she seems all about the job now. She doesn't have any pictures of anyone in her office, not even her parents. It's very organized and very cold—"

"And you aren't allowed to touch anything," Barrett quipped, chuckling as he finished my sentence with a familiar line from *Ferris Bueller*.

I laughed and then continued. "She didn't have a ring on her finger. She's demanding and feared at the office. Her co-workers are actually more afraid of her than their bosses. And when I walked into the conference room to meet everyone, she was ripping the bosses a new one because they hired me instead of promoting one of the executives like they said they were going to do."

"Wow," he stated in a shocked tone. "That doesn't sound like her at all. She would have never ripped anyone back in high school."

I readjusted myself at the memory of her ranting in those heels of hers and that tight-as-fuck skirt that highlighted her legs and hips. "I know . . ."

Barrett sneered. "You were turned on by it, weren't you?"

"I can't help it!" I admitted, laughing. "This is P.J. we're talking about here. She was always independent and I loved that about her, but seeing her demand respect from others and stand up for her co-workers was hot. And the way she was dressed didn't help matters. She had these heels on and this tight skirt that went down to her knees, and—"

"You know, just because she doesn't have a ring on her finger doesn't mean she's not in a relationship with someone."

"Barrett," I said, shaking my head. "You forget that I know what she looks like when she's happy and in love, and the woman I saw today was neither."

He was quiet for a few seconds before speaking again. "I just don't want to see you get hurt again. You were a mess after you guys broke up, and you haven't had a serious relationship since then because you ruin any relationship that starts to become serious because the woman's not Paige. That's not healthy."

I knew that what he was saying was partially true, because I *was* a mess after Paige stopped talking to me. But the crap about the other relationships was bull; I didn't ruin them, I just wasn't interested in anyone else. "I can't just stop having feelings for her."

"But you can't make her love you back either," he retorted. "At some point, you're going to have to move on. You don't even know her anymore."

"I want to get to know her again." I tossed the plate of untouched lasagna onto the coffee table in front of me and ran my hand over the back of my neck. He was starting to piss me off. I didn't need him worried about me; I needed his support as my best friend.

So, I bribed him with the four things I knew would get him back on Team Paige.

"Zoey. Ryce. Quinn. Ziggy."

"What about them?" he asked sharply.

"The only reason you're with Zoey today is because of Paige. You would have never met her otherwise and you know it. You're happily married with three beautiful little girls because of Paige. Don't hate her because of me. We have no idea what happened after we went off to school or what made her push us all away, but I want to find out. Now's my chance, but I need your support. I don't need you reminding me of the past or telling me not to go through with this. I want her, even if it's going to be a challenge. I've already experienced not having her, so she can't really do any more damage."

"Fine. I don't hate her," he admitted grudgingly.

I picked my plate back up and smiled. "Good, and if the situation was reversed, and this was you and Zoey, what would you do?"

Barrett was quiet again for a moment, and I knew he was thinking about it, reversing our roles as if it was he who didn't have Zoey anymore. He finally cleared his throat and stated, "I'd do anything to get her back."

"Exactly."

"But you're not the only person she hurt," he reiterated. "Zoey lost her best friend and she has no idea why. We lost the two best friends we've ever had as a couple. Do you know how hard it is to find another couple you both get along with, to do stuff with together and actually have a good time? It's like a needle in a haystack. It has sucked not having the two of you together. You know I'll support you no matter what because you're my best friend. But if you bring her back into our lives, she better not hurt my wife or ruin our marriage."

"Got it."

"Okay."

My smile widened. "Thanks, man."

"Yeah, yeah." On his end, I could hear the slam of a door closing and next came the sound of three different girly voices all excited to see their dad. "Well, my girls are home and ready to eat. I've got to go. Good luck. I think you're gonna need it!"

***

The next day after work, I walked into Jones Jym in complete awe of the place. It was an athlete's dream workout facility—even better than the one I frequented during college ball. It had multiple floors of equipment and machines, and several trainers on staff. The place buzzed with people who were eager to sweat away their workday. Since moving to the city, I'd yet to find a gym to join, and a guy at work named Owen had given me the name of the gym he and several of his athletic clients used.

I signed up and paid the membership fee. The lady at the front desk gave me a keycard and all the necessary information that came with becoming a member, and then she had a young guy give me a tour of the place. It wasn't until we got to the floor with the pool that I recognized the body swimming toward the other end.

Paige was doing laps in a one-piece black swimsuit. Seeing her in the water reminded me of the times we spent swimming and the bikinis she used to wear, especially the ones I enjoyed taking off of her.

"Dude," the kid said, shaking his head. "Don't even bother. That lady is like the ice queen around here. She specifically requests the pool to herself, and the only reason she gets it is because she's friends with the boss."

"I see," I commented, never taking my eyes off her. *Ice queen, huh?* That was a new nickname for her I hadn't heard around work yet. "If you don't mind, I think I can take it from here. I appreciate you showing me around."

"Just doing my job." He shrugged and picked up a few towels that had been tossed to the side before heading toward the door. "Have a good day."

"You too."

I was alone with her. It was like one of my teenage wet dreams come to life all over again: Paige all wet in a swimsuit. Except this time, she was in a one-piece that covered way too much of her, but I really didn't mind. The suit molded to her, showing off her excellently toned body and how much she still cared for it.

As she swam toward the end of the pool nearest me, I walked to the edge and squatted down to watch her. She pushed harder and harder through the water, kicking her legs and pumping her arms fast toward me. When she got closer, instead of somersaulting against the wall and pushing back to the other end, she reached for the edge and accidentally grabbed my shoe.

"What the hell?" she sputtered as she removed her goggles and moved into a standing position. She brushed her hair out of her face and peered back at me with a pissed off gleam in her eye. "What are you doing in here, Drake? I requested time in the pool to myself."

"I know," I said, smiling. "But I was getting the Jones Jym tour since I'm a new member and when I saw you swimming, I thought I'd say hi."

She rolled her eyes and ticked a brow up at me. "You joined my gym?"

"I didn't realize it was *your* gym. I thought it was open to everybody."

She sighed. "You know what I mean. How did you know I worked out here?"

"Well, if you must know, I asked Owen his opinion on the gyms around the city, and he suggested this one. Your name was never even brought up."

"Goddammit, Owen," she muttered under her breath loud enough for me to hear.

Amused, I stepped back as she lifted herself out of the pool. I admired the body that I missed in an unhealthy manner, feeling suffocated in my three-piece suit as my eyes roamed. She grabbed a towel and started to dry off, and all I could do was stand there and watch. Her suit dipped low in the front, exposing the contours of her breasts, and it was cut high on the thighs to show off her legs and the cheeks of her taut ass peeking out the backside. It wasn't like the one-piece suits with the ugly floral prints. No, this black beaut was one I imagined myself stripping off of her in a slow, seductive manner until I had her begging me to get her out of it.

"Don't," she stated harshly, knocking me back to the present.

"What?" I asked, confused as I refocused my attention to her face, where her eyes were narrowed on me, brows furrowed in annoyance.

She used to love it when I watched her like this.

She wrapped one towel around herself and knotted it, and then proceeded to wring her hair out with another towel. "You don't get to look at me like that anymore."

I cocked my head to the side and shot her a mischievous smile. "Do you realize what you're wearing? How am I supposed to not look at you in a swimsuit? Do you remember all the good times we had with you in—and out—of a bikini? Because I do."

"I can tell." She nodded toward the slight bulge in my pants and tossed the towel in the used barrel. Slipping her feet into a pair of sandals, she threw her bag over her shoulder and made her way over to me. She tugged on my loosened tie and pulled me forward with a playful smile lingering on her lips as she ran her fingers over the silky material. "I remember that one night we decided to go skinny dipping," she stated, her voice taking on a sensual tone that hypnotized me. "You helped me out of my suit, taking your sweet time untying the strings and sliding my bottoms down my legs, and then you took off your shorts." She laughed softly and then shoved me away from her. "But the water was so cold that your genitals shriveled up to unnoticeable proportions."

"Hey, it was really fucking cold!" I exclaimed defensively.

Reaching for the door, her laugh turned devious. "Don't ever interrupt my swim session again, Wilkins."

"Don't act like that's the only swimming memory you have, Abram!" I called back.

Like hell I was going to let her have the last word. One glance at my groin, and I knew the skinny dipping story still had the same damn effect that it had back when we were kids.

Fuck. Getting her back was going to be more of a challenge than I thought, but I'd endure every embarrassing story she recalled about me if it meant hearing her laugh like that again.

***

Once I was back in dry clothes, I brushed off my run-in with Drake—even though it was the most fun I'd had with a guy in years—and searched the gym for my friend, Cash Donovan. He was the only other single person in our group of friends, and the notorious man-whore of our gang. I regularly prayed for the woman he'd eventually talk into marrying him someday. The PR firm had a gala coming up this weekend, and he had always been my go-to date for events I was obligated to attend, especially the work-related ones. Cash was good-looking and one hell of a charmer, so he was the perfect date to any event because he could talk to anybody. So, when I finally found him kickboxing, I put on my best smile and walked over.

He jabbed with his right arm and then glanced my way. "I know that smile, Paige. What do you want?"

"I have a tiny favor to ask," I said sweetly.

"No," he said, catching the punching bag. He wiped the sweat off his face with a towel and shook his head at me. "Whatever it is, the answer is no."

Ugh, he's going to make me beg. "Please, Cash. The firm has their annual New Year gala this weekend, and I have to bring a date. It's mandatory that all staff bring someone with them."

"So, go find a guy to take with you." He opened his water bottle and took a long swig. "You know, like an actual date."

I rolled my eyes. "It's not like you haven't benefitted from this event in the past. You have your own radio show. Attending my firm's gala has given you an in with the musicians that attend to get them on your show. It's a win-win."

"That's not the point," he argued. "If I'm going to go on a date, I expect sex at the end of the night or at least a chance to cop a feel while making out. In the past, you've never put out or even let me touch your ass."

"It's a work event, of course I'm not going to let you touch my ass." I wrinkled my nose. "Just go with me. I really don't want to go through the hassle of trying to find a date on such short notice."

He stared at me closely, so I worked my magic by batting my baby blue eyes and giving him a slight pout. "Pplleeaassee . . ."

"Fine," he said flatly, dropping his water bottle back down onto the mat. "But this is the last time, Paige. I've been doing this shit since college, and I'm tired of it. It's not like you can't find a date. You're a hot, smart, successful woman. There are plenty of guys in this city who are into that."

"I know, I know," I commented, as I made myself a reminder on my phone to pick up my dress and book a car. "Just be ready on Saturday by six o'clock. I'll have a car pick us up."

He swiped my phone from my hands to get my attention and gave me a cocky smile. "I'm serious. Last. Time. Unless we're going to have sex at the end of the night."

"Absolutely not."

"That's what I thought," he said, placing the phone back in my hand. "You're welcome, by the way."

"Thank you, Johnny!" I slipped my phone in my purse and gave him a chaste kiss on the cheek. "I owe you one."

He grunted. "No, you owe me a thousand by now."

"Oh, and wear a tuxedo!" I called over my shoulder as I waved good-bye to him. "Preferably black with a silver vest because my dress is silver."

"Woman!" he groaned loudly. "You know how much I hate wearing tuxedos. Why do we have to match?"

"Because I said so!"

Chapter Three

Saturday night, as Cash meandered around the ballroom talking to people he knew at the gala, I endured the unfortunate aftermath of greeting one of Owen's clients. This guy was in the major leagues and liked to refer to his sexual encounters in baseball terms. His penis was the bat, and a grand slam was some orgy with four gold diggers. He proudly talked about his women like he talked about his baseball stats, as if either would impress me.

I downed the rest of my champagne, hoping it'd give me an excuse to walk away and get another, but just as he started in on his recent workout regimen, a strong hand wrapped around my waist and pulled me away from the blabbing idiot.

"Care to dance?" Cash laughed, leading me onto the dance floor. "Thought you might need saving from Bill Buckner back there."

"Definitely." I wrapped my arms around his shoulders and his hands settled on my waist as Adele's single from the last James Bond movie played. "That's the last time I ever say hi to that guy. He wouldn't stop talking about the women he's *scored*."

"Mookie is the biggest joke in baseball," Cash stated with a smile. "Last year, he blew the playoffs by letting a fly ball drop in center—hence the Buckner reference."

"I'm not surprised," I replied with an eye roll. We swayed silently for a while and I admired Cash in his tux. He'd worn a black tux and silver vest, just like I'd asked, though he opted not to wear the matching bowtie. He'd left the top few buttons on his shirt undone and styled his short, reddish brown hair in a way that made it look sexy and effortless. He cleaned up so well that if I hadn't known him, I'd almost be attracted to him, but his trail of women prevented that from ever happening. "So, how many women have given you their phone numbers tonight?"

"Three," he answered, proudly. "But one was a twofer, so really, the count is up to four. Supposedly, she has a friend who's never been in a threesome, and you know me and my no-woman-left-behind policy."

"You make me sick." I laughed. "How do you know her friend's even a woman? It could be a guy."

The smile from his face dropped as he stared back at me. "You just look for ways to bring me down, don't you?"

"No!" I exclaimed, giving him a playful squeeze. "I'm just making sure you consider all your options."

"Sure, sure," he retorted. "You know, I'm not the only one who should consider their options. There's a guy on my nine o'clock—your three—who hasn't been able to take his eyes off you tonight."

Turning my head to the right, I found Drake standing with a group of people, but he wasn't listening to whatever they were talking about; he was watching Cash and me dance.

I gave Cash my full attention and faked a confident smile. "That's our new senior account manager."

He wagged his eyebrows eagerly. "Well, I think the new guy sees something he likes, especially with you wearing that."

"It's just a dress," I replied, taking a deep breath and rolling my shoulders back. I'd be lying if I said I didn't spend a lot of time getting ready tonight, but perfection took time. Yes, it was *just a dress*, but when I put it on earlier, it came to life. I was a strong believer in women making their outfits look good or bad, and tonight, I looked and felt like a goddess. My dress was a silver strapless Calvin Klein gown that hugged my body all the way down to my hips, where it flowed into a floor-length skirt. I paired the sparkling ensemble with silver Louboutins and diamond stud earrings, and straightened my blond bob into a sharp, silky smooth style that framed my face. My makeup was light—a soft pink for my lips and cheeks and black mascara for my lashes.

But I also spent a lot of time getting ready because of Drake. He hadn't seen me this dressed up since his senior prom, and for some reason, buried deep down, I still had this need to impress him. That's when I knew for certain that I still had feelings for him: when I looked in the mirror earlier tonight and thought, *I wonder what Drake will think*.

"Ooh," Cash murmured. "Looks like new guy is on his way over to cut in."

"W-what!" I stammered nervously. "You cannot let him dance with me. I'm serious, Cash. Do not let him cut in."

"Why not? He's a good-looking guy."

"So, you dance with him then."

"Hey, I'm man enough to admit when there's a guy in the room as good-looking as myself," he said confidently. "But that's where I draw the line."

"Oh, God," I muttered, rolling my eyes. "How will we ever get you out of the building later?"

His lips perked up into an amused smirk. "The guy is interested in you. I'm making you dance with him, so maybe I don't have to go to any more of these stupid galas. I think we can both agree that tonight has been a total bore."

"That's not the point," I cursed under my breath just as a throat cleared behind me, causing a shiver to trickle down my spine.

"Hey," Drake said, smiling at me. He glanced at Cash and motioned to me. "Mind if I cut in?"

Cash shook his head, and my stomach flipped when he handed me over to Drake. "She's all yours."

"Thanks." Drake effortlessly positioned us how we always used to dance as the song changed to an Eric Church hit. He placed my left hand around his neck, then with one hand around my waist and the other holding my right hand, he began to sway us. I was tucked in so close to him that he invaded all of my senses. His navy tuxedo enhanced his beautiful eyes, making them appear bluer. Breathing in his cologne and dancing with him to a song about a good old country boy felt like coming home after being gone for a long time. My eyes lingered on his mouth, knowing he'd taste like spearmint gum, even though I had no intentions of kissing him. Holding on to him felt like I was clutching on for dear life because he'd eventually let go and leave me with only memories of him.

I looked up into his eyes and realized he was staring at me, watching closely as I checked him out, so I said, "You had to cut in?"

"Well, since you've been avoiding me all night," he commented knowingly. "Yes, I did."

"I haven't been avoiding you. I've been busy networking."

He nodded in disbelief. "Mhmm."

I rolled my eyes, even though I had been overly conscious of his whereabouts throughout the evening. I wouldn't necessarily say I was trying to avoid him though. I'd made an attempt to keep business and pleasure separate, because I knew at some point tonight, if we interacted, we'd end up here. Dancing together. And it both scared and thrilled me at the same time.

"Are you and that guy together?"

Taken aback by his question, I shook my head. "Not that it's any of your business, but no, Cash and I are not together. We're just friends."

"With any benefits?"

"No," I answered, laughing lightly. To think he actually thought Cash and I were a couple made me smile; it meant he still cared. "You know, I don't remember Drake Wilkins being so nosy."

He laughed, his eyes studying every inch of my face. "That's because back then I already had the woman every other guy in the room wanted."

"Speaking of," I began, choosing to ignore his charming comment, "Which one of these women did you bring with you tonight?"

His brows furrowed in confusion. "None of them."

"What? You came alone?" I asked, startled by his response. "How did you manage that? It's mandatory for us to bring a date."

"Well, I guess the Banger Sisters failed to mention that rule to me."

Laughter fell from my lips at the reference to our bosses.

He smiled. "Nice nickname for them, by the way. I heard you were the mastermind behind that one."

"Thank you," I said proudly, with a nonchalant shrug.

"So," Drake started, before he twirled me out and spun me back into him and pulled us close again. "When are we going to have that talk?"

Just like that, we were back to that impending talk. The needle of guilt threaded through my veins, stressing how much I owed him. My smile fell as I bowed my head, unable to look at him when I answered, "I don't know, Drake."

"Do you not want to talk to me?" he asked curiously.

"I do," I stated, glancing back up at him in reassurance. "But this is all a little overwhelming. I go from not having you in my life, not seeing you every day, not—"

"Thinking about me?"

God, no.

I shook my head and held his stare. "The exact opposite, actually. I've thought about you a lot over the years. I still think about you. But it terrifies me to have that talk with you. To finally know what you've been up to, if you've been happy, where you've been and with whom. It scares me."

"You don't think I'm scared?" he asked rhetorically. "The first thing I searched for when I saw you again was a ring, and I thank God that I didn't find one because if there's one thing I've learned over the past ten years, Paige, it's that you're irreplaceable. I believed it when we were young, but I know it now."

Tears pooled in my eyes with his sweet words, and I quickly tried blinking them away before one of them fell. Over his shoulder, I caught Trish and Mercedes watching us from the edge of the dance floor. "Drake, did they tell you co-workers aren't allowed to date at S&E?"

He sighed. "Yes, but I'd gladly get fired if that's what it takes to be with you. I'm not going to let a job or anything stand in my way."

I looked away, knowing a tear was about to fall. "You don't even know me anymore."

"But I want a chance to get to know you again," he reassured, brushing away the wetness with his thumb. "I don't care how much it scares me. All I care about is you. There's nothing you could tell me that would make me change my mind."

Yes . . . there is something.

"We will talk," I said as the song came to an end. "I promise."

"You have nothing to worry about, I swear." He grabbed my hand tightly and laid it over his heart so I could feel the intensity of it racing beneath his clothes. "We may have aged a bit, but I'm the same guy in here."

I nodded, unable to say the same about myself.

He broke away from me, smiling. "Will you at least introduce me to your friend?"

Though the thought of mixing my past with my present also scared the hell out of me, I located Cash near our table, watching us closely like the nosy son of a bitch he was. I'd spent most of my life trying to leave the past behind, but now that it was standing right in front of me, that was going to be harder to do, especially with the meddling company I kept now.

I smiled weakly and nodded at Drake. "Sure."

My palms started to sweat as I led us over to where Cash was standing, praying he wouldn't ask Drake a bunch of questions.

"Cash," I said, gesturing to Drake. "I'd like you to meet S&E's newest employee, Drake Wilkins. Drake, this is my good friend, Cash Donovan."

"Nice to meet you," Drake offered, shaking Cash's hand.

"Likewise," Cash replied. "Wilkins . . . you wouldn't happen to be related to Lennox Wilkins, would you?"

Drake laughed and shot me a proud look. "I am. She's my little sister."

"Ah," Cash said, smiling. "Then you're probably her publicist too, and I'm going to be the pain in the ass that keeps hounding you for a chance to have her as a guest on my radio show."

"Radio, huh?" Drake mused. "She hasn't done any radio interviews yet, but we've had plenty asking for her."

Cash put his hands in his pockets. "Well then, what do I have to do to be the first radio jockey to interview her?"

I laughed, shaking my head. "Aren't you glad I introduced you, Drake? Cash is like the Ryan Seacrest of the East Coast."

He smiled at me and then gave Cash his attention. "Give me your card, and you'll be the first to know when Lennox is ready for a radio interview."

Cash pulled his card out from the inside pocket of his jacket and handed it over to Drake. "I'm holding you to that, man."

"You've got my word," Drake replied, "but only because you're friends with Paige."

"Finally!" Cash exclaimed, wrapping his arm around my shoulders. "My friendship with you has paid off!"

"Ha, ha. Very funny." I rolled my eyes at him as Drake continued laughing. Grabbing Cash's wrist, I pulled his sleeve up to look at the time on his watch. It wasn't even midnight yet, but I was ready to go home. Every year, the gala wiped me out, but tonight, I was especially ready to get the hell out of here. From all the networking with clients and co-workers, to my slow dance with Drake, to Cash giving Drake his business card, I was a bundle of fried nerves just waiting for a bed. "Well boys, it is time for this girl to go home."

"Yes," Cash said dramatically, "because the town car might turn into a pumpkin if we don't get you home on time."

I threw my elbow into his side. "Smartass."

Drake laughed and gave Cash a pat on the shoulder. "Well, it was nice meeting you, Cash."

"Same to you, man. I look forward to your call." Cash gave me a playful squeeze and then broke away from me. "I'm going to go get our coats."

"Thanks." He walked away, leaving Drake and me alone once again.

"He seems like a good guy."

I nodded. "He is. We met during college and have stayed friends ever since."

"Well, I'm glad you're just friends." When he leaned in toward me, his warm voice and close proximity caused goosebumps to flourish down my neck as he whispered in my ear, "You look amazing tonight. Thanks for the dance, P.J."

Before I could reply, he turned and walked toward Trish and Mercedes, who were both watching us intently. They obviously hadn't liked the new guy giving someone else attention besides them. At S&E, new employees were expected to spend their first week kissing the bosses' asses. But I knew Drake wasn't that type of person; he'd never been a kiss-ass. However, he was good under pressure and smoothing over hostile environments, like the one we were in now with our bosses probably wondering what the hell was going on between us.

Well, join the club, girls, because I don't even know!

***

Cash was surprisingly quiet after we left the gala. We were headed to my place first, most likely because he wasn't ready to go home yet unlike me. I could feel him staring at me from across the seat. Out of all my friends, he and Elly knew me the best, and right now, I knew he was curious about Drake.

"Just ask whatever it is you're wanting to know," I finally said, glancing over my shoulder at him.

A smile crept into his cheeks, showing off his dimples. "You know him, don't you? I can't believe you know Lennox Wilkins' brother and failed to tell me!"

I sighed and continued to watch the snow falling outside the car window. "Yeah, I do."

"How?" he asked, curiosity lingering in his voice. "I was serious when I said he couldn't take his eyes off you. From the moment we walked in together, he was watching. So, who is he?"

Remembering how great it felt to be back in his arms, I wrapped my arms around my stomach, unsure of how to answer the question. Drake Wilkins was so many things to me, but I wasn't sure if I was ready to tell Cash, or any of my other friends for that matter. They'd want to know the whole story, and that couldn't happen when Drake didn't even know it.

I had no idea how I was going to tell him.

"Drake and I went to high school together," I answered truthfully.

"And?" Cash pushed further. "I'm supposed to believe that you two *just* went to high school together? Acquaintances don't dance that close, Paige."

"Fine." I shrugged. "We may have dated back then."

"Aha!" he exclaimed loudly, chuckling to himself. "So, you've seen each other naked. That explains the tension between you two."

"Seriously?" I deadpanned. "Is it always about sex with you?"

"No," he quipped, "but I have been a little worried about you. Even during college, you'd pushed away any guy that'd give you attention, and now, you still ask your friends to be your date to events. You know, it's okay to let someone in and feel things for them, even an ex."

"We broke up a long time ago, but I never really let him go. If you knew why, I think you'd understand, but it's just something I can't talk about. At least not yet." The car pulled to the curb of my building, and I peered over at Cash and smiled weakly. "Thanks for coming with me tonight. I really appreciate it."

"You bet," he said, placing his hand on my shoulder. "For what it's worth, I thought you guys looked good together. So, whatever happened, whatever it is you can't talk about, don't let it ruin your future."

I already have, I thought as I leaned in and kissed him on the cheek. "Don't do anything stupid tonight, Johnny."

"Where's the fun in that?" he teased.

Shaking my head, I stepped away from the curb and shut the door. The car started to pull back on to the street, so I turned around and stared up at the night sky with its beautiful snowflakes falling down on me. Then I made my way up the steps to my building and the few floors up to my apartment. Locking the door behind me, I grabbed my phone out of my purse and set it on the counter before heading down the hallway toward my room. I was more than eager to get out of these heels.

And even more ready to be alone.

No more phone. No more clients and co-workers. No more networking. No more friends asking me about my past.

My energy was shot.

I took a seat on the edge of my queen-sized bed and pushed my heels off with my toes. The relief that flooded the balls of my feet felt liberating, like they'd just been freed from a designer jailhouse. From the bed, I stared over at my closet, feeling exhausted as the night replayed over in my mind. Dancing with Drake again felt wonderful, but our conversation was one that would haunt me—like the trunk in my closet had ever since Drake's reappearance. I knew I should just take off the dress, hang it up in its garment bag, and close the closet door, but I couldn't. Above the hangers of clothes was a trunk filled with memories of our time spent together and apart. Memories that I had tucked away in the back of my closet because I loved them too much to throw them away, but was too haunted by them to share them with anyone else.

So, I tiptoed into my walk-in closet, grabbed the heavy container, and brought it back to my bed. Maybe going through it would help rid myself of the guilt until I actually had to tell him.

Or at least purge myself of the emotional buildup currently lodged in my throat. I usually kept up a perfect façade for the people around me, pretending like I had everything under control, when really, I was a chaotic mess of remorse and grief hiding behind a strong work ethic and designer clothes.

Hiking up my skirt, I crawled on top of my comforter and took a deep breath as I scooted the box closer to me. I hadn't opened it in years; that's how much some of the items in here scared me. The act of opening it had been taunting me all week, because I knew when I finally did, it'd cause me unimaginable pain.

But tonight, I felt like bleeding.

I punched in the four-digit code to the lock, my son's birthday—0223—which just so happened to be Elly's due date, too.

The hinge released the top from its lock and I pulled it all the way open. One glance at the items inside and tears quickly overtook my vision. I grabbed Drake's hoodie with our school mascot on it and slipped it on over my dress. Lifting the gray cotton material up to my nose, I took a whiff of it and smiled because somehow it still smelled like him. I peered inside again and took out a pile of pictures of us. They ranged from us posing for our mothers at events like the school dances and homecoming, to pictures we'd taken when we were alone together. There were a lot of pictures of us just lying together or kissing. Others captured moments where we were being silly in a photo booth at the local fair or in the car with Barrett and Zoey. We were young in the pictures, but there was no denying how we felt in them.

"We were so in love back then," I cried softly.

Setting the pictures to the side, I grabbed all the corsages he'd ever given me. The miniature roses were wilted, but the elastic and ribbons were all still intact. They looked like crap now and no longer smelled, but I could still remember how gorgeous I thought they were each time he put one of them on my wrist.

Next, I pulled out all the letters he'd sent during his first year of college, after I stopped answering his calls and emails. There were ten of them, but right now, I didn't have the courage to reread them. So, I laid them next to the pictures.

The rest of the items in the top portion of the trunk were gifts he'd given me throughout the years or treasures that he'd left in my room that I'd saved. Like all the beautiful jewelry, the now-empty bottles of perfume, and all the vases that once held the flowers he'd sent me. The empty bottle of vodka we stole from his parents and polished off one weekend when they were away. All of the CDs and movies we enjoyed together, and a copy of his favorite book: *Friday Night Lights* by H.G. Bissinger.

The last item was his class ring that I could still fit two of my fingers through.

Wiping the tears from my cheeks, I slipped the ring off and set it on top of the book. I removed the top shelf from the trunk, tossed it on the floor, and then took another uneasy breath as I glanced in at all the items that filled the bottom half.

That was all it took for me to completely lose it. Sobs wracked my body as I pulled out his onesies and held them against my chest. I attempted to find his sweet, baby scent in them but couldn't, which only hurt worse, knowing that he hadn't even worn some of them. I grabbed the booties and tiny socks that he barely had a chance to wear, and the blankets and hats my mom and nana had knitted for him that they'd never get to see him in. Grasping the soft baby books I used to read to him and the wrist and foot rattles he enjoyed, I cried harder.

I'd kept it all, even the positive pregnancy test.

The rest of the trunk was filled with pictures of him. There were so many pictures of me with my pregnant belly, sonograms, and then even more of him after his birth. Dad had kept his promise and documented every aspect of his grandson's life. The VHS tape and the DVD that he'd made later on were both in the trunk as well as the journal he made me keep that detailed my pregnancy. I had his birth certificate and the birth announcement card the hospital had given me.

And I had his death certificate, too.

Lying back on the bed, chest aching from all the tears, I covered myself with one of his baby blankets and clutched my favorite picture of him between my fingers. I'd taken it after coming home from the hospital, when my parents had finally left us alone in my bedroom-turned-nursery. I'd captured a picture of him in my arms, staring back at me as we quietly admired one another. The only thing I could do now was imagine the weight of him in my arms.

"If I could give my life to bring you back, I would in a heartbeat, so your dad could meet you and get to know the beautiful boy we created together."

But I couldn't, and it made me feel helpless, handcuffed to my anguish, knowing I couldn't bring him back and how much Drake would hate me after he learned what I'd done.

"I should've n-n-never kept you a secret from him," I sobbed, running my fingers over the picture, remembering the softness of his skin. "I'm s-so sorry. I should've told him."

I cried over my one, true regret, surrounded by memories of its victims.

I cried for the girl who lost the two greatest loves of her life, and the woman who still felt incredibly empty without them.

I cried, wearing Drake's hoodie over a designer gown, my makeup a smeary mess running down my face.

I cried until exhaustion took over and my eyes were too heavy to stay open.

Chapter Four

Drake

The following night, I found the upscale restaurant that Lennox had visited a few weeks ago with friends, and decided to grab dinner by myself. She went out to eat all the time and she always managed to find places I hadn't tried yet. She'd told me about Upland on Park Avenue and how much she thought I'd enjoy it. What she didn't know was that I'd enjoy it more if she didn't run around New York City like it was some sort of playground. Her and her friends' arrival had been captured and documented all over the Internet. I still wasn't comfortable with my younger sister in the public eye, with every move she made followed by more people, but she was chasing her dream of becoming a singer and that's all that mattered. She had talent, and with talent came notoriety.

Walking into the restaurant, I automatically appreciated its low-key, spacious interior. It was quiet enough that diners could carry on conversations amongst themselves without having to shout, but still energetic as the staff served drinks and dinners. The sound of laughter coming from different parts of the room created some background noise as people enjoyed their meals. There were only a few tables empty and the hostess had a handful of people waiting to be seated.

At least Lennox has great taste, I thought. Since moving to the city, I hadn't enjoyed eating out as much because most places were loud and crowded. Upland was the exact opposite. Though it was filled with patrons, its environment was roomy enough. I only hoped its food was as good as its ambience.

"Sir," the hostess said. "Will it just be you tonight?"

"Wilkins!" a voice shouted behind me.

"Excuse me," I said to the hostess. Turning around, I found Cash Donovan walking toward me. "Hey, Cash."

"Hey," he replied. "Good to see you again, man. Did you have a good time last night?"

"It was all right," I said with a shrug. "Those types of events really aren't my thing, but it's part of the job, I guess."

"I know what you mean." He glanced over his shoulder and then back at me. "So, are you meeting someone for dinner?"

I shook my head. "No, I just thought I'd grab a bite to eat. Didn't really feel like cooking for myself."

"Then you should join us," he stated, "Paige and our friends are sitting in the back. We just placed our orders."

The need to get to know Paige and who she was now made me want to join them, but if she wasn't ready to talk to me, I doubted she'd like me barging in on her dinner with friends. "Thanks, but I don't think—"

"Nonsense!" Cash interjected, ignoring my hesitation. "You're joining us."

Okay, then.

Cash told the hostess about their addition and she said she'd notify their waitress to add another place setting. Then he waved his hand and I followed him on back. Nerves settled in my stomach with each step. I was about to meet the people she hung out with now, and if I wanted a place in her life, I needed them to like me.

When we arrived at the table, I was shocked to see there were nine other people seated with Paige. For some reason, I thought it might be just her, Cash, and a couple of other people. I never imagined a group that needed more than one table.

"Look who I found on my way back from the restroom!" Cash exclaimed, patting me on the back.

"And who is this?" a woman asked in a friendly tone.

Paige spoke up. "Drake Wilkins, my newest co-worker. Cash met him last night at the gala."

"Paige and Drake also went to high school together," Cash added.

"Holy shit, he is gorgeous."

The group turned their eyes to the petite brunette sitting next to Paige and laughed.

"Okay, from the looks on all your faces, I can tell I said that out loud, but I am not even sorry," she stated, before pointing a finger at me. "Look at him! He looks like Superman in *Man of Steel*—the *hot* superman."

"He kind of does," the redhead agreed, studying me closely.

"Henry Cavill is more muscular though," another brunette said, peeking over at the guy next to her with all the tattoos. "What? I had to fit him in one of my tuxedos a few years ago."

The blonde next to her nodded. "But his blue eyes are way better than Henry's."

"Hey!" the guy next to her said in an offended tone. "I have blue eyes."

She laughed and patted him on the chest. "I know, Fletcher. I sleep with them every night."

"Guys!" Paige exclaimed, shaking her head. "Please stop comparing Drake to some actor we don't even know!"

The group quieted as Cash instructed the waitress to seat me between him and Paige. I shrugged out of my coat before taking my seat and then looked over at Paige. "He doesn't take no for an answer, does he?"

Thankfully, she laughed and shook her head. "No, he doesn't."

Cash sat down beside me and proceeded to introduce me to everyone at the table by explaining to me how they knew Paige and what they did for a living. By the time we got back around to her, I was overloaded with names and descriptions, but still thrilled that Paige had surrounded herself with what seemed like a tight-knit group of people. Even if the women did have some weird infatuation with that Superman guy.

"So, we finally have someone who knows a little background on our girl, Paige," Tessa said, smiling at me.

"Yes!" Harper exclaimed with a clap of her hands. "You have to tell us everything you know."

Paige shook her head and replied, "No, he doesn't."

"Oh, come on, Paige," Elly encouraged, leaning into Carter's side.

"You know everything about everyone," Bayler added.

"Exactly," Carter said, agreeing with his sister. "What was Paige like in high school, Drake?"

"Well," I started, smiling at her. She appeared nervous, taking a deep breath as she ran her hand through her short hair, obviously still not a fan of being the center of attention. But what she didn't realize was that her friends were asking me to talk about my favorite subject. "She was loved by everyone. She was on the honor roll, and a great athlete. She still holds the school record for the 1500-meter run. She was head cheerleader as a junior, and—"

"A cheerleader!" Cash interjected, overly amused. "Guys, can you imagine Paige as a cheerleader?"

"A great runner, yes," Maverick replied.

"But a cheerleader?" Carter mused, shaking his head. "Sorry, Paige."

Fletcher laughed. "I can imagine her in the skirt and bloomers, but with that kind of peppiness? Hell no."

Bayler pinched him, and he grimaced in pain.

"Hey, he asked!"

"You didn't have to answer," she retorted.

"I'm not really that surprised," Justin stated with a shrug. "Paige is a great leader, and cheering apparently requires that."

The gang chuckled at his response and Paige leaned over and quietly said, "Justin didn't go to high school. He started college at the age of fourteen, so he's kind of clueless on these things."

"Gotcha."

"What else!" Elly said, waving her hand at me to continue. She shot Paige a silly face, wrinkling her nose and sticking out her tongue as she laughed. "I am loving this!"

"Okay, well, she had a great group of friends, and she dated the hottest guy in school."

"Ooh, what was his name?" Tessa asked eagerly.

I looked her way and then winked. "You're lookin' at him."

Everyone at the table laughed, with the exception of Paige, who rolled her eyes. "Okay, okay, that's enough."

"No way!" Harper said, shaking her head. She threaded her hand through Maverick's and then asked, "How long did you guys date?"

"Three years," I answered nostalgically, "I was the luckiest son of a bitch back then."

Paige's smile weakened slightly, which in turn made me more conscious of my words. She wasn't comfortable with the turn of the conversation, and I was starting to feel the same way. While her unease was brought on by the fact that her friends were being nosy, mine grew from the bothersome fact that I was the one telling them about us instead of her.

"What happened?" Elly asked.

"We broke up," Paige replied earnestly, gazing around the table at her friends. "He was headed to college, and I had one year of school still left."

The table went silent, and fortunately the waitress came over and took my order before it dragged out too long and became even more uncomfortable. I couldn't stop thinking about Paige's answer though. She didn't tell them that I broke up with her; she made it seem like it was a mutual decision. It certainly didn't feel like a mutual decision at the time. I remember feeling as if I was breaking both of our hearts at the same time and ruining all the plans we'd ever made together.

"So, any more dirt on Paige?" Bayler asked.

"She really doesn't have a lot of dirt, per se. We grew up in Bedford and went to a pretty prestigious school. It wasn't private, but extracurricular activities weren't cheap. So, if you got in trouble, you paid big time by not being able to participate, and your family paid, too. If you did something bad, that reflected back on your parents. With Paige's dad being an author—"

"Wait, your dad writes books?" Carter asked in disbelief. "What does he write?"

"He writes mysteries and horrors," I said, answering for her as I peered around the table and took in the others' shocked faces. *How are these people her friends and they have no idea what her parents do?* The thought irritated me, especially since she used to be such good friends with her parents. "Anyway, Bedford is all about country class and money, so we didn't get in trouble a lot. My parents ran a successful dairy farm and Paige's parents had her dad's image to uphold. Sure, we did things and never got caught, but if you're looking for dirt on Paige, you won't find much."

"I can't get over the fact that she was a cheerleader!" Cash announced, bursting with laughter. "That's enough dirt on her to last a lifetime. You know, if you have a photograph of her in said cheerleading uniform, that'd be even better."

"Yes!" Fletcher said, before tossing back the rest of his whiskey. "I want to see proof!"

"Guys," Paige groaned, shaking her head. "Enough already. It was years ago."

"I'm more shocked over her dad being a writer," Justin admitted, his brows furrowed. "What are some of his titles?"

"Me too," Carter said curiously. "Does he know Stephen King?"

"He's written a lot of books," Paige answered, fully annoyed as her cell phone started ringing inside her purse. "And yes, he does know King."

"King," Carter mocked with an amused grin on his face. "Look at her calling Stephen King by just his last name like she knows him."

"He's her godfather, so I would hope she knows him," I replied.

"Stephen King is your godfather!" Carter exclaimed excitedly, staring at Paige.

"Paige," Elly said in a serious tone, glaring at the phone in Paige's hand. "Can't you ignore it this one time. We're enjoying a nice dinner together."

"It's work so no, I can't, and our food hasn't even arrived yet." Paige pushed away from the table. "If you'll excuse me, I need to take this."

I watched her leave the table, and I felt as frustrated as she did. The people around this table knew nothing about her, yet she called them her friends. They had no idea that some Friday nights we'd spent just hanging out with Cal and Rachel Abram, watching movies and eating popcorn, like they were two of our friends instead of her parents. They had no idea that the master of horror was her godparent and also one of her dad's friends. They knew nothing about me or our past relationship. Why she'd want to keep them in the dark about everything pissed me off, especially when they made it perfectly clear that she knew plenty about the rest of them.

"I'm sorry," Elly said, grabbing my attention. "We probably shouldn't have interrogated you like that."

I shook my head and smiled at her. "Don't worry about it. I don't mind. Paige is a topic I enjoy discussing."

"What name does her dad write under?" Carter asked, typing away on his phone. "I'm trying to look him up on Goodreads. It's Cal Abram, right?"

"That's her dad's name, but he writes under C.R. Abram."

Carter deadpanned as he dropped his phone on the table. "Seriously? I've been a fan of his work for years! I read a lot of it during college, and I even have my students read his books for our contemporary horror lesson."

"Can you tell he's an English professor?" Bayler asked sarcastically, rolling her eyes at her brother. "Hey fan-boy, calm it down over there."

I laughed. "I'm honestly surprised you guys didn't know that already."

"Paige is pretty private about her life," Tessa said with a shrug. "That's just how we've always known her to be, so you shouldn't be surprised."

Well, I still am because that's not how she used to be.

I stood from my seat, eager to speak to Paige alone. "If you'll excuse me, I'm going to go check on her."

I headed in the direction of the restrooms and found her talking on her phone. She was pacing back and forth, with a serious look on her face as she listened to the person on the other end. As I got closer, I listened in and silently praised the tight jeans that seemed to be painted on her magnificent set of legs.

She looked more like the Paige Abram I used to know in her jeans, silk blouse and boots than the Paige Abram at the office in her designer suits and heels.

"Look, I know you want to know more about her upcoming line, but I'm her publicist and I don't even know. If I had an answer for you, I'd give it to you, but for now, all I can tell you is that she is currently focused on her family." She sighed. "No comment. Good-bye."

She ended the conversation and slipped her phone into the back pocket of her jeans.

"What was so important that you needed to interrupt dinner?" I asked.

She spun around and narrowed her eyes at me. "That was a reporter wondering about Harper's next clothing line. When it was going to be out and what they could expect from it. She just had a baby last October, and they're already rumoring her to be pregnant again. If it was a call regarding anyone else, I probably would've let it go, but if it's about my friends and their privacy, I take it and I shut it down."

She started to walk past me, but I grabbed her bicep, stopping her, and then murmured into her ear. "You and I need to talk in private. Now."

"Fine," she said, turning back toward the bathrooms. She led us into the third door, the stall specifically for families, and locked the door behind us. "What do you want? I swear, I will give you anything to stop talking about me to my friends. Just name it."

"What the hell is going on with you? How do your friends not know anything about you?" I snapped, waving my arms in frustration. "I shouldn't have to tell your friends who you are, or who you used to be because you're clearly not the girl I used to know. She used to tell everyone about her dad's books and promote the hell out of him. Your friends don't even know who he is, and they're fans of his! You used to be best friends with your parents, and your friends barely know their names." Kneading a hand over the back of my neck, I stopped and put my hands on my hips as I stared back at her, looking for any sign of emotion from her. With her lips pursed together, she gave me nothing back but a blank stare.

I wanted her to be just as pissed off as I felt, but at the same time, I wanted to kiss her—I wanted to remind her of who we used to be together. I wanted a reaction from her. Moving closer, I grabbed her chin and tilted her head up so she had to look me in the eyes. "How could they not know about me, Paige? How could you not tell them about me, about us? Did I not mean anything to you? Because you meant everything to me. I didn't go off to college and forget about you. All of my college buddies know who you are. They saw pictures of you, of us together, and they heard all about our time together. Hell, I got heat most of the time because I couldn't stop talking about you." Slowly, I slid my fingers up across her cheek, through her soft hair and then held the back of her neck and asked, "Tell me . . . how could your friends not know about us?"

Finally, her eyes glossed over with unshed tears. "Did it ever occur to you that you meant so much to me that I couldn't talk about you? You were the love of my life, Drake, but one of the greatest losses I've ever experienced. They didn't know because it hurt to think about you, to talk about you, to look at pictures of you, of us together. They didn't know about who I was then because so much of me was you. So, it's not that I didn't want them to know about you. College was my chance for a clean slate. I wasn't Drake Wilkins' girlfriend anymore. I was just Paige Abram, and that's who they got to know. The girl I was without you."

"Paige . . ." I leaned my forehead against hers and sighed, feeling as if she had a chokehold on my heart. "There's so much more I want to know. If it was so hard for you, why did you stop talking to me? And what's the deal with your parents?"

"I know," she insisted, clutching on to my sweater. "And I'll tell you. I'll do whatever you want. You want to go out on a date; I'll go. You want to hang out at one of our places; let's do it. But I do not want to have that conversation in a restaurant bathroom or at a table with all my friends. I just can't sit through listening to you tell them any more about me. They don't need to know that I only became a cheerleader so that I wouldn't miss any of your football games. Do you understand what I'm saying? Everything about me then was about you, all that I was centered around you."

That was the exact reason I broke up with her, so I don't know why it hurt to know that I was right; she needed to find herself without me. She did exactly what I asked her to do, but I never expected to be completely cut out of her life because of it. I pulled away from her, nodding. "I get it. Would you prefer it if I just left?"

She smiled weakly, blinking away the emotion from her eyes, and then shook her head. "You can't leave. They like you."

"Only because I know you," I said smartly.

She cupped the side of my face in her hand and sighed. "You're the only person who truly does."

Then she turned around and headed for the door, but before she got too far, I called out, "Friday."

"What?" she asked, glancing back at me over her shoulder. "Friday?"

"You're coming over to my place next Friday for dinner, and we're talking."

"Is that so?" she asked, perking a brow.

"You said whatever I wanted."

"Okay."

We exited the bathroom together and headed back to our table. As we walked, I asked her the other question that was still bothering me. "Why did you tell them our breakup was mutual?"

"Because it was mutual," she answered honestly. "I let you go just as much as you let me go."

Worst decision I ever made, I thought, taking my seat again.

The waitress brought all of our food out and began placing everyone's meals in front of them, and then we all started to dig in.

"Is everything okay with work?" Elly asked, eyeing the two of us.

"Yeah," Paige said, nodding. "I just received another call about Harper's next project."

Harper groaned from the other end of the table. "I'm so sorry, Paige. I know people want to know what I'm working on, but I'm just not ready to put it out there."

"Don't apologize. You have every right to keep it to yourself," Paige insisted, taking a drink of her water. "But you should also know that there is a rumor that you and Maverick are expecting again."

"What!" she shrieked. "We just had Seghen a few months ago."

"Aren't you supposed to wait a few months after giving birth to have sex again?" Tessa asked.

"Unfortunately, yes," Maverick muttered.

"Ah," Cash teased, patting him on the shoulder. "Tired of your hand, buddy?"

"He doesn't need his hand when he has my mouth," Harper quipped, glaring back at Cash.

Maverick laughed, gave her a hard kiss on the lips, and then smiled. "You heard the woman."

"Okay, okay," Carter said, hushing everyone's laughter. "Enough about my sister's sex life."

"Wait, so how did the rumor get started?" Harper asked.

Paige set her fork down and sighed. "Supposedly, someone overheard you in a store a few weeks ago saying something about expecting."

Harper looked down at her sister. "That had to be the day we went out."

Bayler giggled into her glass. "We were talking about Elly and Carter expecting!"

"I know," Harper said, shaking her head. "Oh well. I guess there are worse rumors that could be going around."

Forks and knives chimed against plates as we all continued devouring our meals. I'd ordered the smoked chicken, and so far, I was enjoying its mixture of garlic and asparagus. There wasn't much I wouldn't eat. Beside me, Paige worked on her Caesar salad, and it gave me a sense of relief, knowing she still preferred salads over most dishes. I spent the remainder of my dinner appreciating the company around the table. With Elly eating for two, she took a bite of Carter's dinner every chance he gave her. Fletcher and Bayler didn't share food, but Maverick and Harper enjoyed eating off of one another's plates. As for Justin and Tessa, they didn't share, but I presumed it was because he ordered the same thing whenever he came here.

Back when we dated, Paige and I used to share our meals, while Barrett and Zoey argued over how long it took her to make a decision on what she wanted. Now, Barrett and Zoey were just happy if they made it through a dinner without the kids making a mess. I sat next to Paige wishing we could be like the couples around the table with us.

Times have certainly changed.

"So, Drake," Cash started. "Do you play basketball?"

Paige snickered into a napkin and shook her head.

"Hey," I said, pointing my fork at her. "I can play basketball. I'm just much better at football."

The group laughed, and then Cash continued, "We usually play some pickup games after work or on the weekends at the gym, if you're interested. It wouldn't hurt us to have an extra guy, now that Justin's out."

"I'm not out," Justin stated.

"You're not supposed to be playing," Maverick said. "Physical therapy hasn't released you yet."

"What happened?" I asked, immediately gaining the attention of the whole table. "If you don't mind me asking."

The somber looks on everyone's faces made me regret asking the question, but Paige eventually spoke up. "Justin took a gunshot to the shoulder last month during the shooting at NYU."

"I'm so sorry, man," I said, looking down the table at him.

He nodded as Tessa wrapped her fingers through his. "Thanks, but it could have been a lot worse. I'm just happy to still be here."

"And he's ready to get back to doing everything he used to do," Tessa added encouragingly. "Like playing ball."

I laughed. "Well, if you guys need an extra, I don't mind playing. But I am warning you, I'm not that great."

"That's okay," Fletcher commented, pointing at Carter. "He's not too great either."

"Come on, guys," Carter called out, shaking his head. "I'm not that bad."

"Your pregnant wife is better than you," Maverick remarked.

"Her dad is an NBA legend, she should be better than me!" Carter exclaimed. Then he looked over at Elly and shrugged. "I don't know why I keep having to defend myself on this matter. I suck at basketball. The end."

The table laughed at his surrender, and I leaned over to Paige and quietly asked, "So, who's her dad?"

"Keith Evans."

"Holy shit," I muttered, shaking my head.

"Anyway, we usually all work out at Maverick's gym," Cash explained. "And then pick up a few games against other members who are around, or we'll just play some two-on-three. Are you a member of Jones Jym?"

"Yeah, I actually just joined last week." I looked over at Maverick and commended him on his gym. "Your facility is sick, man. I've worked out in some nice gyms during my football days, but yours is probably the biggest, well-designed place I've been in."

"Thanks," Maverick said proudly. "It's been a long time coming, but we're all pretty proud of it. I wouldn't have been able to do it without the support of these guys. Where'd you play football?"

"USC," I answered, gaining a round of impressed nods from the guys.

Maverick leaned his elbows on the table and snapped his fingers at me. "I knew you looked familiar! I still remember that bowl game where you threw the winning touchdown but got hit so hard that—"

"Mav," Paige said curtly, glaring at him.

"It's okay," I stated, touching her leg underneath the table. Her eyes flickered with sympathy, and I knew right then that she'd watched the game that ended my football career—the dream that both she and I had worked so hard for me to chase. Turning my attention back to Maverick, I smiled regretfully. "I did get hit pretty hard after the throw."

"You didn't move on the field," he said, shaking his head. "Your helmet came off, and they had to take you out on a stretcher."

"Our son is never playing football," Elly whispered loudly to Carter.

"Yes, he is," Carter argued.

"What happened after they took you off the field?" Tessa asked curiously.

With their eyes trained on me, I sat back in my seat and shrugged. "I don't really know. I remember not being able to move after the hit, and then after that, I woke up in a hospital room where I was told I'd suffered from a severe concussion. They couldn't find any damage to any brain tissue, but several doctors warned me that the risk of suffering from another major hit would likely cause permanent brain damage. I'd never been hit like that during high school ball or even the first few years of college, but all it took was one hard hit to end it. I made the decision to walk away from football while I still could."

"Nope," Elly whispered, shaking her head at Carter. "He's not playing football."

I laughed lightly. "It's really not as scary as everyone makes it out to be. As long as you teach him to take care of himself, he'll be fine. My family and friends knew I was done the minute they saw me get hit. My coaches and teammates saw it, too. I wasn't that stubborn kid who bottled up every injury just to keep on playing. That's the difference between football players. Some push themselves or get pushed to keep on going, while others have a great support system that understands them. We all had dreams of me going pro, but life is more important than some high-paying job."

"Well said," Maverick said, lifting his glass to me. "I'm sorry it ended that way though. You had one hell of an arm."

"Thanks."

As our waitress stopped by to remove our dirty plates and leave our checks, a knot twisted in my stomach as it dawned on me that the evening was concluding. I wasn't ready to leave. I was having a good time hanging out with Paige and her friends, despite my initial anger over the fact that they didn't really know her. I understood why she hadn't told them, but I also wished they could've known her back then. She used to be so much more carefree than the woman she was now, but life had a funny way of hardening all of us when we least expected it. I used to be the kid with the golden arm, but now I could barely sit through watching an entire game on TV.

We paid for our meals and then gathered outside of the restaurant in our coats and gloves. "Thanks for inviting me to join you guys for dinner. It was nice meeting all of you."

"Same to you," Fletcher said, shaking my hand.

"Don't forget about basketball," Cash stated.

The rest of them said their good-byes and left in a couple of cabs while Paige hung back with me. We were finally alone in front of the restaurant, and even though it was freezing, I couldn't imagine a better place to be than out in the cold with her. Bundled up in her black coat and matching gloves, she pulled her hood up over her beautiful blond hair as the snow started to fall again.

"You have a great group of friends," I stated, stuffing my hands into my coat pockets.

"Thanks. They are pretty great," she agreed, rubbing her hands together. "Nosy, but loyal as hell."

Taking a deep breath, I studied the pinkish tone of her pale skin and the way she trembled from the cold, bouncing on the balls of her feet, just like she used to whenever she was cold. "It was good to see you tonight, too. I'm more excited about next Friday though. Are you still a fan of clam chowder?"

The smile on her face widened. "Why? Do you have some of Lilian Wilkins' famous soup?"

I laughed, shaking my head. "No, but she might've taught me how to make it."

"Shut. Up!" she exclaimed, smacking my arm. "*You* know how to make clam chowder as good as your mom's?"

"You say that like you don't believe me."

"Maybe I don't."

Stepping closer to her, I leaned in and teased her. "I guess you'll find out next Friday."

"Drake Wilkins," she cursed, poking me in the chest. "You better not be joking! It's impossible to find clam chowder like your mom's here in the city. I haven't had the homemade kind in years!"

Holding my hands out to my side, I conceded, "When have I ever joked about clam chowder?"

"True." She let go of me and stepped back. "Some things haven't changed, I guess."

"No," I said, admiring the rosy color of her cheeks and the excitement shimmering in her eyes. "And that's a good thing." It was nice to see her get so riled up about one of her favorite meals—a welcome reminder that I wasn't just hung up on someone from the past; my girl was still in there somewhere.

I saw a cab coming our way, so I hailed it for her. Once it came to a stop at the curb, I opened the door for her. "I'll see you at work tomorrow."

"See you." She took a seat, and I closed the door behind her. But before the cab sped off, she rolled down her window. "Hey, D-Dub?"

My smile spread at the sound of my nickname falling from her lips. "Yeah?"

"Good night."

"'Night, P.J."

Chapter Five

Friday night came quicker than I expected. As in, I was pacing in front of his apartment door, trying to figure a way out of doing this tonight. It was too soon. Way too soon. He'd just come back into my life a week ago. I wasn't ready to have *the talk* with him. He had one of the greatest hearts I'd ever had the opportunity to know, and I was certain telling him about our son would shatter it.

It would break him, and he'd hate me forever.

The anxiety nearly crippled me, but the trepidation of spending an evening alone with him almost overshadowed it. My mind didn't want to go through with tonight—it begged anyone to call with an emergency to get me out of this—but my heart knew I'd survive; that I'd get through it because I'd been through worse.

Reaching inside my jacket, I placed my hand over the tattoo etched into the left side of my ribcage—the one I got years ago in his memory. I had to do this for him. He deserved for his dad to know him.

"You can do this. The plan may have been to tell him years ago, but you have a new plan now, to tell him tonight. So, deep breaths, Paige," I muttered softly to myself as I stepped up to Drake's door and knocked. "You can do this."

Within seconds, the door opened up, and Drake greeted me looking better than ever, wearing a nice pair of dark jeans and a gray flannel button-up over a simple white tee, with a kitchen towel thrown over his right shoulder. "Hey, come on in."

"Thanks," I said, walking over the threshold into his gorgeous apartment. I didn't expect anything less from a Wilkins. Unlike most places in New York, Drake's place was spread out and spacious, with floor-to-ceiling windows and an open concept, making it feel less like an apartment and more like a home. It was the type of place I pictured him living in, not too small or crowded, but not overly outrageous like he could afford. His furnishings were clean and perfectly placed, just like Lilian Wilkins taught her children to treat a home. "Your place is really nice."

"Lennox helped me find it," he said, smiling. He reached for my coat, so I let him help me out of it. "You look beautiful tonight."

The blush came before I could stop it, and I chastised myself for it. I'd paired my favorite skinny jeans with my most comfortable brown boots and a fitted pink sweater that made me feel confident, so I knew I looked good. But I couldn't start letting him charm me into blushing and feeling awestruck over every little thing he said or did. If I was going to get through tonight, I couldn't let him get to me. "It smells good in here."

He chuckled as he led us into the kitchen, where I noticed a pot already sitting on the stove. "The chowder is ready whenever you are."

"You know you're up against some serious competition, right?" I teased, leaning against the countertop. "Your mom's chowder has won awards."

"I know, I know," he laughed, opening up the fridge. "What would you like to drink?"

"I'll just take some water, please." Using the ladle, I scooped up a cup, took a whiff of it, and nearly had an orgasm—that's how much I loved homemade clam chowder. My stomach growled, so I grabbed myself a plate and a spoon, and that's when I noticed the bread. He'd even made the bread bowls for the chowder to go in, knowing that using a regular ceramic bowl was just plain wrong. "You even made bread bowls?"

"Impressive, right?" he stated proudly as he set the dining table.

"Very." Drake never cooked when we dated, but we were just teenagers then. It was easier and more intimate to go out to a restaurant than to cook dinner for each other at home. "Lilian would be proud."

"She is," he said, grabbing a plate and a bread bowl. "I had to call and ask her a question when I was working on the bread."

"Ah, I see," I said, nodding. I ladled two full cups of chowder into my bread bowl so that it was overflowing and dipped the bread top into it.

"I already set the toppings and our drinks on the table."

"Great." I headed over to the small dining table he had off of the kitchen and sat down. He'd set the table with all of my favorite toppings: bacon bits, croutons, and oyster crackers. He had a glass of water for each of us, and a candle lit in the middle of the round table. As he walked over to join me, I watched that same confident swagger he had carried as a teen run through his body. Now it had a ruggedness to it that made me squeeze my thighs together. He wasn't the star athlete anymore, but rather the manly guy in the kitchen who knew how to impress a woman by cooking her favorite meal.

And I liked it.

A lot.

"What?" he asked with a playful shrug. "It's just food, Paige."

"If I have an orgasm during my first bite, I'm blaming you."

"Please, do." He smiled as he lifted his water glass. "To you, Paige Abram."

"To me?" I said in disbelief, raising my glass to his. "Why me?"

"May you orgasm with every bite of your homemade clam chowder," he teased, tapping his glass against mine. "It's been far too long since I've seen you orgasm."

With my face flushed from laughing, I couldn't help it anymore. He'd been knocking on my heart's door ever since he came back into my life, and I couldn't keep him standing outside in the cold any longer. I never could control the way he made me feel; I wasn't sure why I thought time would change that.

"Well, go ahead," he encouraged, resting his elbows on the table in anticipation. "Try it. Let me know what you think."

"Okay," I said eagerly as I sprinkled a handful of toppings over the creamy goodness. I scooped up a spoonful and brought it up to my lips where I finally took my first bite.

"Oh. My. God," I moaned, wiggling in my seat in celebration as I closed my eyes and my taste buds savored all the delicious flavors coming together. Opening my eyes, I found him watching me, so I smiled back and took another bite. "It's absolutely perfect, Drake."

"I'm glad you approve," he said, picking up his spoon. "I told you I could cook."

"You never used to cook," I quipped with a perk of my brow. "Look at us, talking with our mouths full at the dinner table. Lilian would have our asses."

He laughed out loud and nearly spit out a cracker. "You're right. She would."

I took a sip of my water and crossed my legs under the table. "So, did you tell her you were cooking for me tonight?"

He wiped his mouth with his napkin and nodded. "Yeah, she asked what the occasion was, so now she thinks this is some sort of date."

I tore off a piece of bread and dunked it into my chowder, ignoring the word *date* altogether. I wasn't sure what classified an evening as a date or not. I hadn't been on a date in years.

"I tried telling her it wasn't," he added with another shrug. "But you know how moms are. I'm pretty sure she's spending her evening going through all the old pictures she still has of us together."

I laughed lightly. "If I would've told my mom, she'd be doing the same."

"Speaking of parents," he said, pointing at me with his spoon. "Tell me what happened with yours. Why aren't you close with them anymore?"

Because I made them keep a secret from you and it backfired, I thought, swallowing another bite along with the truth. "We just grew apart after I went off to college. I was on my own then, busy with school, and making new friends, and they were off starting the third part of their life together, where they didn't have to constantly worry about me."

"But they still did," he stated surely, taking a swig of his water. "I don't think parents ever stop worrying about their kids, even when they're adults."

"Yeah," I said with a nod. "But you know what I mean, they just weren't as involved as they were in high school."

He nodded and dumped a few more croutons into his soup. "Well, that's too bad. I always enjoyed hanging out with your parents."

"They've always loved you," I said, smiling around my spoon.

"So, I'm still their favorite?" he asked, proudly amused. "Good to know."

"You didn't have any competition," I answered, rolling my eyes.

"Are you telling me you never brought home any other guys?" he asked, popping a piece of bread into his mouth. "Are we moving on to *that* subject now?"

I laughed. "Yeah, I guess we are. How many girls did you bring home?"

"Oh, no, you first," he said, shaking his finger at me. "Not one?"

I'd only brought one boy home other than Drake and it'd been our son. I shook my head. "Nope."

He sat back in his chair in shock and wiped his mouth again. "You can't be serious. There had to be at least one."

"I didn't date in college."

His brows furrowed slightly. "So, are you saying you just hooked up with guys instead?"

"God, no," I said in appalled tone. "You know I would never do that."

He leaned his elbows on the table again and studied me closely, staring into my eyes and eventually lingering on my mouth. "Please don't lie to me."

I gulped down the knot in my throat, regretful of the lie I'd already told. "Why would I lie about that?"

"Because you don't want to upset me?"

"Why would that upset you?" I asked, leaning into him. I brushed my thumb along the stubble of his jaw and smiled.

"I'm here with you, Drake, eating your delicious meal. No guy has ever cooked for me."

He dropped his head and stared down into his bowl. "I've brought a couple of girls home to meet my family."

"I know," I said respectfully.

"What do you mean, you know?" he asked skeptically.

I spooned the last of my soup into my mouth and then quickly swallowed. "You brought a date to Barrett and Zoey's wedding."

"You were there?" he asked, clearly shocked. "They told me they didn't invite you."

Setting my spoon to the side, I pressed my napkin to my lips and then placed it back in my lap. "Maybe they didn't want you to know. You were obviously with someone else at the time, so maybe they didn't want the knowledge of me possibly attending to bother you."

"It wouldn't have bothered me," he admitted harshly. "It bothers me that they lied to me about it."

I nodded silently, broke off another piece of bread and stuffed it in my mouth.

"So, you came to their wedding?"

"Of course," I said, remembering how gorgeous Zoey looked in her mermaid wedding dress. "Barrett couldn't take his eyes off of her that day. I wasn't able to stay for the whole thing because I had an incident with a client come up and I had to leave, but I was there long enough for the ceremony. It was really beautiful."

"Yeah, it was," he said nostalgically. "I wish I would've known you were there."

"Drake, you were with another woman," I stated, shaking my head. "It's probably best that you didn't. I don't know if it was serious or not, but—"

"I've never been serious with anyone but you."

"Okay, but you looked happy that day, too," I confessed, because he had. With the tall, thin blonde on his arm, he'd looked really happy. "Don't be upset with Zoey and Barrett if they didn't want to screw that up for you."

"I guess you're right," he said, pushing his plate away. "I just always imagined us celebrating their wedding together. Have you seen pictures of their kids?"

Wordlessly, I shook my head. He grabbed my hand and led me over to the living room, decorated with framed photographs of his family and friends.

He grabbed a picture off of his end table and handed it to me. The three little girls in the picture were all dressed in matching purple dresses. "Can you believe it? Barrett has three little girls! This is them last Easter."

I smiled as I sat down on the nearby couch and examined the young faces smiling back at me. "They are so beautiful. The older two look so much like Zoey, it's crazy."

"I know," he said, excitement evident in his tone as he took a seat next to me. "The oldest is Ryce, and then there's Quinn, and the youngest is Ziggy. Zigs takes after Barrett the most. She's such a little spitfire."

Taking in Ziggy's appearance, I laughed. She had her arms crossed over her chest, refusing to smile, just like Barrett used to do whenever Zoey tried to get him to take a picture with her. "You're right. She gets her attitude from her daddy."

"She calls me Uncle Quack even though she can say Drake," he added, rolling his eyes. "Barrett taught her that crap."

I handed the picture back over to him, and he continued. "I still remember the day Ryce was born. Barrett was flipping out because they were going to have to do a C-section on Zoey, when they were hoping to have her naturally. Everything was fine, but I'd never seen him freak out like that before. You know him. He never really lets anything get to him, but the day Ryce came into the world, he was an absolute mess until they put that little girl in his arms and he knew Zoey was doing well."

My chest ached as I listened to him talk about the little girls he called nieces, telling me their birth stories and all about their personalities, when he didn't even know his own son's birth story or personality. Brushing a piece of hair behind my ear, the ache around my heart pounded harder. He was so involved in the girls' lives and had so many pictures of them around his apartment, when he had none of his son. The pure joy of being their uncle radiated from him as he spoke, and it nearly gutted me. I always knew he'd be great with children. Drake had a charm to his personality that drew people to him, so I wasn't surprised that he had a living room full of memories with Zoey and Barrett and their adorable family. By the time he stopped talking though, my stomach was tight with nerves, remembering our boy. He would have been a few years older than Ryce now. Zoey and I had always talked about having kids together, how we hoped they'd grow up and become friends like we did. It hurt knowing that'd never happen now.

"What's wrong?" Drake asked as I sighed audibly.

"Nothing," I lied, shaking my head. I managed to keep the tears at bay, but I felt like my heart was a second away from shattering. How was I supposed to tell him the truth? I'd kept something precious from him, and hearing him speak so fondly of Barrett's girls reiterated how wrong I'd been to do what I did.

"Paige," he said soothingly, scooting closer to me. He cupped my cheek and then ran his hand through my short hair before resting his arm on the back of the couch. "Why'd you stop talking to Zoey and Barrett? They were your friends, too, you know."

Just tell him.

"I thought it would be easier if they didn't have to pick a side," I lied, leaning back into the cushions. "I know our breakup was hard on them, especially since the four of us did everything together. Then the three of you went off to college and I didn't, so it just felt like the right thing to do was to step away and let you have them."

"But maybe they needed you," he replied in a comforting tone. "Did you know they almost broke up a few times after we did? I mean, they fought all the time when they were together, but after we broke up, it seemed like they fought a lot more. I used to think it was because Zoey didn't have you anymore. You were her person back then, the one friend she could always lean on. And then you just disappeared on her . . . on all of us."

"I didn't know that," I replied softly as the guilt slithered through the knots in my belly. I didn't want Zoey and Barrett to tell Drake about my pregnancy, so I'd kept them in the dark about it, too. But when I lost our son, I shut down completely and pushed them away, instead of coming out with the truth like I should have. How was I supposed to tell Drake that though? Words could not describe how much our boy meant to me, or the impact of his loss.

"They're happy now," he continued, sporting a weak smile. "But I still think Zoey misses you."

"Why do you say that?" I asked curiously.

"Because she's never really found a new best friend," he answered. "You have all these new friends here in the city, but back home, Zoey doesn't have anyone she's close with. She has her little girls, her hair salon, and Barrett. That's it."

"She shouldn't miss me," I mumbled, clutching my hands together in my lap. "I treated her like shit after we broke up."

"That's the thing though, you don't get to choose how people feel about you," Drake said, running a hand along my shoulder. "Just because you pushed her away a long time ago, doesn't mean she stopped caring about you. I know I didn't."

Tell him. You have to tell him. Now.

Swallowing back the tears, I turned to face him and nearly fell apart when I saw the sincerity in his eyes. He still loved me—it was evident in everything he did, from the meal he'd cook to the memories he'd never let go of, but especially in the way he spoke about me. Like I'd never done anything wrong in his eyes, even though I had. I'd really fucked up so much that what I was about to tell him would ruin him. I'd take every ounce of candor he had and turn it into hate, and I'd deserve it. So, I reached out and touched his face one more time, though I'd never forget it. How could I, when he'd passed on all the same beautiful features to our little boy. Drake was my favorite piece of art, admirable because he represented the mostly joyful time in my life and the absolute hardest.

"Do you remember the day we broke up?" I asked in a timid voice.

His brows furrowed as he stared back at me solemnly and took my hand in his. "Yeah, I do."

He started tracing the lines of my palms with his finger, and I sighed, feeling more unease as a chill ran down my spine. "I came over to your house that day to tell you some—"

"Hold that thought," he interjected, leaning forward. He pulled his vibrating phone out of his back pocket and answered. "Owen, what's up?"

Excusing himself from the couch, he carried the conversation into the dining room, where he began cleaning up the remains of our dinner, leaving me to sit alone with the guilt that had been tormenting me for years. Placing my head in my shaking hands, I shuddered. "I can't do this."

Standing from the couch, I took a deep breath and exhaled as I stretched my arms and neck, trying my best to work the nerves out of my body.

But it didn't work, so I began to pace.

I walked over to his mantle and admired the memories it held. There was a football signed by all of his USC teammates, dated the year they won the bowl game. Photos of family and friends surrounded the ball, but one specific picture caught my eye. It was a picture of us. My arm was around his waist, his around my shoulder, but instead of smiling for the camera, we were staring at one another, like the camera wasn't even there. Right after it had been taken, Drake had kissed the hell out of me, unable to hold back any longer, literally taking my breath away and sweeping me off my feet as he carried me back to his truck. It'd been the summer before his senior year, and God, how I missed that summer. I missed the crazy, unadulterated passion that he brought out in me, and the adventures he'd taken me on that eventually led to us ending up in the back of his truck naked under the stars. I hadn't been kissed like that in years. Hell, I hadn't been touched by another human being in years, too afraid of the consequences—consequences that I understood now.

In no way could I ever think of our son as a mistake, but he wasn't planned either. I was just a kid when I had him, but I grew up quickly after I lost him. Sex wasn't something I could take lightly anymore. It wasn't something I could do for fun. It wasn't a way to relieve stress or scratch an itch. It meant sharing a piece of myself with somebody I loved. It was an act that could result in creating another life—a life that could be taken at any moment without consent.

And I wasn't willing to risk that again.

At least not yet.

Glancing over my shoulder, I found him watching me, appearing content as he meandered around his kitchen. He smiled at me as he spoke, eliciting a smile back from me in return. A single moment like that with him, and I was taken back to when we were young—when a shared smile emulated so much love and affection, words weren't necessary.

I wanted more than just moments with him again.

"I'm sorry," he said, slipping his phone back into his pocket. "Owen's having a little trouble with a client not abiding by his contract."

"It's okay," I said in a throaty voice.

He saw the picture in my hands and took it from me. "This picture of us is one of my favorites. Do you remember that summer?"

"I don't think I could ever forget it," I replied honestly, laughing lightly. "I am a little surprised to see myself on your mantle, though."

He placed the picture back in its spot and then shot me a smile. "You're part of my story, whether you like it or not. I'm going to have pictures of you lying around. Do you not have any of me anymore?"

Following him back to the couch, I sat down and turned toward him. "I do."

"But they're probably in some sacred box in your closet, right?" he teased.

God, if he only knew about that trunk.

"Yeah," I said solemnly with a nod. "Something like that."

"What did I do wrong?" he asked, his eyes skimming over every inch of my face, trying to find answers.

Shaking my head, I reached for his hand. "It was nothing you did."

He exhaled a frustrated sigh and bowed his head. "Did you meet someone else, then?"

I wasn't sure how to answer him, because I had met another guy, but not in the way he was asking. Our son had stolen my heart faster than Drake had because he was part of both of us—the result of our love. But if I didn't have the tits to tell Drake about his son yet, I'd tell him about the other guy in my life.

He stared at me, patiently awaiting an answer, even though I knew it was killing him to ask. "You could have told me you'd met someone instead of pushing me away and ignoring me. You could have told me you were done."

But I wasn't done, I thought. *Not even close.*

"I did meet someone else," I said truthfully, with a weak smile.

His jaw clenched, as if it pained him to hear my answer. "Did you love him?"

"Yes." I threaded my fingers through his and held on to him tightly. "But not the same way I loved you. I was still very much in love with you even when I was with him, and he knew it."

Puzzled, he furrowed his brows in surprise. "He did?"

"I told him everything about you and showed him pictures of us. He knew all about our relationship and every memory I still have of it. He was never jealous of you, and that's one of the reasons I loved him." I peered down at our joined hands and continued. "But then I lost him, and it was like I went numb after that. Then I almost lost you too during that football game. When you didn't move, I thought I had. I heard reports about possible brain damage and thought, 'What if he's not the Drake I used to know anymore? What if he doesn't remember me?'"

"Even if it had affected my mind," he brought my hand up to his mouth and kissed the top of it, "I like to believe one touch from you would have easily brought back all my memories . . . because it does, even now."

I sighed, blinking back tears. "I think I've been numb ever since, until a few weeks ago when I saw you again in that conference room. I'd thrown everything that reminded me of you into a box, and I hadn't opened it until last week. Not because I didn't want to, but because I couldn't. I have never been done with you, Drake."

"Come here," he whispered, pulling me into him. He wrapped his arms around me, and pressed his lips against my temple. "I used to get so drunk that I'd spend the night telling stories about you. I'd hook up with faceless girls and imagine they were you, and then I'd hate myself afterward. I'd call and you wouldn't answer. I'd email and get no response. When I called and got the message that your number was no longer in service, it nearly killed me. Then I got hurt during that game, and my first thought wasn't, 'Will I ever play ball again?' It was, 'Where's Paige?' That was when I stopped trying to contact you. I finished my schooling, moved back to Bedford and helped Lennox with her music and Barrett with his construction business for a while before finding a job here in the city."

Pulling back, he cradled the back of my neck and dried my cheeks with his thumbs. His warm eyes studied my face as a smile graced his. "We went from planning our future together to not being together at all, and I've hated every second of it."

"Me too."

"I still need you just as much as I needed you then. Now, here you are, and all I can think about is kissing you."

I licked my lips and then whispered warily. "So, kiss me."

His smile grew and then he angled my head to the right slightly. I could feel my body tremble as his mouth hovered over mine and the spice of his cologne surrounded us. "Close your eyes."

My eyelids fluttered shut, eagerly obeying his command, and then I sucked in a deep breath.

"Relax," he said, massaging the back of my neck with his talented hands. "It's just me. You know me."

I nodded, anxiously waiting in the dark. "I know."

His soft lips pressed into the curve of my neck and sucked hard, sending an explosion of sensations trailing down my skin, igniting goosebumps in its wake. He continued his journey north, his nose leading the way, applying a bunch of nibbles to my jawline that caused a moan to fall from my lips.

"There's my girl," he said proudly, his voice deep with need.

Latching on to his shoulders, I felt him draw me into his lap, my knees on either side of his hips. Our lips reunited, quickly resurrecting a craving, one of giddiness and sensual tension that came along with a need I hadn't experienced in years. Like the deprived beings we were, we sucked and bit, teased and invited, and silently begged the other to never, ever stop kissing. Drake's tongue tangled around mine, eliciting another desperate whimper as it reminded me just how well he remembered me. The array of sensations swimming inside of me needed him closer. Much, much closer. Like no-clothes-between-us closer. Digging my nails into his skin, my legs trembled as I rocked my hips against his rigid length nestled between my legs. I felt like I'd been doused in arousal and ignited by the only match that could spark this kind of pleasure through my body. And that spark's name was Drake.

"Holy shit," he muttered against my mouth, breathing heavily.

"Right?" I sighed, opening my eyes to take in the destruction. His eyes and flesh mirrored mine, dancing with excitement and flushed with rebirth. The sound of us both trying to catch our breaths filled the living room. His lips were wet and mine felt equally swollen, but the pound of need throbbing at the apex of my thighs reminded me that the storm hadn't passed yet.

Skimming his hands down my sides, they settled on my waist as he shot me a cocky grin. "Are we done talking?"

"Yes," I answered, ignoring the voice inside my head telling me to stop. I was certain that this wasn't a good idea, but no amount of self-control could stop us now.

He kissed me harder than before, as if he was imprinting his lips onto mine. They were already his though, they always had been. He tasted like my favorite home-cooked meal, long-awaited but always satisfying. My greedy hands trailed the length of his chiseled chest, down to the abs that I could still feel through his t-shirt. God, how I'd missed this body and its lips, and the amazing feelings they elicited. Our kiss felt like it was resuscitating us, liberating us from the chokehold of our past as my lips collided with his and pleasure flourished from within. I wanted more of him—the only person who could make me feel so alive—and goddamn it felt good to feel this way again. To want somebody. To feel the incessant need throbbing between my thighs. To feel his heart kick-start with as much adrenaline as mine. It'd always been this way with us. We'd kiss and the world faded away, leaving only us and our desire for more. It was a blessing to know that we still had it—the passion, our spark—and I prayed we'd never lose it.

"I've missed you, P.J.," he said, running his hands up and down my back as he tugged on my ear lobe with his teeth. "I've missed you so damn much."

"Me too," I replied breathlessly, tossing my head back to give him better access. I snaked my fingers through his dark, soft strands and studied him through hooded lids, completely mesmerized by the intense, heated look in his eyes. "Who knew homemade clam chowder would lead to a make-out session?"

His laughed vibrated against my skin. "I did."

"Of course," I said softly as he sucked on the tender flesh of my neck.

He pulled away and kissed me chastely on the mouth. Then he relaxed into the back of the couch and brushed his thumbs along the bottom edge of my breasts, all the while never taking his eyes off my face. "You got even more beautiful with age. You know that, right?"

Leaning in, I cupped his cheeks and then kissed him slowly. "Thank you. So did you."

As he captured my lips again, I felt his hands dive underneath the material of my sweater and the camisole beneath it. Self-consciously, I pulled away quickly and took his hands in mine.

"Everything all right?" he asked, confusion lingering in his tone. "Did I push too far?"

"No," I reassured, shaking my head. "Well, maybe."

Make up your mind.

"Okay," he said understandingly, entwining his fingers with mine. "No under-the-clothes action tonight."

I nodded, ashamed of myself. His touch felt amazing, but I didn't want him to feel my stomach. I still had the stretch marks that no amount of working out and eating healthy would ever take away. Part of me loved them, because they reminded me that he was once with me. But the other part of me had a hard time looking at them because they emphasized that he was gone.

Drake probably wouldn't even notice them if I let him touch me, but I wasn't ready to take that chance.

"I'm sorry," I said, placing my head on his shoulder.

"Don't be," he replied, rubbing my back in a soothing manner. "If you're not ready, I'll respect that."

He didn't understand my apology, but I wasn't prepared to elaborate on why I was really apologizing. No woman should ever be ashamed or self-conscious of her stretch marks. She should wear them proudly because there are women out there who don't have any and really wish they did.

Somedays, I admired them, while other days, I couldn't look at myself in the mirror without crying.

What kind of mother does that make me?

Lifting my head, I smiled weakly at Drake and caressed the stubble along his jaw. "I should go."

"No," he pleaded, placing his hand over mine. "Please don't go. We don't have curfews anymore, or the risk of our parents walking in on us."

I laughed as I crawled off his lap and stood in front of him, but he never let go of my hand. So, I leaned back down, kissed him once more, and smiled appreciatively. "Thank you for making my favorite soup."

"When will I get to see you again?" he asked before pressing his lips to my knuckles and letting them go.

"On the weekends, my friends and I frequent one of Fletcher's bars called Judge's," I explained. "We'll be there tomorrow night."

Standing from the couch, he grabbed my coat and helped me into it. "Can I bring Barrett and Zoey? They could use a night away from the kids. Even if it is a night in the city."

"They can come." I playfully nudged him. "You still don't like the city?"

"Compared to the country? Hell no," he retorted, shaking his head. "Are you telling me you do? That if you had to pick a place, the city or the Massey Estate, you'd choose the city?"

"Hmm." I contemplated my options for a moment as I knotted the ties on my peacoat. The Massey Estate had been our spot growing up. I had dreams of buying the place and remodeling it to make it more modern. I hadn't been there in years, wasn't even sure what had happened to it, but it still held a special place in my heart that couldn't be compared to the city.

"I'm going to start questioning your morals if it's taking you this long to answer."

I laughed, pressing a kiss to his cheek. "You know I'll always choose the Massey Estate. That'll never change."

"Good." He wrapped his arms around my waist and smiled. "So, where do we go from here?"

Settling my arms over his shoulders, I sighed and ran my fingers through the black hairs on the back of his neck. His fair complexion created such a beautiful contrast against the inky shade of his hair and blue eyes, I couldn't imagine pushing him away again. I'd already tried to cut ties with him once and that hadn't worked. When he learned about our son, he probably wouldn't want anything to do with me anymore, which was understandable. So, for now, I'd take him as long as I could have him.

"Let me rephrase that," he said, searching my eyes for answers. "How do you feel about this? About me? I know work may be an issue, but I want to give us a shot again, Paige. I know it won't be like before, but I don't want it to be. We're older now. We can make our own decisions. And I choose you."

For now . . .

"What do you want?" he asked, his voice taking on a nervous tone.

Behind him, the picture of Barrett and Zoey Gallagher and their adorable family caught my eye. Then I thought of my other friends and how they were doing the same thing—sharing a life with someone they loved and starting families. I wasn't sure if I'd ever be strong enough to have another child, but the person I wanted to share my life with was inevitable.

"I want you," I confessed, smiling back at him. It was the most honest answer I'd given him all night.

"Really?" he asked incredulously, gripping me tighter.

Laughing, I nodded. "Yes, really."

He tugged me forward, cupping my face with both hands, but before he followed through with a kiss, he challenged, "Promise me, we'll do things right this time around."

"I promise," I lied, certain there wasn't an ounce of right in my behavior.

Chapter Six

Drake

"I can't believe you didn't tell me."

"We didn't think she'd actually come!" Barrett said, rolling his eyes. "Zoey insisted on inviting her. Like you said, Paige is the reason we're together."

I had said that. *Dammit.*

"How does anyone drive in this goddamn city!" Barrett shouted, flipping off a cab. It was Saturday evening, and Barrett and I were on our way to Judge's. Zoey had decided to stay home with the girls, according to Barrett. So, now I was riding shotgun, listening to him bitch about the traffic the entire way to the bar as I questioned him about his wedding.

"You're my best friend," I said, leaning against the door. "You're supposed to tell me when you invite my ex to your wedding. That's man code 101."

"If you had sex with me on a regular basis, I'd tell you anything." Barrett slammed on the brakes as the light ahead of us turned red. He looked over at me and laughed. "Sorry, man, but once you put a ring on it, the man codes don't exist anymore. The wedding was years ago, just let it go."

"I know," I said, nodding understandingly.

Once the light turned green, Barrett skidded into a nearby parking garage, fishtailed on some ice, and threw his truck into park. The bar was only a block away, so we climbed out and started heading that way. To say I was anxious was an understatement. I already craved a drink, just to settle the nerves tightening in my stomach. Last night, I had her in my arms, kissing her, but I wasn't sure how she'd act when we were around her friends.

"I thought you said last night went well," Barrett said, shooting me a worried glance. "Why are you all jittery?"

"It did." Or at least I thought it did. I treaded on the snow-covered sidewalk and ran a hand through my hair. "I think I'm nervous."

"Wow," he joked. "I don't think I've ever seen you nervous before, not even during football season."

I glared at him and stuffed my hands in my coat pocket. "I just don't want to screw this up with her."

He sighed, his breath visible in the cold. "Look, I know this isn't how you guys planned it. You were the ones who wanted to settle down and start a family someday, not Zoey and me. But this is the hand life dealt you two. You can't worry over the outcome. Just deal with it."

The further we walked, the more I thought about how different our lives had gone—or the hands we were dealt, in Barrett's words. He and Zoey had fought all the time during their high school relationship, breaking up every other weekend over the stupidest shit. While Paige and I had a more stable relationship, occasionally fighting but never to the point of breaking up. They never planned for anything, while we dreamed of our future and the things we wanted to do together. Maybe they were more realistic than we were, but none of that mattered now. The Gallaghers had dealt with all the drama that ensued between them and the unplanned pregnancy that eventually brought along Ryce. It didn't matter what came up, Barrett and Zoey handled it in their own way.

"Are you happy?" I asked him as we approached the bar.

He nodded, brows furrowed. "Yeah, I'm happy. Why wouldn't I be?"

"Life's thrown a lot at you and Zoey," I mentioned with a shrug. "You said you guys never wanted to settle down or start a family, and you've done both."

"We never talked about the future, no," he said, as we traipsed through the brisk air. "But that doesn't mean we couldn't handle it. I love my girls, more than anything in this world, so yes, I am very happy with my life. Was I terrified the day I married Zoey? Hell yes, I was. Were we ready to have kids? God, no, but no one is ever ready. Life is what you make it, man, and I've been busy making the most of mine. I wish you'd do the same."

He grabbed the door to the bar and held it open for me. "Now, let's get you in there and get you a drink."

I smiled, trying my best to ignore the pressure weighing on my chest. "Thanks, Bare."

"You have nothing to be nervous about, my friend," he reassured, patting me on the shoulder as I walked past him. "You know her better than anyone else."

Inhaling a deep, confident breath, I exhaled. "You're damn right I do."

Walking into Judge's was like walking into a bar back in Bedford. For a Saturday night, it wasn't overly packed. The bar was surrounded, but there were plenty of empty tables and booths for people. TVs were set up to watch various games. Pool tables and dartboards offered extra entertainment. It even had a stage and a dance floor. Scanning the area, I found Paige's friends near the bar, laughing at something Cash had said while he bartended. But what instantly grabbed my attention was the laugh coming from the gorgeous blonde in the tight black jeans and silky blue top that matched her eyes.

I watched her turn around at the sound of the door shutting behind me, and a smile spread across her face, relieving me of any nerves.

She set her glass on the table and then, in a pair of tall high-heeled boots that made her appear even sexier, she sauntered over to us. Her warm, floral scent invaded my senses, announcing her presence and relaxing me further.

"I'm glad you guys came," she said, giving me a quick peck on the cheek. She held her arms out to Barrett and waved him in for a hug. "Barrett Gallagher, come here."

He smiled as he wrapped his stocky arms around her small frame. "It's good to see you again, Paige."

She pulled away from him and then looked around impatiently. "Where's Zoey?"

"She decided to stay home with the girls," he said with a purse of his lips.

Settling my hand on the small of her back, I noticed her friends staring at us and then motioned to Barrett. "Paige, why don't you introduce Barrett to everyone while I grab us a couple of drinks?"

"Okay," she said, leading him off toward her friends.

I made my way over to the bar and nodded at Cash. "Hey, man."

"Hey!" he said, wiping down the countertop. "Who's your friend?"

"Barrett Gallagher. Paige and I went to school with him," I said, leaning against the bar.

"What are you guys drinking tonight?"

"I'll have a blue label on the rocks and he'll take a Budweiser."

Cash nodded. "Coming right up."

As he got our drinks ready, I watched Paige and Barrett. She'd already introduced him to the guys, who were intensely watching a game on one of the flat screens, and now she had him over by the women. He was showing off pictures of his family, and I could see it in his face how happy he really was. Even at a table full of beautiful women, he still only thought about the four women he had back at home.

"Here you go, Wilkins," Cash said, setting the drinks on the countertop.

"Can I just start a tab?" I asked, putting my billfold back in my pocket.

He waved me off. "This is Haney's place. We don't pay to drink here."

"Just start a tab for me, man," I said, shaking my head. "I wouldn't feel right about not paying for our drinks."

"HANEY!" Cash called out, signaling for him to come over to the bar.

Fletcher came over and looked between the two of us. "What's going on?"

"Wilkins, here, wants to start a tab."

Fletcher laughed and Cash quickly joined in, making me feel like a real dick for not knowing what was so damn funny.

"What?" I asked.

Fletcher composed himself and then scooted our drinks closer to me. "You banked in a three-pointer today, you deserve free drinks for the rest of the night after such a monumental disgrace."

The embarrassment from this morning's basketball game came rushing back as I grabbed our drinks and shook my head at them. "Hey, at least I scored!"

They continued laughing at me as I walked away with our drinks in hand. I found Paige and Barrett sitting at a table near her friends and headed that way, greeting the rest of the gang as I walked by.

I handed Barrett his beer, and then took a seat next to Paige. The two of them looked as if they were trying to contain their laughter. "You guys heard about the bank shot, didn't you?"

She leaned over and kissed me on the cheek. "Yeah, the guys told us."

"I would have paid good money to see you play basketball," Barrett laughed, taking a drink of his beer.

"Shut the hell up, Gallagher. Like you'd be any better," I said, shaking my head. I glanced over at Paige, who was still giggling to herself. "It was the embarrassment of my athletic career."

"Not everyone can be LeBron James," she said encouragingly, rubbing my arm.

"Maverick could give him a run for his money." I brushed her short strands away so I could kiss her neck. I caught a stronger whiff of her delicious perfume and felt myself jerk in response as I ran my nose up to her ear. It was different from the perfume I used to buy her back in high school. More floral and feminine. "You smell so damn good. What is that scent?"

"Thank you," she said, shivering from my touch. "It's Calvin Klein."

"Well, keep that stuff around," I said, smiling at her. "I'm a fan."

She laughed, bringing her drink up to her lips. "I'll remember that."

"What are you drinking?" I asked, eyeing the clear concoction in her wine glass.

"Mango Moscato," she answered proudly. "You?"

Barrett scoffed next to me as I answered. "Johnnie Walker."

"Scotch?" Paige said, wrinkling her nose. "You're a scotch drinker now? When did that happen?"

Barrett busted into a fit of laughter and toasted his mug up in the air at her. "Good question."

I rolled my eyes at him and answered Paige. "My teammates got me a bottle of it after we won the bowl game. I've been a fan of it ever since."

"Yuck," she said, shaking her head. "I can't drink scotch."

"Speaking of," I said, nudging her under the table with my leg. "When did you become a wine drinker? We always had to have vodka for you and Zoey."

"True." Barrett nodded in agreement. "Do you remember that time they made us get the ingredients for that one drink that stained our hands . . . God, what the hell was that shit called?"

"Sweet Tarts," Paige answered, laughing.

My stomach clenched at the memory of that night. "That crap was nasty."

"No, it wasn't!" Paige argued, shaking her head. "It was good."

"What wasn't good was waking up the next morning with that crap still on my hands," Barrett said, lifting his palms. "I had purple and red Kool-Aid stains on my hands for the entire weekend."

I nodded in agreement. "I remember telling Duke and Lilian that we'd been working on an art project for school."

"My parents knew," Barrett admitted, with a shrug. "There was no point in lying to my mom. I couldn't get away with anything."

Paige smiled into her wine glass and then peeked up to find Barrett and me watching her. "What? Zoey and I weren't the ones with the evidence on our hands. All we ever suffered from were the hangovers the next morning."

"Man," Barrett stated with a smile as he relaxed back in his seat. "The shit we did for them back then."

"I know," I said, narrowing my eyes at Paige. "We always stole the alcohol from my parents. Found stuff to mix it with at Barrett's house. You'd think we would've gotten a little more appreciation for it."

"Right!" he exclaimed, jokingly.

Paige teased her boot up the inside of my calf and quipped, "I think you guys received plenty of thanks back then."

I grabbed her foot underneath the table and smiled. "Well, thank God I didn't have to steal any of Lilian's wine. She would have had my hide over her wine."

"Your mom does like her wine," Barrett agreed.

Paige sighed and stared into her glass wistfully. "I started drinking wine after I turned twenty-one. I'd buy something different whenever we'd stop in at the liquor store, and wine just seemed to become my new favorite. But I'll still drink vodka on occasion."

"Zoey would be proud," Barrett commended, wiping the condensation off his glass. "She's still a fan of vodka. We had to start locking it up because Ryce thought it was water and almost drank some of it. You know you're in the midst of parenthood when you have to start locking shit up."

"You're going to have to put your alcohol under some military-grade lockdown once the girls get into high school," I stated. "If they're anything like Zoey, she could pick a lock to anything."

The smile from Barrett's face fell and he pulled his phone out of his pocket. "You're right."

"What are you doing?" I asked, amused.

"I'm texting Zoey to remind me to get a better lock for the liquor cabinet."

I glanced over at Paige, who was fingering the rim of her wine glass and reading something on her phone. "Hey."

She blinked and smiled back at me. "Hey."

"Everything okay?"

"Yeah," she said, closing the app. "I was just reading an email about a client."

"Put the phone away," I said, nudging her again under the table. "Or else I'm going to put music on and make you dance with me."

"No," she begged, shaking her head. "You wouldn't. This isn't high school anymore, Drake."

Barrett laughed from across the table, knowing full well that I'd fucking do it. "That doesn't matter to him."

I quickly downed the rest of my scotch and jumped up from my seat. I was just planning on going to the restroom, but if she continued to refuse, I was going to do what I always did at the dances in high school. I'd request some stupid song and dedicate it to her, so everyone would make her get out on the dance floor with me. At first, she'd be pissed, but by the time we started dancing, she'd end up laughing and staying out there with me. Kids took dances way too seriously in high school. The boys were worried about where to put their hands and how to lead, and the girls were worried about whether or not they'd be asked to dance. So, I started a fun way to break through the cluster-fuck of emotions and awkwardness.

Now, I was curious to see if she'd still do it.

"Seriously, I am not dancing with you to some stupid song," she said before taking a sip of her wine. She glared at me, her blue eyes like ice. "Don't even think about it."

Barrett leaned in and asked her, "You do realize who you're talking to, right?"

"Yes," she said, rolling her eyes. "But we're adults now."

Smiling, I walked over to her and lifted her chin before laying an easy kiss on her lips. "Rein it in, woman. I'm just going to the restroom."

She grabbed my sweater and pulled me close. "You better be."

"And if I'm not?" I challenged with a raise of my brows.

"Drake!" She pushed me away from her with a hard shove, and Barrett and I started laughing, knowing I was going to get her out on that dance floor before we left here tonight.

I turned toward the restrooms, my grin widening with each step as my plan formed.

***

Paige

"He hasn't changed a bit," I mumbled, smiling as I watched Drake walk away.

"Did you expect him to change?" Barrett asked, watching me intently.

Ever since he'd walked into the bar with Drake, I'd felt some animosity from Barrett. He had every right to feel that way toward me now. I was fully aware that I hadn't just messed with Drake's life by doing what I'd done, but Barrett and Zoey's too.

"No," I said honestly, looking down into my wine glass. "Not really."

He rested his elbows on the table, and I could feel his eyes on me. "You've changed though."

Glancing up at him, I nodded. "Yeah, I have."

It wasn't a question. He was stating that he already knew I wasn't the same. I wasn't sure how to feel about that. Drake and Barrett were still close, so I'd figured they'd talked about me. But I wasn't prepared for the guilt that came along with seeing Barrett again, especially after what Drake had told me about him and Zoey. How they'd had trouble after we broke up, and everything about their lives now.

The Barrett Gallagher I knew had always been a quiet but fun guy. He was tall and built, and he had a sweet side to him that was still quite evident by the way he proudly talked about his girls earlier. He never once flirted with any of my girlfriends, respecting Zoey even when she wasn't around, which I loved. Even though we weren't close anymore, I still wanted her to be happy, and Barrett had definitely followed through on that. He hadn't changed much since high school, except for the way he regarded me now.

Like I was someone he didn't know anymore.

"Zoey didn't come tonight because of me, right?" I asked, pursing my lips together.

Barrett nodded and then took a swig of his beer. "She wasn't sure how she felt about seeing you again and meeting your new friends."

I deserved her uneasiness toward me now. "I get it."

"Your friends seem like nice people, Paige, but you have to realize that she was more worried about seeing you again. You hurt her, but she misses you. She hasn't really made any new friends except the imaginary ones our daughters hang out with from time to time."

I smiled at that last bit as he laughed. "I know I hurt her, but I just couldn't—"

"Couldn't what?" he asked inquisitively. "You couldn't pick up the phone and call? That's all it would've taken, and you couldn't do that?"

"At the time? No," I said, shaking my head. From one parent to another, if Barrett really knew why, I doubt he'd be grilling me right now. "I couldn't. I was in a really bad place, and I didn't want to drag anyone else into it."

Confusion marred his features as his brows furrowed. "What are you talking about? Why were you in a bad place?"

Shaking my head, I finished the rest of my wine but couldn't look at him as I answered. "Forget I said anything, Barrett."

"No," he said harshly. "I'm not going to just let it go. I want to know why."

Looking back at him, I mentally demanded my armor to stay in place. "I can't tell you why."

He sat back in his chair, staring back at me in disbelief. "Because you haven't told Drake yet, right?"

I nodded silently.

"Why haven't you told him?" he asked.

"Because he's going to hate me once I tell him," I said truthfully. "When I do, I hope you're there for him because he's going to need you."

"No, he won't." Placing his mug back on the tabletop, he smiled weakly and shook his head at me. "He's only ever needed you."

The guilt burned inside my throat, making me wish I had another glass of wine to put out the flames. I picked up my empty glass to take back to the bar and get another, but before I got up, a familiar song from an iconic movie came through the speakers.

"Oh, no . . ."

"Barrett Gallagher, please get your ass out here!" Drake yelled from the middle of the dance floor.

The surrounding patrons stopped their conversations to watch Drake.

Barrett stood from his seat and chugged the rest of his beer. "And you thought he'd make you dance?"

"I cannot believe he put this on!" I stated excitedly.

"It's a good thing I wore my boots!" he exclaimed as he headed toward the dance floor.

Barrett stood next to Drake, and then they started doing the dance they learned specifically for Zoey and me back in the day. Most of it was from the end of the scene in *Footloose* where Ren teaches Willard how to dance, but the rest of it, they'd made up themselves. And apparently they still remembered it!

"Ohmigawd, Paige!" Elly exclaimed as she waddled over to me, clapping along to the song. "Are you seeing this? You didn't tell me he knew the *Footloose* dance!"

I laughed, shaking my head. "I honestly thought he would have forgotten it by now."

"This is awesome," Carter laughed. "Barrett's pretty good, too, for a bigger guy."

I nodded. "I know."

They continued their line dancing as some other people joined in and the rest of the bar clapped for them, myself included. Tessa, Bayler, and Harper danced next to their guys and sang along with Deniece Williams. I couldn't take my eyes off Drake as he laughed along with Barrett and smiled my way.

"I love him," Elly said, squeezing my arm. "Seriously, marry him tomorrow."

"Easy there," I laughed, knowing Elly's obsession with the oldies. "I think you're more over the moon about the song and what movie it's from."

"If he lip-syncs "Twist and Shout," I'll divorce Carter for him," Elly stated in a serious tone.

"Don't say anything or he will," I warned.

"Hey," Carter said defensively, wrapping his arm around Elly's shoulders. "I can do that."

"But you can't do that!" Elly exclaimed jokingly, pointing to Drake and Barrett.

He laughed, shaking his head at her ridiculousness before kissing her.

As the song came to an end, the bar exploded into ovations for the guys, and they both bowed before Drake patted Barrett on the back, excusing him from the dance floor. Drake caught my attention and crooked his finger at me. I felt my face heat with excitement, but I still felt bashful when he called me out to dance.

"No," I said to him.

"Come on, Paige!" Elly begged, pulling me out of my seat. "He wants to dance with you!"

"GET OUT THERE!" Tessa shouted at me from the bar.

The next song started and Shaggy's distinctive voice resonated from the speakers. I smiled as I started toward the dance floor, feeling a little embarrassed but overjoyed at the same time. Drake met me halfway and grabbed my hand, leading me onto the dance floor. Then he pulled my arms up around his shoulders and rested his forehead against mine as he swayed us along to the reggae beat and lip-synced the words to me.

Eventually, he took my hands and spun me out. When he pulled me back, he anchored his hands to my hips so my back was up against his front as we moved. His warm breath against my ear tickled, sending shivers down my spine. He started singing the chorus to me, and the rest of the bar and its patrons faded away. It was just him and me, out there on the dance floor, grinding to a song we'd danced to numerous times throughout high school.

"You mad?" he asked, chuckling into my ear.

I put my hands over his, which were still planted on my waist. "How can I be mad when you picked this song?"

"I thought you might like it," he said, pressing a kiss beneath my ear. "You're still my angel, you know."

"And you are still so ridiculously handsome," I said, turning to face him. I wrapped my arms around his neck and covered his lips with mine. The bar erupted into another round of applause as the song ended. When I broke away from our kiss and opened my eyes, I found all of my friends with their significant others around us.

The fun quickly diminished when Elly and Carter were walking back to their seats and I noticed her stop and hold her belly. Carter paused and looked back at her with a worried expression on his face.

"Elly," I called out, rushing over to her side with Drake trailing close behind.

"What's wrong?" he asked.

She shook her head, holding her hand up to stop the onslaught of questions from all of us. She took a couple of deep breaths, but according to the grimace on her face, she was still in pain.

"Talk to me, Goose," Maverick coaxed, squatting down in front of her. "Are you okay?"

"I'll be fine," she said with a curt nod. "It's just Braxton Hicks."

"We should probably get you home, babe," Carter said, rubbing her back. "I know you don't want to go, but the doctor said—"

"Carter, I probably just need to sit down for a little bit," she retorted, smiling at him. "I'm fine, really."

I didn't want to give my opinion, but I was worried about her. I had no idea she was even experiencing Braxton Hicks contractions, but why would she tell me? I was the friend who'd been avoiding her for most of her pregnancy because it reminded me too much of my own. I didn't deserve to give my opinion on the matter at hand now. But if I were her, I'd go home and lie down. Even though I never suffered from them, I'd read enough about pregnancy prior to giving birth to know that Braxton Hicks usually subsided once you changed positions.

"Fine," Carter said, giving in to her. "But please take it easy. No more dancing. Just water and talking."

"Okay," she said cheerfully, giving him a kiss. Then she leaned in close and whispered something in his ear, and the worried expression on his face quickly morphed into a smile as they kissed again.

The rest of the gang went back to their seats as Drake and I headed over to our table, where Barrett was still sitting. He had another beer and two new drinks for us already on the table.

"Is she going to be okay?" he asked, nodding at Elly.

"Yeah," Drake said with a smile. "Just some Braxton Hicks."

"Zoey had those with all three girls," Barrett said, shaking his head. "As if regular labor isn't bad enough, women have to experience that crap beforehand, too."

I took a drink of my wine, still unable to take my eyes off of Elly. She was my best friend, and I wanted nothing but the easiest pregnancy for her.

"When's she due?" Drake asked, pulling my attention back to our table.

"February twenty-third," I answered.

"Just around the corner," he said excitedly. "Do they know what they're having?"

I sighed, and chastised myself for dodging her these past few months. When I looked over at the two of them, I noticed Drake pleasantly awaiting my answer, but Barrett's head was cocked to the side, inquisitively watching me. "They're having a boy."

"Nice," Drake stated, taking a sip of his scotch. He nudged Barrett on the arm and laughed. "So, how about that dancing, Barrett? When's the last time we did that?"

Barrett laughed. "Um, senior prom?"

"Probably," he said, nodding.

"I haven't danced like that in a long time," Barrett said, shaking his head. "I downed a water the minute I got off the dance floor."

I excused myself from the table and carried my wine with me over to Elly's table. While I welcomed the distraction the guys provided by talking about something other than pregnancies, I wanted to make sure she was really okay.

Taking a seat next to her, I smiled at the rest of our girlfriends as I laid my head on her shoulder.

"Are you really okay?" I asked, taking a deep breath.

She patted me on the cheek and laughed. "Yes, I am. You know I wouldn't be here if I wasn't."

"Okay, good," I said, smiling up at her.

"Since we've got you here," Elly teased, playfully pinching my cheek. "How could you keep all of Drake's awesomeness a secret for all these years? He's so hot!"

"Yes. He. Is!" Tessa gushed, chewing on the straw from her cocktail.

Bayler nodded as she took a sip of hers. "He's one hell of a dancer, too."

"You know what I love about him?" Harper started, smiling over at Drake before giving us her attention again. "I love how he lights up the room. Look at that dance floor now.

There are a handful of people out there now who probably would've never gotten out of their seats if it weren't for him starting something. He's just so much fun."

"So, how did *you* end up with him?" Bayler quipped, nudging my side.

"Hey!" I retorted, lifting my head to glare at her. "I can have fun."

"Mhmm," Bayler teased.

"And," Harper continued, her eyes glimmering with excitement, "for the first time, Paige isn't spending a Saturday night with her phone glued to her hand!"

"Amen to that!" Tessa agreed, nodding. "You work too much."

"Well," Elly said, looping her arm through mine, "I hope you're having fun with that tall, sexy hunk of high school sweetheart."

I laughed and rolled my eyes at her. "We're taking things slow."

"I've seen you two kiss numerous times tonight," Tessa pointed out, narrowing her eyes at me.

"He's completely smitten with you," Harper added.

Bayler smiled. "Don't lie to us, Paige."

"I'm not lying!" I exclaimed, holding my hands up in defense. "We haven't done anything else. We work together and it's not allowed, so—"

"So, I work for Fletcher," Bayler stated with a shrug. "What does that have to do with anything?"

"It's a rule at their firm that co-workers can't date," Elly explained.

"Then get a new job," Bayler concluded.

I smiled at her. "Are you saying that if you weren't allowed to be with Fletcher, you'd find a different pastry shop to bake at?"

"Yes," she said determinedly, glancing over at him. "Because it's Fletcher. A job is a job. I wouldn't risk losing him over it."

"She's right," Harper said with a knowing smile. "You have a great portfolio of clients, Paige. You could easily get on with any other PR firm here in the city."

"It is kind of fun sneaking around though," Bayler added with a shimmy of her shoulders. "Back when we were keeping things a secret from all of you guys, Fletcher and I had a lot of fun."

Tessa grimaced. "Now, I really question whether or not I should ever buy anything from your shop."

"We've never done it in the shop!" Bayler exclaimed loud enough to gain the guys' attention. "Really, we haven't."

"It was fun until it blew up in your face," Harper remarked, and then turned toward me. "Don't take advice from her."

I laughed at the sisters and then looked at Elly, who'd been watching me. "What?"

"I do think he's good for you," she said with a yawn. "And it has been nice not having you on the phone all night."

"Thanks."

"But when you do start doing the dirty stuff," she added, as she slowly gathered up her things. "You better tell us all the details. I want a high school review versus a post-high school review."

"I wonder if he's gotten bigger," Tessa said curiously. "Does length change as they age?"

"Stamina," Bayler said, nodding enthusiastically. "Stamina totally changes with age."

"Guys," Harper stated, slamming her empty glass down on the table. "How about we just tell her we're excited for her and leave it at that for once?"

"Thank you!" I announced, standing from my seat to help Elly up. "Are you and Carter getting ready to leave?"

"Yeah," she said with another yawn. "I just can't do late nights anymore."

"We can't either," Harper said, peering down at her watch. "We should probably get home to Seghen, too."

Harper excused herself to find Maverick as Carter helped Elly into her coat. Fletcher and Justin took over their seats next to Tessa and Bayler as I made my way back over to the guys.

Taking my seat next to Drake, Barrett looked at his phone and said, "I should get back home to Zoey and the girls. I told her I wouldn't be too late."

"I understand, man," Drake said, nodding. He smiled at me and I could tell he was a little buzzed by the glazed look in his eyes. "Do you guys remember when we used to start the party around this time?"

Barrett laughed. "Just thinking about that makes me tired."

"Yeah, we're too old for that now," I said, caressing his light scruff. "You're looking a little sleepy, too."

"Are you ready to go?" he asked, reaching for my hand.

"I'm ready whenever you are."

I helped him up out of his seat even though he was still sober enough to stand on his own. We put our jackets on and followed Barrett to the door. I waved good-bye to the remainder of our group and then we walked out into the cold January night.

"I can give you guys a ride home if you want," Barrett offered, handing me his phone. "Just plug your address into my GPS."

I quickly typed it in and handed his phone back to him, and then Drake took my hand. "Did you have fun tonight?"

"Yeah," I said, resting my head on his shoulder. "Did you?"

"Yep," he said, pressing his lips to my head. "But Barrett and I concluded that we shouldn't dance like that anymore. We're too old to be doing that shit."

I smacked him on the chest playfully and laughed. "You're not too old!"

"Yes, we are!" Barrett announced in front of us. "Especially in this cold weather. I'm going to be aching like a mother tomorrow."

"I'll be thirty-one this year, P.J.," Drake said, shaking his head. "Can you believe that? I felt like I was twenty in there tonight."

"Another reason why you should keep dancing," I said, before kissing him on the cheek. Harper was right. He had ignited the room tonight with his impromptu dance. But he'd always been that way. A school dance didn't kickoff until Drake Wilkins did something ridiculous, which usually included me. "The girls all loved it, you know. I'm pretty sure Elly's going to make you teach it to Carter. She has a thing for classic movies and old songs."

"I'm too old!" he exclaimed. "Like Barrett said, I'll probably feel it tomorrow."

"What would Zoey say, Barrett?" I asked. "Would she think you're too old?"

"Ha!" he stated loudly as we walked into the parking garage. "She loves that dance. She'd never want us to quit doing it. She'll be upset that she missed it tonight."

"I'm really surprised you remembered it," I said to Drake.

"How could I forget it when I know you love it?" he asked, opening the back door of the truck for me. He gave me a hand climbing in since I was in heels and then he jumped in behind me.

Barrett turned over the engine and quickly flipped on the heat. Smiling, he glanced in the rearview mirror and asked, "Where to first? Paige's place or yours?"

"Paige's," Drake said, pulling me closer to him. He drew my legs over his lap and ran his hands up and down them in an attempt to warm me up. Then he leaned in and placed a kiss right below my ear before asking, "What would you think about me staying the night? I don't expect anything to happen. I just want to sleep next to you again."

God, I'd love that. Some of my best nights of sleep had occurred in that man's arms, and I wasn't about to pass it up.

I slid my hands inside his coat and answered in a soft voice, "I think that sounds good."

Barrett put the truck in reverse and started out of the garage. We stayed mostly silent on the drive back to my apartment, too tired to make any more conversation. That was something I'd always loved about Drake, aside from his fun, adventurous side. He didn't always have to be doing something to have a good time. We could lie together and watch the stars, or cuddle in his truck and listen to music.

I wished it could be as simple as it was back then.

When Barrett finally pulled over to the curb outside my building, Drake hopped out of the backseat and gave me a hand to help me out. Barrett rolled down the passenger side window and said good-bye to me.

"It was good to see you, Barrett," I said, smiling back at him. "I hope you make it home okay."

"Thanks."

Then Drake leaned in to speak to him, and from the tone of Barrett's voice, I could tell he wasn't happy with our arrangement. But Drake backed away from the truck smiling and then waved to him.

"He's not thrilled with you staying with me?" I asked as we climbed the stairs to my apartment.

Drake scratched the back of his head and sighed. "He's just worried about me."

"I understand," I said with a nod. "He's your best friend. He has a right to be."

"It's more than that," he said as I slipped my key in and unlocked the door. He followed me into the darkness of my apartment and then locked the door behind him.

Removing his coat, he tossed it on the nearby chair as I laid my coat, purse and phone on the kitchen counter. I'd checked my phone only once tonight, so I checked it once more and switched it to silent mode when I noticed all the missed calls and email notifications.

Work can wait until tomorrow, I thought, remembering what Bayler had said about her job.

"Barrett doesn't want me to get hurt again," Drake continued, following me down the hall to my room.

I flipped the light on and sat on the edge of my bed to remove my boots. The reminder that I was going to hurt him felt like a cold smack in the face as he sauntered over to me with that adorable smile on his face. He knelt down to help me with my shoes.

"I don't want to hurt you," I whispered, unable to look him in the eyes.

"I know," he said, placing both boots on the floor next to him. Still kneeling, he moved closer, in between my thighs, running his hands up my legs until they rested on my hips. The sincere gleam in his eyes made me wish I hadn't agreed to let him stay the night with me. It was almost too much, keeping this secret from him but wanting him around all the time, knowing full well that I was going to destroy us the second I told him.

"But you know what?" he stated before leaning in to kiss me. The spearmint flavor of his gum was evident this time, a staple in his teenage kisses that I used to thoroughly enjoy. I couldn't help the smile that spread across my face.

"What?" I asked, snaking my fingers through his hair.

"I'm probably going to hurt you again someday," he started, skimming his fingers up my sides. "And you're probably going to hurt me. But I will keep coming back to you because you're worth the pain. You matter. Who we are together matters."

The weight of his words made my chest sore, because I knew there was a kind of pain that nobody should ever endure. The circle of life shouldn't happen with a parent burying their child. Life wasn't supposed to happen that way, but sometimes it did, and the pain was so unbearable that one would try to keep it hidden from their closest family and friends by not telling them about it. They'd keep a secret from the other parent just so they didn't have to know that kind of pain.

"I love you," he confessed, pressing another kiss to my lips. "I will always love you."

Part of me wished he'd drunk more tonight so that I could blame his words on the scotch. I didn't deserve to hear his sweet nothings or have his strong hands touching me. But I reveled in them nonetheless, because I felt the same toward him. There wasn't anyone else who could ever make me feel so alive and loved as Drake Wilkins.

"I love you, too," I stated honestly.

"But sometimes people hurt the ones they love," he said confidently, brushing my hair out of my face. "How we handle the pain is what's important."

I nodded, silently agreeing with him. I hoped he remembered that when he eventually found out about our son. In my mind, I imagined him losing it, yelling words he never thought he'd say to me, and then never wanting anything to do with me again. I'd thought about his reaction so much, it crippled me from actually telling him.

"Let's get ready for bed," he said with a long yawn.

I pulled him up off the floor, grabbed my pajamas and headed in to my master bath. He'd seen me naked a lot, but I wasn't ready for him to see my body now. As a guy, he probably wouldn't notice all the things I noticed, but he'd definitely question my tattoo.

"I'm going to wash my face real quick and brush my teeth, then the bathroom's all yours." I glanced back at him and saw him pull the navy sweater over his head, revealing a set of abs that were still masterfully etched into his stomach.

He ran his hand through his hair, righting it into its natural state again, and then he started unbuckling his jeans. "Okay."

I closed the bathroom door behind me and leaned against it, unable to get my emotions in check. One minute, I was feeling guilty and sad, but then one glimpse of him taking off his clothes had me all sorts of hot and bothered and extremely worried about sleeping next to him.

You've slept with him plenty of times, I thought, mentally giving myself a pep talk as I stared into the mirror. *You can do this without letting anything happen.*

I grabbed my face wash and scrubbed the makeup off my skin, and then I brushed my teeth, ridding the taste of mango from my mouth. Slipping out of my clothes, I grabbed my pajamas—an old t-shirt from high school and a pair of shorts—and quickly threw them on. I used the toilet before heading back into my room, where Drake Wilkins was standing in nothing but a pair of boxer briefs.

Holy shit, I thought, taking in the sight of his muscles encased in all that beautiful, creamy skin.

"My turn?" he asked.

"Y-yeah," I stuttered, unable to take my eyes off his chest. He had so much chest hair now. "I laid out an extra toothbrush for you."

"Thanks," he said, kissing me on the cheek. "Nice shirt, by the way. Go, Foxes!"

I laughed, glancing down at our high school mascot printed on the front of my tee. When I lifted my head back up, I noticed the soft ambience of my bedroom. He'd already cut the overhead light and turned on the bedside lamp. He'd turned down the covers and had the bed all ready for us.

"I'm really not trying to put the moves on you," he said from inside the bathroom, the door still wide open for me to see him brushing his teeth. "I know it looks like that from the turn-down service and lighting, but your bed's just soft as hell and I'm ready to sleep in it."

I giggled as I crawled into bed, naturally taking the right side like I always did. When he closed the door to take a piss—thank God—I pulled the covers up and laid my head down on the pillow.

A few seconds later, he walked back into the room, and again, my breath caught at the sight of him. He'd never had that much chest hair back in high school, but good lord, it looked sexy as hell on him now. The strong muscles of his arms and legs were thicker, but not too big for his lean, solid frame. He moved with the athletic grace he'd always carried, that same cocky swagger that emphasized his confidence. He was still so agile and seductive that I had to throw the covers over my head to hide my blush.

"Ugh!" I scoffed, muffling my frustration into the pillow.

He laughed as he crawled in beside me and turned the lamp off. "What's wrong?"

"You got so much hotter!" I announced, turning to face him.

Even in the dark, I could tell he was smiling by the sound of his chuckle right next to me. His arms slid around my waist and pulled me against him, my head resting on his shoulder.

"Seriously," I said, running my hand up the rigidity of his abs, through the wilderness of his chest hair. "When did all this hair come in?"

He chuckled again and grabbed my hand, threading his fingers through mine. "A while ago. I had hair there in high school."

"But not this much." I tried to go back to my petting, but he had a tight hold on me. "I think your pecks got bigger, too."

Every inch of him had intensified since our youth, and I wanted to explore.

"Why won't you let me touch you?" I asked, curling up next to him.

"Because I haven't been touched by you in years," he said in a frustrated tone, tangling his legs with mine. "And unless you plan to finish what you start, I can't have your hands all over me yet."

I bit back a smile, trying my best to contain my laughter, but I eventually let it go and received a smack on the ass for it.

"You have no idea how painful blue balls are," he stated, turning us so that we were on our sides, spooning. He threw an arm over my waist and linked our hands back together. His other hand moved my hair away from my neck, and he proceeded to trail kisses from my ear down to my collarbone. "I want to touch you so bad. I want to reunite with this body and get to know you all over again. But I won't. Not until you're ready. With the amount of clothes you're still wearing and the fact that you had to change in the bathroom, I know you're not ready."

"I'm sorry," I murmured, lifting our joined hands to my lips to kiss his.

"You don't have to apologize," he said, nuzzling my neck. "I'm quite fond of cuddling with you."

So, that's what we did. In the darkness of my room, under the warm, soft, cream-colored sheets of my bed, Drake and I settled into each other like we'd done so many times before, drifting off to the sound of our breaths getting heavier and heavier until sleep finally took us.

Chapter Seven

Paige

The following week was a complete disaster. There was no other way to describe it. I had clients doing all sorts of shit that ended up in the media, and not in a positive way. There was the singer who had a wardrobe malfunction while she was drunk at a club. An actor who was caught cheating on his equally talented actress girlfriend. And finally, the model who'd been caught with drugs.

I was a second away from losing my shit with Mr. Cheating Asshole when Skye walked into my office.

"Jason, stop talking," I said, placing him on hold. I looked up at Skye and sighed. "Please tell me you have some good news for me. It's Friday."

"Uh," she said, biting her lip nervously. "Your mother called. You're supposed to call her back."

"That's not good news!" I exclaimed, pushing away from my desk. My mother only called my office when she desperately needed to get ahold of me and I wasn't picking up my cell. "I'll call her back once I get off the phone with Jason."

"Okay." Skye left my office quickly, knowing I wasn't in the mood for a snarky remark from her. A moment later, I heard her greet Drake as he walked into our office. "I wouldn't go in there if I were you, she's been dealing with idiots all day and her mother just called."

"I'll take my chances," he said, chuckling to himself. He moved into my doorway with his brows perked up in interest. "Bad day?"

"Close the door," I said, plopping back down in my chair. I resumed my call with Jason as Drake took a seat on the other side of my desk. "Jason, how do you not know whether or not you two were still together? Were the words 'done' and 'break up' used in the same sentence or not? If they weren't, you cheated on her. Simple as that."

"I don't know! We just had a fight!" he exclaimed. "What's the big deal? It's not like we were going to last anyway."

"The big deal is, you have a movie coming out in a few months and nobody is going to want to go see a movie with a cheating asshole in it as the lead character."

"But my character doesn't cheat in the movie," he stated in a confused tone.

"BUT YOU DO IN REAL LIFE!" I shouted, shaking my head. "I'm more worried about your career than I am about your relationship status. I don't care who you rub uglies with, but when you do something to make yourself look bad, I care. This cheating incident is making you look really bad."

"I wasn't thinking, okay?" he admitted.

I stabbed the hold button and rolled my eyes at Drake as he started laughing. "He was thinking all right, just with the wrong brain."

"I love listening in on your calls," he laughed.

I resumed the call again. "You need to issue an apology. I know, I know. You don't want to do that, but you have to. Your fan base will appreciate you more for it, and it will give you a chance to redeem yourself with people who aren't a fan of your work."

"Fine," he replied sharply.

"I'll work on something with Skye and have her get it to you this afternoon."

"Thanks, Paige," he grumbled before hanging up the phone.

Taking a deep breath, I relaxed back into my chair and exhaled. "I hope your day has been better than mine."

"Eh, not really," Drake said with a shrug. "Mookie is giving Owen trouble. I think we're going to be letting him out of his contract soon. He's not worth the headache."

"Good," I said, grabbing the stress ball off my desk. Squeezing the hell out of it, I imagined the tension exiting my body through my fingertips with each compress. "I heard his baseball career is going down the shitter anyway."

"Yeah, that's part of the problem," Drake said, eyeing the gray ball in my hand. "You have a stress ball?"

"Yes," I said, digging my nails into the foam material. "Did you just hear the phone conversation I had? People like Jason are the reason I need a stress ball, or else I'd probably be running rampant around the city, killing celebrities over their stupidity."

As he burst out laughing, he put his feet up on my desk. "Have you called your mom back yet?"

"No," I wailed, leaning my head back against my chair. "She never calls me at work."

"You should call her back then," he said, handing me the receiver.

Reluctantly, I took it and dialed my mother's number. It rang two times before she picked up.

"Paige," she said, her usually pleasant voice tight with tension. "I'm sorry to bother you at work, but—"

"You're not bothering me, Mom," I interjected. "What's going on?"

She sighed into the phone but remained silent for a long time, which in turn increased the weight of concern on my chest. "I just wanted to let you know that Nana passed away yesterday."

The stress ball fell from my hand as I swiveled around in my chair to face the dull gray clouds hovering over the city. I was named after my Nana Jane, but I hadn't seen or spoken to her in years. She'd been diagnosed with Alzheimer's shortly before I found out I was pregnant, and it progressively worsened after that. It got so bad that she couldn't remember that I lost my son. Whenever I'd visit her, she'd ask where he was and if she could hold him. It was unbearable, knowing the elderly woman who'd once showered me with love had completely disappeared into this stranger who caused me so much pain. I couldn't stand to be around her anymore. I loved her, and I knew she loved my son, but I couldn't take answering her questions about him or explaining his death over and over to her every time I visited. So, I stopped visiting her, and my family knew why.

Clearing my throat, I asked my mom, "When's the funeral?"

"It isn't until Wednesday," she answered. "Grandpa said she wanted to be cremated, so he's respecting her wishes and having her memorial after that."

"Okay," I said, nodding. "I'll be home this weekend then, if that's all right."

"Of course," she said kindly. "I'm so sorry, sweetie."

"Me too, Mom," I answered honestly. It was sad to hear that she'd passed, but at the same time, I was grateful that the disease wasn't killing her anymore. She was in a better place now, where she could remember every part of her life without issue. And I liked to imagine her in a place where she could be reunited with my son, the boy she'd always asked about. "Please give Dad my condolences, too."

"I will," she said. "He knew it was coming, but it's still hard losing a loved one."

Mom had lost her parents years ago, so I knew she was remembering them now. "I know."

"Do you have any idea when we can expect you?" she asked, a hint of excitement evident in her tone. "It's been so long since you've been home."

I smiled weakly. "I'm not sure. Maybe tomorrow night. I need to get some things taken care of here at work, and then go home and pack."

"Okay," she said. "Well, I should let you get back to work then. Be sure to keep an eye on the weather before you head north. I heard it might snow again."

"I will."

"Love you."

"Love you too, Mom," I said, before ending the call.

I stared blankly out the window, trying to remember a time when my nana wasn't forgetful, and the first thought that came to my mind was the day I gave birth. She and Grandpa had visited us in the hospital, showering him with all sorts of baby gifts. She held my boy in her arms and told him how much he looked like his handsome daddy—she had always been fond of Drake. Then she proceeded to congratulate me. Neither she nor Grandpa were ever upset at the prospect of their granddaughter giving birth at such a young age.

"Paige?" Drake asked, pulling me out of my thoughts. "Everything okay?"

I shook my head as I spun back around to face him. "My nana passed away yesterday."

"I'm sorry to hear that." Reaching across my desk, he grabbed my hand and kissed it. "Nana Jane was a pretty great woman."

I smiled at his words. "Yeah, she was. The funeral is Wednesday. I'll need to see if someone can cover my clients while I'm gone. Skye will be able to do most of the work, but just in case something comes up with her."

"I'll see what I can do."

"Thanks," I offered, letting go of his hand. "I told my mom I'd be there tomorrow night."

"That actually works out," he said, standing from his desk. He leaned against the edge of my desk and smiled down at me. "Lilian's invited us over for a family dinner tomorrow night, if you're interested. If you don't want to now, I understand, but that's what I'd initially come in here to ask you."

"I'm going home to see my family," I said with a shrug. "Might as well see yours while I'm there, too."

"Great," he said, comforting me with a kiss. "I'll let her know we'll be there, but if you don't feel up to it later, that's fine. She'll understand. I'll let her know about Nana, too."

"I should get back to work," I said, eyeing the colorful mirage of post-its covering my desk. "I have an apology to draft for a cheating client."

"Do you want to drive out to Bedford together?"

"I don't have a car now that I'm in the city," I confessed. "I was planning on renting one."

"No," he said adamantly, shaking his head. "We'll take Old Blue."

"You still have Old Blue?" I asked in disbelief, surprised that the old Chevy had lasted this long.

"Yep, and I will never get rid of him!" he proclaimed proudly, pushing away from my desk. "We'll pick you up tomorrow afternoon. How does that sound?"

"Perfect."

***

The next day, Drake cranked Old Blue's steering wheel to the left and turned into my parents' driveway. His sentiment toward that truck was one of the many traits I admired about him. His family had money. He could've been driving the latest, most expensive model, but he chose to drive the old blue Chevy truck his grandpa had left him in his will years ago. It made me appreciate the man behind the steering wheel even more. The drive had taken longer than expected with the snowfall we had the night before and the artifact we used to get here. But Drake had made the time go by easily, cranking up the music, allowing both of us to sing as loud as possible to the songs on the radio. Now that we were back in Bedford, the reason we were here came creeping back into my mind.

Nana's funeral.

He parked his truck behind my dad's SUV and then turned toward me. "As much as I want to come in and say hi to everyone, I think I should give you a chance to be with them by yourself."

I nodded, grateful for his consideration. "That'd be good."

"Are we still on for dinner at my parents' tonight?"

"Yes." I grabbed my purse and slung it over my shoulder, and then grabbed the duffel bag that had been sitting between my feet on the floorboard and set it on my lap. "Thank you for the ride home."

He reached across the bench seat and grabbed my chin. "You're welcome."

Then he kissed me, and all of my worries floated away as our lips came together in their familiar dance. I didn't want to get out of the truck. Home had been a nightmare for me. The house sitting in front of us was where I lost our son. My bedroom still had all of his things in it, from his crib and changing table, to all the items we'd bought in preparation for my parenthood. There were diapers sitting in the back of my closet, and bottles and pacifiers and plenty of other items in the drawers of his changing table. My parents had asked once before if they should do something with it all, but I begged them not to remove any of it. I was too attached to it all to get rid of it. This house was not a home to me anymore, and walking into it was like stepping back in time to the worst day of my life.

Drake pressed one more hard kiss to my lips before breaking away and brushing a strand of hair behind my ear. "It's never easy losing a loved one, but I'm here for you, okay? If you need anything, just let me know."

"I will," I said, nodding.

He had no idea how familiar I was with loss. Reaching for the door handle, I sent up a silent prayer, asking God for the strength to walk through that front door.

"I'll pick you up for dinner around six," Drake added.

"See you then," I said, before slamming the old, squeaky door shut.

He waited until I opened the front door to pull out of the driveway. Crossing the threshold, I stepped into my own personal hell. I could hear Mom and Dad talking in the kitchen, so I quietly snuck up the stairs to my bedroom before I had to make conversation with anyone.

I turned the knob to my bedroom and was greeted by its light gray walls. When I found out I was having a boy, I'd decorated my room in light blues and grays, and my parents had bought white furniture to go with it. Laying my purse and duffel on the bed, I walked over to the changing table and pulled out the top drawer. Relief instantly flooded me at the sight of the diapers sitting exactly where I'd left them, along with the baby powder and the nearly spent box of baby wipes. It was all still here.

Running my hand along the white furniture, I smiled when I realized Mom came in here on a regular basis and cleaned. It wasn't just left here to collect dust. For that, I was grateful.

"I didn't even hear you come in," Mom said, leaning against the doorjamb.

"I'm sorry," I said, turning around to face her. "I wanted to put my things up in my room first."

"I was hoping to say hello to Drake, too," she said excitedly, walking into my room. She took a seat on the edge of my full-sized bed and fluffed the pillows. She hadn't changed much over the years. She'd kept her blonde hair long and pulled back out of her face. Her signature outfit of blue jeans and a cardigan was perfectly in place.

"He wanted to give me some time with you guys first." I'd told her he was back in my life, but I hadn't given her any other details. She'd already asked me if I'd told him, and I quickly shut down any more of her questions.

"Well," she said nervously, setting the pillow back in its place. "I'll let you get settled in then."

She started toward the door, but I stopped her before she left. "Mom."

"Yeah, sweetie?" she asked, smiling at me.

"Thank you," I said, looking around my room. "For keeping everything so nice for me."

She walked back over to me with a determined spring in her step, her motherly smile spread across her face, and she pressed a kiss to my forehead. "I'd do anything for you."

Then she let go and left me to unpack. I hung up my dress for the funeral and the rest of the clothes I'd brought with me that needed to be ironed. The three pairs of shoes I'd packed were placed in my closet. As I arranged my toiletries on my vanity, I could hear Dad and Grandpa arguing about something downstairs. So, I left my rearranging for later.

I found them in the kitchen. Dad was pointing at a piece of paper on the countertop and glaring at his dad. Neither of them had seen me walk in, so I turned back into the hall and eavesdropped from there.

"I can't believe you put this in the paper without talking to us first," he said sternly.

"I don't need to discuss things with my family before I do them," Grandpa returned, standing his ground.

"When it pertains to my daughter," Dad retorted, "Yes, you do, Dad."

Grandpa scratched the back of his head and shrugged. "Cal, you can't keep holding her hand through life anymore."

"We haven't been holding her hand!" he snapped, slamming his fist down on the counter. "Don't you think she's been through enough?"

What the hell was on that piece of paper?

"I do," Grandpa said, nodding. "But your mother would have—"

"No!" he interjected, shaking his head. "I don't want to hear it. What Mom wants is irrelevant now. She's dead. She's not going to be reading this. You should have talked to us first."

I couldn't take it anymore; I had to know what the fuck Grandpa put in the newspaper. Rounding the corner, I ignored both of them as I journeyed into the kitchen and grabbed the piece of paper. It was a newspaper clipping, and at the top it had my nana's picture and her name; it was her obituary.

"Paige," Dad said warily, but I waved him off as I read through the article.

Tears formed in my eyes as I came to the list of individuals who had preceded her in death, and I knew what was coming as I read through them.

. . . and great-grandson, Declan Abram Wilkins.

"How could you do this?" I sobbed, tears streaking down my face as I looked up at my grandpa.

"You're not the only one who lost him, Paige. There's a whole other family who doesn't even know about him."

"Y-you think I don't know that?" I cried, waving the paper in my hand. "Is this how you wanted them to find out, by reading his name in her obituary?"

"No, but it's been years," he stated, shaking his head. "And you still act like you're the only person who's allowed to miss him."

I stepped toward the man I was taught to respect and shoved his wife's obituary into his hand, crinkling the paper as anger and agony sliced through me at the same time. "Until you know what it's like to bury your child, you don't get to tell me how to feel or how I'm supposed to act. I know exactly how long it's been."

Grabbing Dad's keys from the island, I ran out of the house, started his vehicle, and sped out of the driveway toward the Wilkins' home. Tears blurred my vision as more continued to fall. My heart ached from the pain of reading his name and knowing there was a real possibility that someone in Drake's family already had, too.

Chapter Eight

Drake

Leaving my room, I bounded down the stairs to find the rest of my family. I hadn't spent a weekend at home in a while, and since Lennox was back, I was looking forward to Paige and all of us getting together tonight. Our family dinners were an event I'd looked forward to on a weekly basis growing up. During high school, Paige often joined us and fit right in, laughing at all of Dad's stupid jokes and praising Mom's cooking. I was excited to have her by my side again tonight.

I turned the corner and walked into the dining room, where I found Mom, Dad and Lennox sitting around the table. Dad had the Saturday newspaper in his hands, but the second he saw me, he placed it on the table and looked at the women in our family. None of them greeted me the way they usually would. Mom should've been hugging me and asking where Paige was, and Lennox should've been giving me shit about the sweater I had on. The joy that had normally lingered here had been sucked away by the tension that filled it now and the worry embedded in my family's features.

"What's going on?" I asked, eyeing the three of them cautiously.

"Drake," Mom stated nervously, standing from her seat. She walked over to me and smiled weakly, and that's when I noticed the tears in her eyes.

"What's wrong?" I asked in an adamant tone. "Why have you been crying?"

She looked away from me in an attempt to blink away the tears blanketing her bright blue eyes. "There's something you need to see."

"Here." Dad slid the newspaper over to me.

Glancing down at the black and white print in front of me, I noticed Jane Abram's picture along with her obituary. "Jane's obituary?"

"Just read it, Drake," Lennox said firmly from across the table.

Leaning over the oak, I placed my hands on the table and proceeded to read her obituary. I read about a familiar, wonderful woman and how much she enjoyed reading and knitting. I read about the woman who was like a grandmother to me back in high school because she knew all of my grandparents had already died. But then I read about her family and friends, and her relatives who'd passed before her, and that's when I saw it.

Declan Abram Wilkins.

My last name was in her obituary, tied to a boy I didn't even know existed. Reading it was like a swift kick in the stomach that hurt so much, I had to read it three more times before it sunk in.

Great-grandson, Declan Abram Wilkins.
Declan Abram Wilkins.
Declan Abram Wilkins.

I kept rereading his name, unable to comprehend how she could've kept him from me. The myriad of emotions felt unreal, like one person shouldn't ever experience this many at once. Anger. Sorrow. Hurt. Disbelief. Grief. My mind couldn't decide how I was supposed to feel. There wasn't one emotion to sum up finding out you had a son and that he'd passed away before you had a chance to meet him. But there was one for finding out the love of your life betrayed you. By the time I'd read it for the fifth time, fury stormed through my system as I crumbled up the paper and threw it off the table. I pushed away from the table, unable to face my family members, kicking over a chair as I went.

"Goddammit!" I shouted furiously, grabbing my head as tears took over my vision. "How could she do this to me? H-how could she not tell me?"

Dad walked up behind me and put his hand on my shoulder. "I don't know, D."

Looking back at him, I noticed the tears pooling in his eyes and completely lost it. The first sob broke through as his arms caught me and wrapped me into a hug.

"I don't know," he repeated in disbelief, rubbing my back.

I looked over at Lennox, who was consoling Mom as she cried on her daughter's shoulder and watched me fall apart. I'd never seen my family so destroyed. Paige didn't just hurt me this time around. I'd never even seen my dad cry until today, and the fact that my little sister was comforting our mother, the woman who constantly nagged us to give her grandchildren, reiterated that the woman I loved had hurt us.

The doorbell started ringing repeatedly, as if someone was pressing it multiple times in a row, so I shrugged out of my Dad's arms and dried my face with my hands. Lennox offered to get the door, and the rest of us stood motionless in the dining room, unable to truly function until I heard her voice.

"Lennox, please!" Paige begged. "I need to explain."

"I don't know if now is the time," my sister replied.

Too pissed off to stop myself, I grabbed the obituary section and left the dining room, with Mom and Dad trailing behind me. Paige stood in our foyer, her makeup smeared from crying, looking almost as bad as I felt. Her blue eyes were bloodshot, and her face was blotchy. Staring at her, I no longer saw the girl I loved; all I saw was the woman who'd kept our son a secret from me.

"How could you?" I snapped, clenching the paper in my fist before dropping it. "We had a son and you couldn't even tell me! My family and I had to read about it in some fucking newspaper? In your grandma's obituary!"

"I know! I know! I'm sorry!" she exclaimed, her hands shaking in front of her. "But I can explain. Please, let me explain."

"You should've explained a long time ago, Paige!" I stepped closer, her tears and her nerves fueling my anger even more. "You should've told me the minute you found out you were pregnant. When was that? When did you know? Was it before or after I left for college?"

She took a deep breath and then answered. "Before."

I scoffed, shaking my head. "So, why didn't you tell me? I wasn't thousands of miles away from you yet."

"I planned on telling you," she stated, running a hand through her hair. "Do you remember the day we broke up? I came over here to tell you something, but—"

"You didn't tell me because we broke up?"

"No," she commented, clearly frustrated. "I didn't tell you because I didn't want you to give up your dream of playing football. We broke up so you could focus on school and football, and I could focus on me. So that's what I did. I planned on telling you that day when I came over here, but once we broke up, the plan changed because I knew what you'd do. You would have given up everything to stay here and be a dad. You would have given up your football scholarship and your academic scholarships to stay here and provide for your little family, and I didn't want you resenting us for the rest of your life for that."

Crossing my arms over my chest, I glared at her. "What was the new plan then, to never tell me?"

"No," she repeated shamefully, bowing her head. "My due date was around spring break, so I planned on telling you after he was born when you were back here on break. I wanted to show you that I could handle parenting alone while you were in college."

"Then what happened?" I asked, swallowing back the tears. "Why wasn't I ever told?"

Pursing her lips together, she looked away as she started crying again. "He came early, February twenty-third, but labor went perfectly fine. He was eight pounds, seven ounces and twenty-one inches long, with a head full of your black hair and your same fair skin tone. He was absolutely perfect."

Listening to her talk about him was like trying to understand a second language; she knew everything I didn't. "Go on..."

She wiped her face and shuddered another breath. "I graduated early so I could prepare. I took the birthing class and read all the baby books because I wanted to know how to do everything and do it right. And the baby books say that when your baby is sleeping, that you're supposed to sleep, too."

I heard my mom let out a sob behind me, but I was unable to take my eyes off Paige.

"One day, a couple of weeks before spring break, I laid Declan down for a nap in his crib," she stated softly, struggling to say the words. She wrapped her arms around herself and slightly shook as she continued. "I made sure there was nothing else in the crib with him, and then I laid down on my bed to rest while he did." Closing her eyes, tears poured from them as she shook her head. "But when I woke up, I knew something was wrong because his cries didn't wake me up like they normally did. I woke up to silence."

Her words made me unsteady on my feet. Placing my hands on my hips, I knew what was coming, and it was so hard to watch her that I started to cry. She visibly shook in front of me, sobbing into her hands, and for the first time since she walked through the door, I wanted to go to her and comfort her.

"W-when I checked on him, he was still lying on his back but he wasn't breathing," she stammered. "I called 9-1-1 and performed CPR, and when the EMTs arrived, they tried to revive him but he was already gone."

The tearful sound of sniffling could be heard around the room, but I still could only look at her. She was the only one in here who understood the insurmountable pain I was feeling right now. It felt like my heart had been ripped out of my chest and thrown on the floor with the newspaper. I thought losing her was bad, but this, hearing about the loss of my son, the boy we created together, was a million times worse.

"The doctors all determined that there was no cause for him to stop breathing. They said it was SIDS—sudden infant death syndrome."

I couldn't breathe anymore, even though I was still alive and trembling, but the shock of it all—learning what'd happened to him—was overwhelming. It no longer mattered that I was hearing about it eleven years later. The wound was fresh, still hemorrhaging.

"You know what the baby books don't tell you?" she continued softly. "They don't tell you that something bad could still happen. They tell you all the ways to prepare for parenthood and what to expect after birth, but they don't tell you how to handle the loss of your child."

I nodded silently.

She took a step toward me and looked me in the eyes. "Please understand, I never wanted you to find out by reading Declan's name in an obituary. I meant to tell you sooner, but the words are difficult to find and even harder to speak. I'm so sorry I didn't tell you when I should have. When I saw you again a few weeks ago, Declan was my first thought. I knew I needed to tell you about him, but again, I didn't know how. But I never wanted you to find out the way you did." She drew her trembling hand up to my face and smiled weakly as she cupped my cheek. "Declan looked exactly like you, and I loved that because it felt like we always had part of you with us. Even though we didn't plan for him, I never once thought of him as a mistake. He's the best thing I've ever done, and I couldn't have had him without you. I will never forgive myself for taking away your chance to know him and hold him and be with him." She took a step back and gazed around at my family and me. "I know sorry isn't enough, but I truly am sorry. You all deserve to get to know him. I know it's not the same, but I kept everything of his. I documented my entire pregnancy and moments with Dec. I took a lot of pictures of him too because I didn't want you to miss anything." She paused for a second and sniffled back more tears. "Losing him was never part of the plan, and if I could give my life to bring him back, I would in a heartbeat."

Gazing back at me, she waited for me to say something. My parents and sister waited, too. But all I could do was imagine it in my head. I didn't picture Paige pregnant with him or the day he was born. I didn't imagine a little boy who looked exactly like me. I imagined the day he died. I saw her the way I used to. Just a teenager, trying to save our baby and calling for help. EMTs were there; they tried to save him. I had more to say to her and much more to ask about him, but I couldn't.

Swallowing back the tears, I wiped an exhausted hand over my face and then said, "I need you to leave."

The words caught her off guard at first, but then she nodded. "Okay."

The four of us watched her leave, exiting our house without another look back at the destruction she caused. She roared in like a tornado and left behind the debris of heartbreak and pain. What hurt the most was that he was gone, and there was no bringing him back. Every man dreamt of having a son, and I never even knew mine existed until now.

When the door closed behind her, I ran up the stairs to my room and slammed the door shut. I lay down on top of my bed, gazed up at the ceiling, and let the sobs flow freely. I caught sight of my football sitting on its shelf and thought about how I'd never get to teach my son how to throw it. Then I saw the picture of Paige and me still sitting on my nightstand, and part of me considered throwing it up against the wall, watching the glass shatter and then tearing the picture into pieces. The same thought passed through my mind the more I looked around my room. I wanted to take everything and throw it—make my room look the same way I felt.

Broken. Destroyed. Helpless.

My chest hurt from all the crying.

My lungs struggled to function properly.

My head ached.

My limbs felt numb.

Exhaustion became the marrow in my bones.

However, I was certain I wouldn't feel better after wrecking my surroundings. It wouldn't fix anything. It wouldn't bring him back. It wouldn't change what'd happened. It wouldn't take back the forgiveness I'd immediately bestowed upon Paige the moment she'd told our son's tragic story. Even after all these years, her pain mirrored my own now, and I could understand how losing him continued to hurt her, which provided my current anguish.

Eventually the tears subsided, and I lay in my room for an hour before Lennox knocked on my door. She walked in and sat on the edge of my bed, wearing the most sympathetic smile on her young face.

"I called Barrett and Zoey," she confessed. "I thought you might need them."

I wanted a time machine more than anything right now, but I nodded silently.

"Mom talked to Rachel Abram," she added.

Her mother's name caught my attention and I stared at Lennox, mutely begging her to continue.

"She stopped by in search of Paige. Mom asked if she had a picture of Declan, and she gave us this one and said they had more."

I noticed Lennox had something in her hands that she kept gazing and smiling at. It looked like a four by six photograph, so I pointed to it and opened my hand.

She placed the photo in my palm and then laid her head down beside mine on the pillow. "Look at him. He's adorable. He really does look just like you."

He did look like me.

The photo showed Paige holding him, and he was swaddled in a blue and white blanket with mini footballs all over it. She wasn't looking at the camera, she was smiling down at our son who was asleep in her arms. They looked beautiful together. She appeared so much younger in the picture than I'd imagined, but she was only eighteen then.

"Will you say something?" Lennox requested, leaning her head on my shoulder. "I'm sorry if the picture upsets you, but I wanted you to see it. To see him. To see her with him. I know you're not physically there, but I like to think of you there in spirit. Did you see what's on the table in the background?"

It was hard to see because of the lighting in the picture, but a framed photo of us sat on the table next to Paige.

For the first time this evening, I smiled. "I guess I was."

Lennox laughed lightly and nudged me. "If this is all we have left of him, we should appreciate it."

"Thanks, Len," I said, admiring the way his tiny hands wrapped around Paige's finger.

She placed a kiss on my forehead before rolling off my bed. "Barrett and Zoey are downstairs. Do you want me to send them up?"

"Sure."

"Are you hungry?"

"No."

She nodded. "Okay."

She left, and before I could have a second to myself again, Barrett and Zoey barged in and took a seat on my bed. They'd clearly been fighting with the shared glare they shot at each another.

"Lennox told us what happened," Barrett said, shaking his head. "I can't believe she kept this from you for eleven years, man. I am so sorry."

I silently nodded, too busy marveling at the picture in my hands. Declan had the same curve of my lips and my nose. We even shared the same "chin butt" that Paige loved so much. Reaching out, I handed the photo to Zoey.

"Oh my gosh," she cooed softly, covering her smile with her hand. "He's precious, Drake."

Barrett leaned over her shoulder to check out the picture and he nudged me in the knee. "Looks just like your ugly ass."

I couldn't muster up the energy to laugh, so I just shook my head at him and stole the picture back from them. Now that I had it, I couldn't stop looking at it. But when I glanced back over at my friends, I noticed them quietly murmuring to one another.

"What?" I croaked, grabbing their attention. When Zoey turned back toward me, she had tears shimmering in her eyes.

"Nothing," Barrett said, nonchalantly shrugging his shoulder.

"Zoey?" I asked, eyeing her as she looked away from me.

She sighed audibly before standing from the bed. "It's just that, it all makes sense now. Why she stopped talking to all of us. She was pregnant and didn't want you to know until after he was born, but then . . . all I'm saying is that, I get why she did what she did."

"She still should have told him from the beginning!" Barrett argued, shaking his head.

"I'm not disagreeing with you there," she said, glaring at her husband. "I just can't imagine what she went through. No, she shouldn't have kept him a secret, but she did and then she lost him. I would have been a wreck had I had Ryce at eighteen and lost her. I wouldn't have known how to tell you, Barrett. Losing a child is a parent's worst nightmare, and it happened to her when she was just a child herself."

"He never got to hold his son," Barrett continued. "Just because she was upset over losing him. That isn't an excuse to withhold information from Drake for the past eleven years and act like it's okay."

Zoey wiped away a fallen tear. "Did we not hear the same version from Lennox? Paige was bawling while she told him. You think she's okay? She will never be okay. Do you think you'd be okay if Ryce or Quinn or Ziggy died tomorrow?"

"Goddammit, Zoey," he growled, standing from the bed. "We came over here to support Drake, not to argue in front of him over his current situation."

Clearing my throat, I looked up at my best friend and saw the wetness glistening in his eyes, so I asked, "Answer the question, Barrett. If one of your girls died tomorrow, how would you feel? How would you act?"

"I don't know!" he exclaimed. "I don't know because I don't want to even think about losing one of them, okay? I don't want to imagine a life where one of them goes before I do."

Zoey wrapped her arms around his waist and gave him a kiss on the cheek. "That's what I mean, Bare. You don't even want to think about it and you're thirty, but try to imagine what she went through being eighteen. I'm not taking her side or anything. I'm just trying to explain that I understand why she pushed us all away, or why she couldn't answer the phone when we called. From one mother to another, I get it."

I understood it the second Paige finished explaining what happened to Declan. It was evident in her tone, in her tears, and how she struggled to explain that she was still mourning his loss. I was just beginning.

"But didn't you say she'd met someone else after you?" Barrett asked me.

Nodding, I replayed that conversation with Paige, the one we'd had at my apartment. I remembered it well because I'd honestly thought she had met someone else back then. But now, thinking back on the exact words she used—*but then I lost him*—I realized I was wrong.

"It was him," I stated clearly, sitting upright as the light bulb finally turned on. Looking over at Zoey and Barrett, I explained. "She didn't meet someone new. She was talking about meeting Declan and loving him in a different way than she loved me, but then she lost him." Resting my elbows on my knees, I sighed and let the epiphany settle in my system. "God, it all makes sense now. She tried telling me that night in my apartment."

"Okay, well, I think she could have tried a little harder," Barrett added bluntly.

I scooted to the edge of my bed and placed my feet on the floor. "I appreciate your support, but this is something I have to get through with her. She's the only one who knows how I feel right now. I don't need you to be on my side, I need you to be on our side. So, please don't be upset with her. You're a parent, and until you experience losing a child, I don't think you should judge how another parent reacts to their loss."

Barrett clenched his jaw but nodded in agreement. "I know."

Zoey smiled weakly at me and then hugged her husband. "I think our work here is done."

"We didn't even do anything besides argue with one another," Barrett objected.

"Sure, we did," Zoey encouraged, nodding toward me. "He's not lying in bed anymore, is he?"

Barrett shook his head at her, but then shot me a grin. "What are you going to do, Drake?"

"I'm going to get to know my son," I said, a hint of sadness lingering in my voice.

"Okay then," he said proudly. "We'll get out of here."

Zoey walked over to me and pressed a kiss to the top of my head as she wrapped her arms around me. "Parenting doesn't get any easier, okay? If you ever want to talk, we're here. We might not know what you're going through, but we fear it every day. Every parent fears it." She ruffled my hair as she pulled away from me. "I know this will be the hardest thing you and Paige go through together, but if you love her like I know you do, don't ever stop fighting for her."

"Yeah, we need a couple to do things with again," Barrett added playfully, sliding his arm over his wife's shoulders. "So, you know, we're really pulling for you guys."

I laughed as Zoey punched him in the gut and chastised him for the insensitive comment.

"Hey!" he exclaimed as they walked out of my room together. "I made him laugh. We got him out of bed and made him laugh."

"Shut up!" she groaned, her voice carrying through the hall.

Alone again, I went back to admiring the picture Lennox gave me, except this time, I analyzed my son's mother. I couldn't get over how young she appeared. She was wearing my high school hoodie, and her long blonde hair was pulled back into a low ponytail that lay over her shoulder. No makeup, no jewelry. Just some sweats and our boy in her arms. I'd loved her in so many different ways throughout the years. I loved her as a teenager, when I didn't have a clue about how relationships worked, but found myself hooked on the beautiful blonde with the gorgeous smile. As a man who missed her so much that he figured out how to make bread bowls for her, I fell in love with her again. Now, as I held this picture in my hands, I knew I was falling in love with her all over again. As the father of our son, I was mesmerized by the woman who'd brought him into the world.

Chapter Nine

After Drake asked me to leave, I drove straight to the cemetery where Declan was buried. I felt drained—though no amount of tears could drain me of the guilt. I hadn't visited his grave in years, mostly because I didn't think I needed to; I kept him with me all the time. In my heart. In my mind. Memories of him were my survival now. But right now, I felt like we needed each other. I'd pulled the quilt out of Dad's trunk and laid it on the ground with me next to Declan's marker. I'd done this for weeks after his death. Every day, I'd get up, throw on some sweats, and come to the cemetery, too afraid to leave him alone because I'd thought never coming here meant letting him go.

Now, I knew I'd never let go of him. Though I wasn't granted as much time with him as I'd hoped, I'd been given enough to hold on forever. I only hoped Drake held on to us, too.

Lying here, I thought about all of the Wilkins' reactions after I told them. Duke stood behind his son with tears in his eyes as he comforted a sobbing Lilian. Lennox couldn't even look me in the eyes, using the electric blue curtain of her long hair to cover her face. But it was Drake's reaction that I remembered the most because I'd imagined it so many times. I'd scripted the conversation in my mind several times in the past, but today, it didn't go the way I'd always thought it would. At first, the look of hate in his eyes was welcomed, because I'd imagined the anger emitting from them, but it was more brutal than I expected. He glared at me like he wanted to physically hurt me. The fury laced in his voice when he spoke shook me to the core because I'd imagined the words, but the bite they carried in reality was harsher than I could've ever mustered in my imagination. The entire conversation was augmented compared to the way I'd imagined it. His voice was as sharp as a knife. His body language reflected the damage I'd caused. The tears he'd shed proved how wrong I'd been.

Even now, a chill ran through me as I thought about it, and it wasn't due to the inches of snow surrounding me as I lie on the ground without a coat. In my jeans, boots, and a sweater, I couldn't even feel the coldness anymore. I could barely breathe when I left the Wilkins' place, too shaken for my organs to work accurately, but after being out here for at least an hour, with tears frozen to my cheeks and my eyes swollen from crying, the guilt that ate away at my stomach bothered me more than the cold.

It wasn't until I heard a car pull up nearby that I opened my eyes and realized how dark it had become outside. Footsteps crunched through the snow, making their way toward me. I already knew who it was.

"I thought I'd find you here," Mom stated, throwing my coat over me. "Dad said you left without your coat or your phone, so when you didn't come back right away, I started to worry."

Pulling the material around my body, I shrugged it on and then slid on my gloves. "Thank you."

She kneeled down next to me and reached for my hand. "How'd it go?"

"It was awful," I confessed, blinking back the tears I didn't deserve to cry. "I'm certain Drake hates me now, but I deserve it. I shouldn't have waited eleven years to tell him."

"You don't deserve it," she stated softly, tightening her grip on me.

I felt like I did. Especially after what Grandpa had said earlier, about how I acted like I was the only one who'd lost him. "Mom, can I ask you a question and you'll be completely honest with me?"

Scanning my face, she nodded with a slight smile. "Of course."

"Do you think I act like I'm the only one who lost him?"

"Sweetie," she sighed, shaking her head. "No, I think you act like a grieving mother. You have a hard time talking about Declan because you miss him so much. You rarely visit us because it's hard for you to be in the same room where he died, yet you refuse to change a thing about the room. You miss him, but you know others miss him, too. I know how hard it is for you to see his pictures around our house, but you've never told us to take them down. People have different ways of coping with loss, Paige, and Grandpa just doesn't agree with yours because he doesn't understand the type of loss you've experienced." She wiped away one of my tears and then continued. "Your dad and I don't even understand it. But we have had a glimpse of it. When Declan died, he took part of you with him. We're not as close as we once were, and I know it's because you feel guilty for asking us to keep him a secret."

"I do," I confessed, staring up at her with tears in my eyes. "I never should have asked you guys to do that. I should have told him a long time ago."

"I know," she said in a comforting voice. "But would that have really changed anything? We'd still mourn him just like we do now. We'd grieve the loss of our daughter who's been hardened by the unfairness of death."

"Mom," I cried as I wrapped my arms around her. She embraced me tightly and kissed me just above my ear. "After he died, I wasn't sure how to act or how to go on, so I just went through the motions of what people my age were doing at the time, and I've been going through them ever since."

When she pulled away, she cupped my face and wiped it dry with her thumbs. "I know, but Paige, at some point, I want you to think about your future. You deserve to be happy again. You need to stop punishing yourself for what happened because it was never your fault. I'm not suggesting you move on or get over him because I know that's impossible, but I do think you need to be able to talk about him and share his memories with others. Was it really the end of the world that Grandpa included him in Nana's obituary? I think you'd want people to remember him."

"I just wish he would have told me so the Wilkins didn't have to learn about him from the newspaper," I said, shaking my head.

"I agree," she said with a nod. "A head's up would have been nice, but there's nothing we can do about it now. I went over to the Wilkins' place first in search of you, and I talked to Lilian. She asked if I had a picture of Declan, so I gave her the one I kept in my purse."

I stared at her in disbelief, anxious to hear Lilian's reaction. "What'd she say?"

Mom smiled proudly. "She said our grandson was handsome, and I agreed with her. She seemed eager to know more about him."

"Oh," I said, relaxing somewhat.

"See," she continued, resting her head on my shoulder. "She wasn't upset with you. I think she understood, as a mother herself. It's easy for a parent to put themselves in your shoes and realize how hard it's been. A parent never stops fearing the worst. Even though you're an adult now and you have your own life in the city, I still worry about you every day. We used to be so close, and I miss that with you. Think about it, if Declan were you and you were me, how would you feel if he never called or visited?"

The answer was easy because I'd thought about it a lot. I had nights where I'd lie in bed and think about what it would have been like watching him grow up. I strongly believed it would have been terrifying. Sure, there would have been joyful times, but overall, I would have been a nervous wreck. "I'd be scared, all the time."

"A parent always is," Mom said, patting my leg. "I wish you'd learn to let people in again. The fear is much more manageable when I know what you're up to."

I smiled weakly and laid my head against hers. "I'll try, Mom."

"Thank you," she said with a pleasant sigh. "So, what are your friends up to? Has Cash found a woman yet?"

I laughed. "No, he's determined to stay single for a while."

"That's a shame. He's too cute to be single. And what about Elly? Is she enjoying married life?"

I thought about my best friend and how her impending due date fell on the same day as Declan's birthday. I'd struggled with it ever since she and Carter announced her pregnancy. I knew it was out of my control, but that didn't stop the pain that ensued whenever I thought about it. "They're actually expecting a little boy February twenty-third."

"Oh," Mom said, lifting her head to look at me. "I know that's got to be hard, but it's also a nice coincidence, don't you think? Have you told her about Declan?"

"No, most of my friends just think pregnancy scares me."

She chuckled at that. "Well, I think you should tell them about him. After all, doesn't one of your other friends have a little girl now?"

"Yeah, Maverick and Harper. She's about three months old. Every time I see her, I want to hold her so bad because it's been so long since I've held a baby, but at the same time, I'm scared to."

"Hold the baby, Paige. You of all people know that life is short, so make the most of it and hold your friend's baby girl and tell them all about Declan," she encouraged, picking herself up off the ground. She smiled down at me and then tipped my chin up to look at her. "I'm going over to Grandpa's to help Dad sort through Nana's things. We'll probably spend the night over there, so the house is yours tonight."

"Okay."

"I love you, Paige," she said, tightening her coat around her body. "But it's getting colder out, so I'd really appreciate it if you headed home soon."

The smile on my face widened as I stood up and gathered the blanket I'd been sitting on. I wrapped an arm around her neck and sighed. "Thanks. I love you too, Mom."

"I'll see you later."

She pulled away from me and headed toward her car, and I waved as she started to drive away. Then I faced Declan's grave and reached my glove-clad hand out to touch the slate granite. On the front, his full name was engraved in cursive letters with his birth and death dates placed underneath it. I'd had a pair of booties etched into the bottom left-hand corner, and on the back, a sleeping lamb was engraved above the inscription, "Beloved son of Drake and Paige."

"He knows now," I whispered, "and I hope you can forgive me for waiting so long to tell him. Just know that we both love you, that'll never change."

***

Once I got back home, I roamed around the house aimlessly for hours until I finally ended up in my bed, wide awake with the lights still on. When I'd first gotten back from the cemetery, I changed out of my clothes and into a pair of yoga pants and Drake's hoodie. I didn't eat, though my stomach grumbled, begging for sustenance. It felt good to feel something other than heartache. It felt good to feel empty. I could already feel myself slipping back into my post-Declan self, where I couldn't sleep for days and the normalcy of everyday tasks such as eating felt tiresome. Tragedy took everything normal and reversed it.

And I hated it. The longer I lay there, the louder my mind screamed at me to get my ass out of bed and eat something. I was a second away from doing so when I heard a strange noise outside my window. It sounded like scratches on the roof. Then came a loud knock on the glass, and I jumped out of bed to find Drake squatting outside on the roof.

I rushed over to the window, quickly unlatched it and slid open the pane. A cold gust of air blew past me as I leaned out the window. "What are you doing here?"

"I saw your light on," he said with a shrug. "Can I come in?"

Stepping away, I gave him space to step into my room, just like he used to do when we were teenagers. He closed the window behind him and locked it before turning and gazing around my bedroom. I tried to imagine what it looked like through his eyes. It looked completely different from the last time he'd been in here. Back then, it'd been decorated in various hues of purple. Now, it looked like a nursery with my full-sized bed and matching dresser at one end and Declan's things at the other.

Walking over to my bed, I curled up on the edge and wrapped my arms around my legs. "I know it looks different."

"Yeah," he stated softly, running his hand along the rail of Declan's crib. He moved about the room determined, checking everything out, and I let him, knowing he deserved this exploration. He opened drawers on the changing table, and spun the football mobile above the crib. He admired the pictures of Declan displayed on the shelves before taking a seat next to me on the bed.

Unsure of how to respond, I sat completely static and held my breath, waiting for him to speak as my eyes skimmed over his appearance. He seemed as exhausted as I felt. His blue eyes were rimmed with red and still slightly swollen from crying. The sweater he'd had on earlier had been exchanged for a thicker hoodie. His hair was unkempt, as if his fingers had been swimming through it. I wasn't sure how he'd react to seeing all of Declan's things, but I hoped it'd bring him peace. I wanted him to appreciate what I'd done with the room, even if it was years ago. Maybe it was morbid that I'd kept it all intact, but I wasn't ashamed of it. I'd kept it all for Drake, so he could see the environment I'd created for Declan.

"It was him, wasn't it?" he finally asked, glancing back at me. "The other guy you met. It was Declan."

"Yes," I replied, mesmerized by the melodic way his name rolled off Drake's tongue. I dropped my feet to the floor and sighed, wiping my sweaty palms on my pants. "I'm sorry I didn't tell—"

"You don't have to apologize anymore," he interjected, shaking his head. "What you've been through—"

"No," I insisted, staring directly at him. The compassion glistening in his eyes made my heart race. The last thing I expected when I watched him crawl through my window was sympathy. I'd spent the past eleven years fearing this confrontation, and here he sat next to me, acting as if he'd already forgiven me.

"Don't make excuses for me," I said, standing from my bed. I began to pace in front of him, shaking my head in disbelief. "Don't be sweet to me now. I don't deserve it. You should hate me for everything I've done. Hell, I hate me for it! So, please don't sit there and forgive what I've done."

He caught me around the waist, effectively shutting me up as he pulled me in between his legs, gripping my hips tightly. He had tears in his eyes as he peered up at me. His hands skimmed up my sides—he smiled when he realized what I was wearing—then he cupped the nape of my neck. "I forgive you because I can't hate you, Paige. Hating you would be easy, and I don't want easy."

I placed my hands on his forearms and bowed my head. "That doesn't excuse what I've done."

"I'm not making excuses for you. I'm stating facts. Isn't it bad enough that we lost him? I don't want to lose you, too."

Gazing back at him, I asked, "What if I'm already lost? I meant what I said when I told you I wasn't the same. Losing Declan changed me."

"I don't expect you to be the same. A few hours ago, I wasn't the same. But I can't hold a grudge over what you did, especially when I can tell the pain of losing him continues to haunt you. I heard it in your voice when you told me. I saw it in your tears. I felt it with each word you said, and I realized that no amount of tears could ever wash away that pain. So, I forgive you, because I'm not sure I could've done it any differently had our roles been reversed."

"You know this pain," he continued, never once taking his eyes off of mine. "The kind that feels like the world is using your heart like it's a stress ball, fisting it until it's shriveled down to barely nothing and then never letting go. I've never felt pain like this until today. But you have. You've felt it for over a decade, and you still feel it, I know you do. You're the only person who knows what I'm feeling right now. Sure, I'm upset that I missed out on so much, that I never got to experience him the same way you did, but what I hate is that you went through it all alone."

A tear streaked down my face at the same time one fell onto his cheek. I never expected his forgiveness, but his words undid me. He described the same pain I'd been experiencing for years. I used to fear hurting him by telling him about Declan's death, but now that he knew, it was a relief sharing the agony with him.

"I had more than one dream back then," he confessed, kneading my skin. "It wasn't just about football. It was about you, too. About us. I dreamed of us building a life together someday. Maybe I never told you that, and all we talked about was my football career. Maybe you knew that, because you were right about how I would've reacted. I wanted you just as much as football, but had you told me you were pregnant, I would have given the football dream up in a heartbeat for the two of you.

"So, I'm still chasing after that dream of us, and all I ask is that you let me. But right now, I'm more interested in learning about our boy than holding a grudge. You think you could help me with that?"

"Yes," I whispered, as a smile spread across my face.

"Good." He dried both of our faces and pulled me down into his lap so that we were facing the rest of my room. "But you're going to have to be honest with me. No more lying."

I nodded. "I know."

"Your friends don't know about Declan, do they? Is that why you didn't tell them about your past?"

"Yeah," I answered truthfully. "They know I'm uncomfortable talking about pregnancy or being around pregnant women, but they think it's because I'm scared of getting pregnant. I haven't been able to spend time with Elly lately because she's pregnant with a boy and her due date is the same as Declan's birthday. When Harper was pregnant, I avoided her for months."

"Do you mind telling me about your pregnancy?" he asked curiously. "There are things I'd like to know, but if you're not comfort—"

"No," I interjected, covering his lips with my hand. "I'll tell you whatever you want to know."

A smile widened across his face, the exhaustion quickly fading away from his features as excitement took over. "Okay . . . how'd you come up with the name Declan?"

"I had names picked for either a boy or a girl," I stated, resting my head on his shoulder, already feeling more relaxed in his arms. "When I found out we were having a boy, I wanted a D name for him since that's what yours started with. I eventually wanted him to be the next D-Dub. So, I picked Declan."

He chuckled. "What was your girl name?"

"Peyton."

"Naming her after a Manning, huh?" he teased, playfully pinching my waist. "I like them both."

I watched him and the carefree expression on his face mirrored mine. I once feared this conversation, telling him in detail about every moment he missed, but now I couldn't remember why. "Dad videotaped everything, and he made me keep a pregnancy journal. I specifically remember him taping the appointment where we found out the gender of the baby. I think he shouted into the camera something like, 'Another gold arm!' He was so excited, he had a USC football jersey made with your name and number on the back."

"Do you still have the jersey?"

"Yeah, it's back in the city. Most of Declan's clothes and things are at my place. The big stuff, like his crib and changing table, I've kept here. Mom and Dad have asked if I wanted the room changed, but I wanted you to see it first. I wanted you to know that Declan was safe, that I provided him a good home."

"I know you did," he said, running his hand up and down my back. "And the truth about your parents? Why are you not close with them anymore?"

I sighed. "For several reasons. I begged them to keep him a secret, and it backfired. I put them in a position where they couldn't share the joy of expecting a grandchild with any of their friends. Mom wanted to throw me a baby shower and I didn't let her. All they ever wanted was for me to tell you, and I didn't listen. I should've listened. After Declan died, I realized all of this, and I felt like I failed them as their daughter. They would have done anything for me, and I couldn't let them celebrate? I couldn't let Mom throw me a baby shower? It was selfish of me."

He rested his hand on my waist. "I don't think that's selfish. They didn't have to listen to you. They were your parents. They could have made you tell my family and me. They could have made you attend a baby shower. But they respected you enough to follow your wishes. Not all parents are that understanding."

"I know," I said, nodding. "They've always been the understanding parents, but after we lost Declan, I couldn't ask them for anything anymore. I couldn't let them be there for me. I pushed them away, but I'm slowly letting them back in because I don't want them to feel as if they've lost me too. I think the only thing that's worse than losing a child is losing a child who isn't dead because you have no idea if they're okay."

He nodded silently, and in the midst of that silence both of our stomachs rumbled with hunger.

"Have you eaten anything since we've been back?" Drake asked.

"No, have you?"

"Nope."

"We should eat then," I suggested, nodding toward the door. "My parents aren't home, but I know the fridge is stocked. I'm sure we can find something."

"Okay."

We stood from the bed, and he followed me out of my bedroom and down the stairs. I turned into the kitchen, but when I didn't hear footsteps following behind me, I peeked in the living room and found him checking out the pictures my parents had hung up. So, I went back to the kitchen and made us a couple of sandwiches. It wasn't anything fancy, but it would work for now.

"Was he a good baby?" Drake asked loudly from the other room. "Or did he fuss a lot?"

I licked a drop of mayonnaise from my finger and smiled. "He was the perfect baby. He'd wake up in the middle of the night, but it wasn't hard getting him back to sleep. He either wanted food or a new diaper, and then he was good until morning."

I plated our sandwiches and grabbed us two glasses of water and placed everything on the kitchen island. Drake walked into the kitchen with a picture frame in his hand. He set it on the countertop before reaching for his sandwich and taking a bite.

"What picture do you have there?" I asked curiously, unable to see the photo from where I sat.

"It's just a picture of you pregnant," he said in between bites. "I was going to ask how far along you were in it."

Ugh, I thought, mentally rolling my eyes as I took a bite of my sandwich. Out of all the pictures in the living room, he focused on the one of my big belly. What was it with guys and their pregnant women? Carter couldn't seem to keep his hands off Elly's belly nowadays, and now Drake was hung up on some picture of me pregnant.

He turned the frame toward me and smiled. "You look like you're about ready to pop here. How far were you?"

I wanted to groan at the sight of my swelled self, but I held back. "That picture was taken right before we left for the hospital. Dad insisted on an in-labor picture. A few hours later, Declan was born."

"That explains the look on your face," he said, chuckling to himself. "You look seriously pissed off here."

"I was in pain and he wanted to stop for a stupid picture!" I exclaimed, rolling my eyes. "It seemed like I couldn't go to the bathroom back then without Dad wanting to document it."

Drake took a drink of water. "Was he ever pissed about you being pregnant? Like when he first found out, did he want to hunt me down and murder me?"

"No." I nearly spit out my food, laughing. "I actually got kind of irritated with Mom and Dad because they weren't upset about it at all. They trusted me with you. They knew we were using protection. They understood how we felt about each other. Dad was upset because I didn't tell you. He made me promise

165

to document everything and let him help capture every moment of my pregnancy."

He smiled and admired the picture again. "Was labor bad? Did it hurt as bad as they say it does?"

"Dad recorded the whole thing, so you can watch it," I stated smartly, after swallowing another bite. "I'm glad I had my mom there. She coached me through most of it. It was painful, but it was worth it. It's the type of pain you don't regret going through."

"I'm glad it went okay," he stated, finishing the rest of his sandwich.

"Me too."

I grabbed our empty plates and rinsed them off in the sink before placing them in the dishwasher. Then I cleaned the island, wiping away any crumbs, while Drake took the picture and put it back where he found it.

"I don't remember your boobs ever being that big," he said in an astonished tone. "Were they like that throughout the entire pregnancy?"

"Pretty much," I muttered, recalling the soreness that came along with their annoying increase in size. I downed the rest of my water and stood at the sink staring down at my body.

"What's wrong?" he asked, wrapping his arms around my waist. "Did I take it too far with the boob comment?"

My first instinct was to lie to him, to tell him nothing was wrong and go on with our night, but I remembered what Mom said at the cemetery, how I needed to start letting people back in. This was a chance for him to see how insecure I was about my body now. So, I told the truth.

"My body has changed, Drake," I confessed, leaning into his chest. "I don't look like the girl you used to date—the one who wore the stringy bikinis and felt no insecurity whatsoever. I'm not the twiggy girl I used to be."

"I know," he said, pressing his lips to the back of my neck.

"I still have stretch marks, and they're not just on my stomach. They're on my boobs and my thighs, too. I have cellulite now. Some days, I can't even look at myself in the mirror without crying because they remind me of what I've lost. While other days, I admire them because they're another beautiful memory of Declan.

"What I'm trying to say is that I'm insecure about my body now. That's why I didn't want you to touch me the other night in your apartment. I loved every minute of being pregnant with Declan, and while I think the marks are attractive, you may not. I have the curves I always dreamed of having back when we were dating. My boobs are bigger, and I actually have hips and an ass now. But I have no idea what to do with them. I haven't let another guy touch me since you."

As the confession spilled from my mouth like word vomit, I hadn't even realized he was touching me. Drake had slipped his hands underneath the hoodie and found my stomach. He slid them along the soft, smooth skin, down the curves of my sides, until settling them just below my belly button. The temperature in the kitchen escalated to an inferno.

"You say those things as if they're going to deter me away from you," he said in a deep, challenging tone as he ran his nose down the length of my neck. He pressed a trail of kisses along my tender flesh before coming to a stop just below my left ear. "I want to see you. All of you, Paige."

Before I had a chance to protest, he lifted me up off the floor and tossed me over his shoulder. He started toward the staircase and carried me up to the second floor.

"What are you doing?" I asked, admiring his sculpted backside as he walked.

"I need a shower," he stated nonchalantly. "You're getting one, too. You kind of stink."

Jaw dropped, I scoffed. "I do not stink!"

"Well," he said, kicking the bathroom door open as he turned on the lights. "Your attitude toward your body stinks. We're going to change it."

"Drake," I warned in a serious tone. "I am not showering with you. Especially not in my parents' home. They shower in this bathroom."

"Then they shouldn't have left you alone in their house," he stated, locking the door behind him. He set me on my feet and began stripping off his clothes. "Take your clothes off."

Crossing my arms over my chest, I stood my ground. "No, I'm not doing this. We've never showered together."

"There's a first time for everything," he said playfully, toeing off his shoes. Once he was barefoot and wearing only his jeans, my eyes fixated on the hard ridges of his obliques. He moved closer to me and uncrossed my arms as he spoke in a soft, seductive voice. "Trust me, Paige. Shower with me."

He reached into the tub and cranked on the hot water before switching it to the showerhead. Reluctantly, I began taking off my clothes one piece at a time as slowly as I possibly could, delaying the inevitable. I was certain I'd get in the shower with him, because I hardly had a record for denying him, but I was still fearful of his reaction. I wanted his hands on me like any straight woman would, but I also didn't want him to see the dimples on my thighs. In the end, my greedy sex drive won the battle over my nagging insecurity.

When I finally got down to my bra and sweatpants, I watched as he undid the buckle on his belt and pushed his jeans down his thighs. His eyes never left mine until he slid his jeans to the side and stepped toward me wearing only a pair of navy boxer briefs.

Steam bellowed around us and the tension in the room thickened. He reached for the band on my sweatpants and slid them to the floor. He smiled at me as his hands reached for my panties and pushed them down over my hips where they landed next to my sweatpants. He skimmed his hands up my sides, stopping briefly over the script tattooed on my side, and then continued back around to my bra and unhooked it. I tore it away from my body and stared down at his briefs.

Taking my hands in his, he gave me a quick kiss on the knuckles, and then encouraged me to remove his underwear. I snaked my hands under the waistband and pushed the cotton material over his ass where my hands lingered over creamy, taut glutes before finally sliding them all the way down to the floor.

"You keep that up, the water's going to get cold," he said, tossing me over his shoulder again, eliciting a scream out of me as he carried us into the shower. He slid the curtain shut behind us and set me down safely under the hot water.

I shut my eyes and tilted my head back into the warm stream, drenching my entire body in water. With my eyes shut, I could pretend I was alone in the shower, but at the same time, I wanted to see his reaction. Stepping out from under the stream, I opened my eyes and found him watching me. His entire presence made me eager for his touch. His eyes roamed fervently over my body. His hands fisted at his sides as if it was taking everything in him not to reach out and touch me. His cock bobbed between his legs, declaring that neither stretch marks nor cellulite would ever change its reaction toward me.

"Paige," he stated in an amazed yet throaty tone. "My God, woman."

"You can take a turn under the water," I said, switching places with him.

He didn't take his time like I had. He dipped under the water for a few seconds and then reached out a hand for me to take. "Come here."

I stepped toward him, and he took me in his arms, his hands settling above the curve of my ass. He flicked his wet hair out of his face and smiled at me.

"Do you mind if I explore?" he asked, a hint of playfulness in his voice.

"Depends on what you mean by *explore*," I said, narrowing my eyes at him.

He chuckled to himself as he bent his head and kissed my neck. "I want to touch you. I want to kiss you. Just my hands and lips on your gorgeous body."

I ran my hands through his chest hair and smiled. "Do I get to explore?"

"You're more than welcome," he replied, skating his hands around to my hips. He lifted my arm and bent down to read my tattoo. "You have a tattoo?"

"For Declan," I stated proudly, smiling as his traced the lettering with his finger.

"Silverstein," he said, recognizing his beloved children's book.

"I used to read *The Giving Tree* to him."

Drake placed a kiss next to the tattoo and then touched it again. "It's beautiful."

He slid his hands down to my stomach, and for a moment, I held my breath. When his lips connected with my wet skin, I exhaled. My insecurities and inhibitions quickly slipped through the drain along with the running water the longer he kissed me. His hands glided over my body gently, taking their time and turning me on all at once. It'd been so long since I had experienced his tender, sweet touch that I leaned against the tiled wall for support as he continued his onslaught, dragging his fingers up the backs of my legs.

My hands found their way into his hair and pushed the strands back out of his face. "That feels good."

"My hands or my mouth?" he asked curiously, devilishly skimming his lips up the inside of my thigh.

Resting my head against the tile, I sighed. "Both."

Rising to his feet, Drake skated his hands up my sides and rested them along my rib cage. "You really haven't let another man touch you, have you?"

"No," I stated honestly, staring back at him.

"Your body is amazing, Paige." He brushed his lips over mine at the same time the pads of his thumbs slid over the swell of my breasts. "You brought life into the world, and the effect motherhood has had on your body is breathtaking. I understand it's sometimes hard to see the marks he left on you." Placing a hand on my stomach's stretch marks, he smiled nostalgically. "But don't ever think I won't find them attractive. He's a part of you and me, and these marks symbolize the life we made together. I can't think of a more beautiful gift than that."

"Drake." I cupped his face in my palms and kissed him hard. I'd dreamed of hearing those words from him, and now that I had, I couldn't think of anything else to say or do but kiss him. He was the reason I hadn't let another man touch me. Nobody else understood me like Drake did, and he definitely hadn't forgotten how we were together either. Our kisses grew rougher as we sought pleasure. He didn't need to touch my breasts to make my nipples pebble for his attention. He didn't need to check to see if I was wet. He knew by the goosebumps covering my flushed skin that I was aroused. He heard it in the sighs that fell from my lips, and saw it in the darkness of my hooded eyes. He felt it in my trembling hands, failing to properly grasp on to him as he continued exploring, his hands and lips igniting a need begging for a release.

Taking his hand, I guided him down between my legs and kissed along his neck. "Touch me. Please."

"P.J.," he groaned, letting his head drop next to mine against the tile as he slipped his fingers inside of me.

Arching into his touch, I relished in the inveigling movement of his fingers. I took his cock in my hand and began stroking him. I remembered how he preferred to be handled, the exact tightness of my grip and the maneuvers that made him go off. He pumped his hips into my hand but kept his attention on me as he thumbed rhythmic circles against my clit that nearly made me slip and fall. We'd touched and teased and sought pleasure regularly during high school, but now our movements were more intense and deliberate. Time had only amplified our need for one another, evolving us into two beings reveling in what they already had etched into their souls.

"Oh, God," I cried, rocking harder against his hand.

"Fuck," he gritted, thrusting his hips faster as he stroked me at the same pace.

I increased my speed of stroking him to keep up with his pace, and within seconds I felt myself fall into a blissful haze as the orgasm undulated through my body. Tension remedied around my spine, uncoiling through my nerves, stimulating a satisfaction I hadn't felt in years.

When I came back to reality, I noticed the creamy substance on my stomach and laughed.

"Well, that's a first," I stated, running my fingers through Drake's release.

"Sorry," he said shamefully, cleaning it off with his hand.

"Don't be," I replied in a sated tone. "I'd rather you come on me instead of the shower my parents use."

"You're right." He laughed loudly, shaking his head. "Way to kill the mood."

I laughed again as he brushed a piece of damp hair off my face and smiled before he leaned in and gave me a chaste kiss. "I just wanted to prove to you that your body is beautiful."

Wrapping my arms around his neck, I nodded. "Point proven. Now, let's get out of here before the water gets chilly."

He moved us under the water and we cleansed ourselves of the day. Drake lathered shampoo and conditioner into my hair while my soapy hands bathed his body. We switched roles and rinsed off before getting out. I shut the water off, and he grabbed us each a towel. We dried off in silence, glancing at one another and smiling. I cleaned the bathroom and grabbed our clothes, and we headed back to my room wrapped in our towels.

At my dresser, I dug through the folded clothes in search of pajamas. I heard Drake close and lock the door to my room, and then he walked over to me, grabbed the clothes out of my hands and tossed them back into the drawer.

"No clothes tonight." He dropped the towel around his waist and smiled as he undid my towel and let it fall next to his. He reached for my hand and led me over to the bed. "Just us."

"Okay," I said, climbing into bed.

He killed the lights and slid under the covers next to me. In my old full-sized bed, there wasn't much room for both of us, but we made it work. He rested his head on the pillow and stretched out before pulling me close. For a while, we laid in silence, surrounded by Declan's things, a weariness settling over us like another blanket on the bed.

"Thank you," he said softly.

"For what?" I asked, confused.

"For letting me back in. I get it now, why everything with us happened the way it did. Now that I know what you were going through at the time, I understand."

I swallowed the guilt that had buried itself deep inside. "You should've been going through it with me though, instead of wondering what you'd done wrong. I should be thanking you, for forgiving me."

He brushed his lips against mine and then yawned. "I'm not going anywhere. You know that, right?"

"Yeah," I answered with a yawn. "I know."

"Good," he replied tiredly, closing his eyes. "Now, let's get some sleep."

Chapter Ten

Drake

The smell of coffee cake woke me up. Rachel Abram's coffee cake was a staple in their household. Most families had normal breakfasts with cereal or toast—something small to start the day—but not the Abrams. There wasn't a weekend that went by back in high school where I didn't enjoy a piece of her coffee cake. If I had to spend the rest of my life eating one meal, it'd be her coffee cake.

With the aroma of spices filling the room, I curled my body around Paige's and watched her sleep. She appeared at peace while she slept, but I understood her life had been anything but calm. In her twenty-nine years, she'd been through more than most people experienced in their entire lifetime. Now, she'd let me in, and I couldn't imagine a better place to be than right next to her. She was the constant in my life. No matter how many miles apart we were or how long we'd gone without speaking to one another, my feelings for her never dwindled. I had no idea where we went from here, but I was eager to find out.

Last night, when I crawled through her window, all I'd hoped for was the woman who'd changed my life forever. I never expected to see our son's possessions in her room. I never pushed her to tell me about him. But thankfully, she opened up and gave me answers. The pride in her voice when she spoke about Declan and her pregnancy was obvious, but the sorrow that lingered in her eyes didn't go unnoticed. The tattoo etched into her skin proved how motherhood had permanently affected her. I never thought I'd see Paige with a tattoo, but the one she had now, along with the effects of pregnancy, looked beautiful on her. I wasn't sure whether or not she wanted another child, but I hoped she did. Last night, I'd memorized the picture of her pregnant with our boy, her belly swollen with life, and I couldn't stop myself from imagining her pregnant again with my child.

But Zoey had been right. Losing Declan had become our biggest hardship, filled with pain and sorrow. Still, I wasn't afraid of a challenge; I hoped Paige wasn't either. I strongly believed we were better off managing our grief together than apart. All we needed was hope.

Brushing her short strands off her neck, I pressed my lips to her soft skin as my hand ran down the curve of her side, causing her to squirm against me. The scent of my favorite food, mixed with her naked body lying next to mine, made it impossible to keep my hard-on under control.

"It's too early," she mumbled, turning on her back to face me. The sheet slid down, exposing her boobs. She opened one eye and shot me a half smile. "What?"

I trailed kisses from the space between her boobs up to her neck, where I nuzzled her. "Do you smell that?"

She inhaled and then laughed lightly, running her fingers through my hair. "Coffee cake. Your favorite."

"Mhmm." I ran my hand back up the length of her body and rested it over her tattoo. "Did you sleep well?"

"I did," she said with a yawn. "Did you?"

"How could I not with you next to me?" I asked rhetorically, kissing her on the lips.

"We aren't doing anything else in my parents' house," she warned, pushing me away from her as she covered herself with the sheet. "Go get your coffee cake. That'll sate you for a while."

"You know me so well," I laughed, crawling out of her bed. I grabbed my clothes from the floor, and she became the voyeur while I dressed. Her blue eyes took in every move I made, from buttoning my jeans to slipping the shirt over my head. She empowered me as she watched, making me feel as if her eyes were mine, even if she looked disappointed that I'd covered up. Leaning over the bed, I gave her another kiss and smiled down at her. "I'll let you get some more sleep, but if you want any cake, don't sleep too long."

She laughed against my mouth. "Knowing Mom, she probably made two cakes, one specifically for you."

"God, I hope so!"

I left her to sleep and hurried down the stairs to find Rachel Abram reading the newspaper at the kitchen island. The second she laid eyes on me, she set the paper down and stood from her bar stool. She walked over to me with a smile, her arms open for a hug.

"Drake Wilkins," she stated in an awestruck voice. "I didn't think it was possible for you to get more handsome!"

Her hand rubbed my back in a motherly way, and I relaxed into her petite frame and squeezed her back. "It's good to see you, Rachel."

"It's been too long," she said, patting me on the cheek as she took in my grown-up features.

She hadn't changed in the years since Paige and I dated. Her personality was as friendly and welcoming as it always had been. To me, she looked like the woman I'd considered a second mother to me back in the day. Time hadn't aged her, but she shared the same blue eyes as her daughter, and when she looked at me, I caught a hint of sadness glistening in them.

"Please, sit down," she said, motioning to the island. "Cal and I saw your truck sitting in the driveway when we got home this morning, so I made the coffee cake that you used to always love. What would you like to drink?"

"Whatever you have is fine," I said, taking a seat across from her at the island. "You know I'm not picky."

"Do you drink coffee now?" she asked, glancing back at me over her shoulder.

"Black would be perfect," I stated with a nod.

She laughed to herself. "Ugh, the same way Cal drinks his. I don't know how you guys drink that strong crap."

I smiled at her as she carried a plate and cup back to the island with her. "I can put down a cup of it, and then I'm done."

"Not Cal," she said, rolling her eyes. "I swear, that man would drink coffee until it took the place of his blood. He's actually been told to cut down on it."

"Is everything okay?" I asked curiously. Paige hadn't mentioned anything about her dad, but then again, we never discussed how our families were doing.

"He's fine," she said, slicing off a piece of cake for me. "It's an age thing. They'd like him to switch to decaf, but he refuses to do that, claiming his writing would suffer if he gave up caffeine."

I laughed into my mug before taking a sip. The burn of the hot beverage jolted my senses as it traveled down my throat. My stomach growled, eager for a bite of her cake more than another swallow of the steaming drink. She handed me a fork and slid the plate across the island to me.

"Eat up."

Pushing the fork into the fresh brown and yellow loaf, I sliced off a bite and slid it into my mouth. The streusel was my favorite part. Hints of brown sugar and cinnamon ignited my taste buds, and the maple glaze already had me craving another piece, bigger than the one she'd given me. Why she bothered giving me a plate when she could have set the pan in front of me instead was a mystery to me.

"Nice to see some things haven't changed," she said, watching me taking another bite.

I pointed my fork down at the cake and swallowed my food. "I've had a lot of coffee cake over the years, and yours is still the best."

She grinned proudly. "Thank you, Drake."

"No," I said, forking up another bite. "Thank you."

She took a sip of her coffee and then her smile dissipated into apprehension. Placing her mug on the countertop, she closed the newspaper and set it to the side before giving me her attention again. "I know yesterday wasn't easy for you, but I do want you to know that Cal and I are very sorry for not handling the situation better. We could have made her tell you back then and we didn't. We—"

"Don't. It's not your fault," I said, shaking my head. I picked a crumb off my empty plate and tossed it in my mouth as a heaviness settled in my chest. I wasn't prepared for an apology from her. "It's nobody's fault. You couldn't have known what was going to happen. You were supporting your daughter, and I respect that."

"Thank you," she said, blinking quickly to avoid crying. "How are you doing?"

I shrugged, taking another sip of my coffee. "I'm not really sure. Yesterday was life-changing. I'm a father now, and it took me a while to wrap my mind around that. When I saw the picture you gave my mom, of Paige holding Declan, our small family became real. Last night, I saw the pictures of Paige pregnant, and I felt joy and sadness at the same time because I'd missed it. I could never blame her though. I love her too much to be upset with her for mourning the loss of our son." I glanced over at Rachel, and she had tears in her eyes as she smiled back at me. "I still love her, but I'm not sure where we go from here."

She reached across the table and grabbed my hand. "You learn everything you can about him. You mourn with her and on your own. You talk about him, and help each other through the grief. Most importantly, you stay patient with one another. I may not understand what you're going through, but I know my daughter."

"Rach, who are you talking—"

Cal Abram stopped in his tracks when he saw me sitting at the island with his wife. He had a cup of coffee in his hand, and the overhead light in the kitchen glistened off of his bald head. In his jeans and Giants hoodie, he looked exactly like the man I'd respected growing up in Bedford.

"Drake," he said excitedly, grinning widely. "Look at you all grown up and drinking coffee."

"Right?" Rachel laughed, waving her husband over toward her. Cal gave her a peck on the cheek and then the two of them gave me their attention again.

"I'm actually here for the cake," I quipped, showing off my empty plate.

Cal laughed, smacking me on the shoulder. "Still have the appetite, I see."

"I doubt that'll ever change," I said, cutting off another piece of cake. "It's good to see you again, even under the circumstances. I'm sorry about your mom."

"It's good to see you, too." He took a seat beside Rachel and set his elbows on the table. "And thank you. Mom had been battling Alzheimer's for years."

My brows furrowed. "I wasn't aware. When was she diagnosed?"

"Shortly before you started college," he answered, refilling his coffee mug. "She declined faster than we expected. We put her in a home around the time Paige had Declan. After he passed, she couldn't remember much. We had trouble getting her to understand that he was no longer with us. She'd ask to see him all the time, which made it difficult for Paige to visit her."

I nodded and watched as Paige stepped into the kitchen. Her hair had been straightened around her oval face, and she had applied minimal makeup. Her jeans molded to her legs and accentuated her ass, and the purple tunic sweater she wore brought out the blue of her eyes. She had on a pair of fuzzy socks—the sort she'd always preferred to wear during the cold weather. Once she grabbed herself a water out of the fridge, she headed toward us.

"Good morning, sweetie," Rachel said, smiling at her daughter.

"Morning, Mom," she returned.

I detected the light scent of her perfume, and pulled her down to sit on my lap.

"Did you enjoy your cake?" she asked, smiling at me.

"Two slices of it," I stated proudly. "Would you like a piece?"

"No, thank you," she said, shaking her head.

"Now, that I have both of you here," Rachel started, placing her coffee in its saucer before wiping her hands on her jeans. She shot us an anxious smile and then continued. "I wanted to let you know that I've invited Drake's parents over today to discuss Declan. They're eager to watch the videos we made and see the pictures we took."

"Mom," Paige sighed, narrowing her eyes at Rachel. "Drake hasn't even had a chance to see everything yet."

"Then the two of you should join us," she offered, her smile widening. "I think it would be good for you to stick around and contribute, Paige. Answer any questions Lilian and Duke may have."

Paige stiffened in my lap, clearly uncomfortable with the plans her mom made, so I comforted her by rubbing my hand up and down her back. I leaned in to her ear and kissed the area below her lobe before whispering, "You can do this, P.J. I want to watch the videos and see the pictures too, and I'd like you by my side when I do."

Her tension vanished with my words, her body relaxing against mine, and she gave me a small smile as she said, "Okay."

"Great!" Rachel exclaimed, hopping down from her barstool. "They should be here any minute, so I'm going to set up some food and drinks in the living room. Cal, you go get all of Declan's stuff."

"Will do," he stated, downing the rest of his coffee.

They rushed out of the kitchen, and Paige shook her head at them. "I'm sorry. This wasn't how I wanted to share him with you, with our parents tagging along."

I chuckled lightly and leaned my forehead against hers. "I know, but I also know my mom is dying to see everything. So, I don't mind."

"I have one condition though," she stated, pulling away from me. She took a deep breath and exhaled, unable to make eye contact with me. "I can't watch the labor video with you."

"Why?" I asked curiously, brows furrowed.

She swallowed hard and shook her head again. "I just can't, Drake."

Taking her chin in my hand, I made her face me. "Why can't you watch it? Explain it to me, Paige."

She reached for my hand and entwined our fingers together. Staring at our joined hands, she said, "I feared the worst during labor, but once they put Declan in my arms, all those fears went away, as if we were invincible together." She blinked away the tears pooling in her eyes and continued. "But we weren't, and I can't hold him anymore. That day was one I will cherish forever, but I prefer not to watch the video because I lived it. I never should have let my fears subside. If I hadn't, maybe he'd still be alive. I would have been too afraid to sleep while he slept." She brought our hands to her lips and kissed them, and then she offered me an ashamed stare. "I promise to do anything else you want, but please don't make me watch it with you."

"Okay," I said sympathetically, wrapping my arms around her tighter. I swallowed down the anger her words fueled. Her notion pissed me off—as if she could have stopped death from taking him by acting paranoid. I wasn't sure how I would manage removing that concept from her mind, but I'd figure it out. In the meantime, I'd support her wishes. "You don't have to watch it with us."

She cupped my face and covered my lips with hers. "Thank you."

The doorbell rang and we heard the sound of our parents greeting one another. Paige and I walked into the living room to find our moms hugging one another while our dads carried on a conversation. They'd always been cordial while we were dating, so it wasn't surprising that they'd picked up right where they left off. When Mom caught sight of Paige, she let go of Rachel and rushed over to us.

"Paige," she said compassionately, wrapping her arms around Paige. "I'm so sorry."

"Me too," Paige replied, smiling weakly as she returned the hug.

Then Mom patted me on the arm comfortingly before taking a seat beside Dad on the couch. Cal and Rachel sat on the love seat, leaving the oversized chair for Paige and me.

"We'll start with the labor video," Rachel stated excitedly, pointing the remote at the TV. "I think it's a good place to start."

I peered over at Paige and she nudged me with her arm. "I'm going to go make some phone calls for work. I'll be back down once it's over, okay?"

I nodded, and then watched her leave the room, praying she'd come back so I didn't have to experience this alone.

"She's not going to stay and watch?" Dad noted.

"No," I stated, not caring to elaborate as I took my place in the chair. Instead, I focused my attention on the TV, and when a young Paige filled the screen, a smile graced my face.

Lying in a hospital bed, she wore the clinical gown, and her long hair was piled on top of her head in a messy bun. She had a machine hooked up to her, and Rachel stood next to her bed making sure she was comfortable.

"Dad," she warned in a younger voice. She appeared sweaty and annoyed. "I swear to God, if you don't get that thing out of my face, I'm going to break it."

He laughed. "You said I could film everything. Labor is part of everything, sweetie."

"Well, I know it has a zoom feature, so you could capture it from far away," she said, rolling her eyes.

Cal panned the camera to Rachel, and she glared at him. "Cal."

"Fine," he said, taking a seat farther away. He used the zoom feature and held the camera on Paige and her mom.

Paige gripped her mom's hand tightly as she endured another painful contraction.

"You're close, Paige," a nurse informed them. "About nine centimeters dilated. When you get to ten, you'll start pushing."

"Oh, God," Paige cried nervously, resting her head back against the pillow. Rachel dotted Paige's forehead with a wet washcloth. "It already hurts, Mom, and nothing's even happened yet."

"It's going to be okay, sweetie," Rachel said in a calm voice. "Just relax and focus on your breathing."

She nodded, and for the next several minutes, the camera showed her taking deep breaths and exhaling them. When the nurse left the room, Paige turned her head toward her mom and asked, "Mom, do you remember what we talked about?"

"I'm not discussing it," she said adamantly, shaking her head. "Because nothing bad is going to happen."

"But he's really early," Paige stated in a worried tone.

"Babies come early and late all the time," Rachel commented. "That doesn't mean something bad is going to happen."

"But what if it does?" she asked. "I need you to promise me—"

"Paige, I love you—"

"And I love him, Mom," she interjected strongly, placing her hands on her belly. "If something happens and they have to decide which one of us to save, promise me you'll make them save him. Promise me you'll let me go."

Rachel looked away from her, as if it pained her to consider choosing anyone over her own daughter, but then she went back to dotting Paige's forehead with the washcloth and whispered, "I promise."

"Thank you."

I wiped the fallen tears off my face and didn't bother glancing around the room at anyone else. I heard their sniffles and the sound of hands stealing tissues from their boxes.

"Okay, Paige," announced the doctor, "you ready to start pushing?"

"N-no, not really," she replied fearfully.

"Well, it's time," he said, taking a seat on the rolling stool at the end of her bed. He scooted in between her legs, and then shot her a caring smile. "You're in good hands, so just focus on pushing and breathing."

Rachel grabbed Paige's hand and kissed her on the forehead. "You can do this. If I could do it when I had you, I know you can do it now."

"Right." Paige nodded furiously. "I can do this."

She started pushing whenever the doctor demanded it. She cried out in agony and then relaxed and focused on matching her breathing to her mom's. Then it would start all over as she began pushing again. She contemplated giving up, sweaty and exhausted from the strenuous labor, but she persevered. It went on for what seemed like forever. I'd never watched such a scene. The pain in her voice terrified me and made me squirm, but her willingness to keep going, despite the pain, amazed me. I couldn't take my eyes off the screen.

I was on the edge of my seat by the time I heard his first cry.

When they placed Declan in her arms, Paige glowed with happiness. She admired him like he was a precious gift, and my God, he was. My boy was this tiny human nestled in a white blanket with thick black hair, resting in my girl's arms. Her tears of joy matched mine now.

"He's beautiful, Paige," Rachel said, smiling down at her grandson.

"I know," Paige stated in an awestruck voice, unable to take her eyes off him. "He looks just like Drake, doesn't he?"

"He does."

A nurse stepped up to the bed and asked, "Do you have a name picked out?"

"Declan," Paige said proudly. "Declan Abram Wilkins."

Relaxing back in the chair, I placed a hand over my chest and felt my heart racing from within as I watched the happiness ensue on the TV screen. The last time I experienced this many emotions at once was yesterday afternoon, when I first learned about him. The pain still wallowed around the joy and excitement though, and I understood why Paige chose not to watch. He wasn't here anymore. While I was thankful they'd recorded it, I wasn't sure if I ever wanted to watch it again.

"Excuse me," I said, standing from my seat.

I left the living room and climbed the stairs two at a time, determined to find Paige. I needed her to soothe the pain running through my veins. Walking into her room, I found her pacing as she spoke to somebody on the phone. When she saw me standing in the doorway, she cut the conversation short and hung up, sliding her cell phone into the back pocket of her jeans.

"I can't believe you did that," I said incredulously, admiring her from across the room.

With a nonchalant shrug, she stated, "Women give birth every day, Drake."

"But it was you, with our boy," I continued, walking toward her. I cupped her face in my hands and kissed her hard. "You asked your mom to let you go."

She gripped the crook of my elbows and sighed. "I was worried one of us wouldn't make it through labor because he was early."

"I'm glad you both made it," I said, kissing her once more. I slid my hands down her neck and shoulders and grabbed her waist for support. "I've never watched anything like that before. It was terrifying and beautiful all at the same time. When I heard his cry for the first time . . . my heart feels like it's going to rip through my chest just thinking about it, Paige."

"I know," she said, wrapping her arms around my shoulders.

I hugged her back tightly and allowed her touch to calm me down. "It hurts."

"I know," she repeated, pressing her lips to my neck.

"Are the other videos that emotional?" I asked hesitantly.

"No," she said, pulling back to smile at me. "They're minor compared to the labor video. Dad mostly videotaped our everyday lives around here. So, it's basically just us holding Declan or interacting with him."

"Okay," I said with a nod. "I think I can handle that."

She grabbed the hoodie I wore last night and a coat for herself, and then reached for my hand and tangled her fingers around mine as she led us toward the window. "How would you feel about escaping right now? We can watch the videos later, when our parents aren't around."

"Sounds excellent," I answered, eyeing the window behind her. I'd lost count of the times I'd escaped with her through this window over the years. "Where did you have in mind?"

She unlatched the window and slid the pane all the way up. Smiling, she tugged me forward and said, "Let's go visit our son."

***

Once we arrived at the cemetery, she directed me toward Declan's grave and we parked. Maybe it was morbid of me, but I was more excited to be here with her than back at her parents' place watching memories. When she got out, I threw a heavier coat on over my hoodie and shut the door behind me. Paige jumped down from the bed of the truck, carrying the blanket I had stowed away in the toolbox.

"I'm surprised you still had this in the toolbox," she said, spreading the material out over the snow-covered ground.

"Yeah." I walked around Declan's headstone, staring at it.

She stopped what she was doing and reached for my hand. "It's hard to pick out a headstone for a child. The funeral director actually said that to me, as if I didn't already know that."

She leaned her head against my shoulder and sighed.

"Am I supposed to think it's beautiful?" I asked curiously, tracing the engraved letters with my finger.

She knelt down beside me on the blanket. "I think it's okay to think that, but I'm the one who picked it out. If you don't like it, we could always have something added to it or have it redone."

I shook my head. "No, I like it just the way it is."

"Lie down here with me," she stated, patting the empty spot next to her.

I lay beside her and stared up at the gray, gloomy sky, entwining my fingers with hers. Despite the cold, it felt peaceful here. The cemetery's quietness, mixed with Paige's presence, soothed me.

"I used to come here every day after he died," she said, scooting closer to me. She laid her head on my shoulder and continued. "I'd just lie here all day with him. I didn't know what else to do. I felt lost without him, but being here helped. It made me feel closer to him. It made me feel like I wasn't letting go."

"What made you stop?" I asked.

"A month after his funeral, I visited my nana at the nursing home she was in for her Alzheimer's. When she saw me, she asked about him. It was the first time someone casually brought him up in a conversation with me. She wanted to see him. She asked if she could hold him. She had no idea that he was gone. The visit was painful. After that, I stopped coming out here to visit his grave, because I realized no matter where I went, he was with me. He was in here."

She placed her hand over her heart as a tear slid down her cheek. I reached over and dried it with my thumb, and she turned to smile at me. "Say something."

I smiled at her and then gazed back up at the sky. "Tell me a happy story."

She sighed and took her time thinking. "One night after my shower, I walked into the living room to find my dad holding Declan and talking to him about football. He was watching a USC game, and giving him a play-by-play commentary of the game. He told Declan all about his football star dad, and how he was going to be like you someday." She laughed lightly and tightened her grip on my hand. "It reminded me of all the times you sat in the living room with Dad, discussing football together."

"Yeah," I said, basking in the pleasant sound of her voice.

She rolled over onto me and laid her arm over my chest, resting her chin on top of her hand as she studied my features. "How are you doing? All we've done is talk about Declan and me. I want to talk about you."

Caressing her cheek, I stared back at her. "I don't know how I'm doing. I haven't had a whole day to process the idea of fatherhood, let alone understand it. My world turned upside down when you told me what happened to him, and I feel like I've been drowning in the pain ever since. I have no idea how to right it, to make this ache in my chest go away. But I do know one thing . . . I miss him. Even though I never held him in my arms, he was mine, and I miss the life he could have had." I ran a hand through her hair and sighed. "I always imagined you'd have my children, but I never thought we'd be sitting at our son's grave."

"I don't think the pain ever goes away," she replied honestly. "It idles in the body until a memory triggers it and disturbs the grieving. I don't think grief ever ends either. It's a constant wave of joy and sorrow, a longing for him that never ceases. Some days the tides will pull you under, drowning you in pain, but they always recede and you manage to catch your breath again, until the next disturbance."

"Well, that's something to look forward to," I quipped sarcastically.

She laughed lightly and then brushed her fingers along the stubble of my jaw. "I've learned to succumb to the grief, to let it take me under whenever it wants. It's easier than fighting it. It's okay to be a mess sometimes. It's okay to miss him. It's okay to sit here in the cemetery with him. It's okay to lie in bed, surrounded by all of his things, and cry yourself to sleep. And it's even okay to act like a normal adult. Grief doesn't have a playbook, Drake. I wish it did, because that would make life a hell of a lot easier."

Propping my arm under my head, I ran my other hand down the curve of her spine, replaying her words over in my head. She had years of experience with grief, while I was on day two of it, so I believed her when she said it was never-ending. The pain was worse than any hit I'd endured during football. I couldn't fake left and then go right, away from the pain. I didn't have a team of linemen protecting me from it.

She was my sole support.

"How'd you manage it alone?"

She scoffed, shaking her head. "I haven't been managing it well at all. It wasn't until you came back into my life that I stopped fighting it because I knew I'd have to tell you about Declan. I've never been able to talk about him and the effect his death has had on me, but you've helped me. It's felt good to finally share him with you."

"I have no idea how to manage this, Paige."

"Neither do I," she said reassuringly, leaning in to kiss me. "But we can figure it out together."

Chapter Eleven

Drake and I spent the days leading up to my nana's funeral discussing Declan. We went through the pictures and watched the remaining videos of him. We even drove back to the city for a day, so he could check out the keepsakes I had in my trunk. Now, we were in my parents' home, following Nana's funeral, surrounded by people who were here to celebrate Jane Abram's life and share stories about her. Our family had invited everyone back to our house for dinner. Conversations were impossible to avoid, making it a feat to replenish our wine intake. Several people had asked Drake and me about Declan, thinking we'd recently lost him, and we didn't bother correcting them. But it wasn't until I saw my group of friends walk through the door that I panicked.

"I didn't know they were coming," I whispered, turning away from them.

Drake caught me around the waist with one hand and waved to them with the other. "We have to tell them."

Glancing over my shoulder, I smiled weakly as Elly spotted me and waddled her way through the crowd, followed by Carter and the rest of the gang. Maverick and Harper had even brought Seghen with them. They had her in a black dress, her chubby baby arms protected from the cold by a black cardigan. Black hose lined her legs and she wore the cutest black dress booties to match. They'd combed over her brunette strands and slipped a black headband on her, its old Hollywood-style feather making her appear even more fashionable. The desire to hold her strengthened, but I restrained myself. Asking to hold her now would likely send my friends into shock, and they already looked as if we were attending Declan's funeral instead of Nana's.

"Hi, guys," I said, wrapping my arms around Drake's waist. "There's food and drinks in the kitchen if you're interested."

"How are you doing?" Elly asked, eyeing me closely, her voice taking on its therapist tone, the question about Declan lingering on the tip of her tongue. I'd witnessed the pity look a lot over the last few hours, and I had known Elly well enough to know that she wanted to ask me the same question everyone else had today: *Why didn't we know you had a son?*

As if everyone who'd ever known my family or me was entitled to such information.

"I'm fine," I answered, gazing around at the others. Their faces matched Elly's, tightening the ball of guilt in my stomach.

"Why don't we head down to the basement?" Drake suggested, smiling at me. "It won't be as crowded, and it will give us some privacy."

"Yes, but please get some food first. We have plenty."

They nodded in agreement and headed toward the kitchen while Drake and I waited on them. Mom quickly made her way over to us, smiling.

"It's nice that your friends came," she said, waving at Elly. "She looks like she's about ready to pop."

"I know," I said, glancing over Mom's shoulder to catch Carter making a plate for himself and Elly, who was waddling beside him and pointing at the various foods as she rubbed her belly. "We're going down to the basement, if that's okay. It's so crowded up here with everybody."

"That's fine, sweetie," Mom said, squeezing my arm. She leaned against me and whispered, "Remember what we talked about. They're your friends. Don't be afraid to open up to them."

"Thanks, Mom," I said, offering her an appreciative smile.

"Ooh, that little girl is darling, too!" she cooed. "Look at her headband!"

I laughed and nodded in agreement. "I know. She looks like a starlet."

"She does," she said, turning her attention back to us. "Well, I'll leave you kids alone. If you need anything, just holler."

"Thanks, Rachel," Drake said, wrapping his arm around my shoulders. "To the basement, P.J."

With the gang close behind us, we headed downstairs, flipping on the lights as we went. The basement to my parents' home was my dad's domain. Dad's writing lair—his words, not mine—was down here, giving him the space and the quiet to focus on his work. The main living area consisted of comfortable, leather furniture for entertaining and bookshelves, crammed with his favorite titles, lining the walls. A large flat-screen TV hung from the wall, and the corner of the room boasted a wet bar. In non-writer terms, it was a man cave.

"I cannot believe I'm in C.R. Abram's house," Carter stated in awe.

I smiled, watching him study the shelves. "I can introduce you to him later, if you want. He'd probably even sign a book for you."

"See," Justin said, glaring at Tessa. "I told you I should've brought my books."

"His mother died," Elly said, rolling her eyes. "He does not need you asking him to sign your books."

They spread out a bit, taking a seat wherever they could find one. Fletcher and Bayler shared the love seat, while Tessa sat on Justin's lap in the recliner. Maverick, Seghen and Harper shared the couch with Cash, and Carter and Elly commandeered the oversized chair and ottoman. Drake stood next to me a few feet away from them, and when I caught him smiling at me, I took a deep breath and confronted my friends.

"I wasn't expecting you guys to come," I stated, smiling at the nine of them. "But I'm really glad you did."

They nodded in silence, some of them opting to shove food in their mouths instead of replying, while others stared at me. Finally, Bayler huffed and stated unabashedly, "Kind of like we weren't expecting to find out you had a son?"

"Bayler!" they chastised loudly, throwing daggers her way.

"Oh, please," she said, rolling her eyes. "Like there's a better way to start this conversation?"

Drake and I actually laughed, which made the rest of them relax back in their seats, easing the tension from the room.

"She's right," Drake said, grinning at Bayler. "There isn't an easy way to talk about Declan."

"I'm sorry I didn't tell you guys before, but . . ." I said, reaching for Drake's hand again. I tangled my fingers around his and continued, "I wasn't telling anyone until I told Drake. He found out on Saturday."

Then I proceeded to tell them our story—the one they hadn't heard yet. It went deeper than just the star quarterback falling in love with the head cheerleader. It spanned over a decade instead of the three years like they'd previously thought. A story filled with heartache and loss, not only for the son we lost but for the dreams it took from us as well. It turned a boy and a girl into a mother and a father, and now, we stood before them as grieving parents. By the time I finished, my girlfriends were wiping away tears and the guys were attempting to blink away the ones glistening in their eyes.

I focused on Harper and Maverick and Elly and Carter, speaking directly to them. "I never meant to make you feel as if I wasn't happy for you during your pregnancies. I know my avoidance has come across as if I wasn't excited for you, but I was. I always have been and I always will be, but I will always miss Declan, too." Walking over to Elly, I crouched down in front of her and touched her swollen belly, her hands covering mine as a sob punctured her. "I miss the feel of him kicking inside of me. I miss how the sound of my voice excited him." Moving on to Harper and Maverick, I took a seat on the arm of the couch beside them and smiled at Seghen. "I miss holding him. I miss hearing his cries, and what each of them meant. I miss soothing him back to serenity and rocking him to sleep. I miss spending lazy days with him. I miss everything about motherhood, and when I look at Seghen, all I want to do is hold her."

Standing, I walked back to Drake, grateful for the encouragement radiating from his outstretched hand. I took it, leaned my head on his shoulder, and gazed around the room at my friends.

"I'll never stop being a mom, but I am trying to express it better. I never want my grief to overshadow your happiness. I never want you guys to tiptoe around the topic of parenthood and children. I want you guys to remember him with me, bring him up whenever you can, and know that I'm always here for you."

Elly attempted to get up from the chair, but her belly made it difficult. Carter took her hands and lifted her out of the chair, and then she waddled over to Drake and me and threw her arms around us.

"I'm so sorry," she cried empathetically. "We're here for you too, you know."

"I know," I whispered, rubbing her back as she sobbed. "I know."

Harper joined her, wrapping her arms around us for a hug, and then the whole gang was around us, with Maverick on the outside holding Seghen. Sniffles and cries could be heard throughout the group, but eventually we caught our breaths and relished in our friendship and the support it offered.

"Hold long are we supposed to hug?" Cash whispered to Carter, interrupting the silence.

"I don't know," Carter snapped, smacking him in the back of the head. "Just shut up."

"I was just asking," Cash said defensively.

His tone made me snicker, breaking the somber moment entirely. We let go of one another and laughed at Cash's remarks. The longer the laughter went on, the harder it fell from us, and it felt redeeming. The guilt from keeping Declan a secret from everyone faded away the more I laughed. Sometimes laughter truly was the best medicine.

"This is why you're single," Bayler teased, shoving Cash in the shoulder. "You don't know when to shut up."

"That's the truth," Justin added.

"Do you ask a bunch of questions during sex?" Fletcher mocked, then his voice took on a breathy tone as he continued, sometimes. Hell, when Barrett and Zoey found out about Declan, they came over and were arguing about our situation because he couldn't wrap his mind around the idea of losing one of his girls. It's impossible for them to empathize with us.

"I'd like to give the support group a chance," he stated firmly, clenching my hands. "I know you don't want to, but you promised me you'd do anything I wanted. This is what I want and I want you with me. I'm not sure if it will help, but I hope it does." Frustrated, he let go of me and sat down on the edge of the bed, placing his elbows on his knees and his head in his hands. The stress of the past few days exuded from him. "Today, when Barrett and Zoey stopped by with the girls, I was afraid to hold them because I thought I'd start crying in front of them. I don't want to fear them. I don't even want to look at them and think bad thoughts, like how unfair it is that this happened to us. I don't want that, Paige."

Kneeling in front of him, I lifted his head and kissed him. "I don't want that either."

He grasped my waist. "You'll go to a support group with me?"

"Yes." I'd turned him into the person I was after Declan's death. Everywhere he looked he saw the death of our boy, and he buried the emotions instead of allowing them to run freely. The only difference now was that he recognized it; I hadn't then. Maybe he wouldn't feel this way had I told him years ago. The regret of that notion ate at me like hunger chomping away at an empty stomach, searching for a sliver of sustenance. "I promise."

Chapter Twelve

The next week we had our first meeting with the SIDS support group. It was a small group of five other couples that meet once a week at a therapist's office a few blocks away from S&E. Drake and I opted to walk the short distance after work, discussing the events of our day and how many clients I added to my hit list. I wished we were headed to the gym instead. A nice, long swim in the pool sounded more appealing and more therapeutic than a support group, but I owed him this.

When we walked into the office, I mentally rolled my eyes at the cliché of chairs set up to form a circle in the middle of the room. Did sitting in a circle make it easier for people to open up?

Doubt it.

Coffee and snacks lined a nearby table, but when I glanced around the room, I noticed nobody had partaken in any refreshments.

Thank God.

"Hello." A woman around my mother's age greeted us. "My name is Sydney, and this is my husband, Jay. We're the leaders of the SIDS group."

I already knew who they were. Once Elly had given us their names, I'd made Skye run a background check on them. Neither of them were therapists. They'd been married for twenty-five years, and lost their firstborn son to SIDS a year after they got married. They went on to have three other children.

"Hi," Drake said, shaking Jay's hand. "I'm Drake, and this is Paige."

I smiled at them politely and then took a seat next to Drake. The other couples were already here and staring at us from around the circle. Sydney and Jay took their seats and started the meeting.

"Everyone, we have a new couple with us today," Sydney said, motioning to Drake and me. "So, I'd like us to go over the one rule we have. We don't judge. We're all suffering a similar loss. It's occurred at various times in our lives, meaning we've all handled it differently. We ask that you keep an open mind, that you think before you speak, and that you lend the support you'd want to receive."

"Well said, Syd," Jay said, smiling at her. "Who would like to share first tonight?"

The woman seated directly across from me raised her hand and smiled at the gentleman beside her. "We'll go."

"Perfect. Chris and Jessie, you have the floor."

"We picked out wedding invitations today," Jessie said, grasping Chris's hand. "We don't know if we're ready to set a date yet, but it felt like a step forward for us."

How do you pick out wedding invitations without having a date set? I thought.

"It's been hard," he said, staring at Jessie. "Harder than we thought it would be."

Jessie's eyes landed on me, and I prayed I masked my confusion, but then Drake spoke up and asked, "You're planning your wedding?"

She nodded as tears pooled in her eyes. "Yes, we had plans to get married after Olivia was born, but . . ."

"We lost her two months later," Chris finished. "We've been putting off our wedding ever since."

"We've set several dates, but we always end up pushing it back." She crossed her legs and fiddled with the gold band of the princess-cut diamond on her left hand. "This time around, we've decided to make decisions on smaller items such as invitations and decorations before nailing down the important ones."

"I think that sounds like a good idea," Drake offered, smiling sympathetically.

"I agree," Sydney added. "You've taken your struggles and turned them into a plan you can manage. It's smart. I hope you stick with it."

"Thanks, Syd," Jessie said.

"Have you decided on your colors yet?" asked the woman next to Jessie.

"We haven't, but we're thinking about pink and navy."

That'll be pretty, I thought.

"Who'd like to share next?" Jay asked, peering around the circle.

The gentleman next to Drake raised his hand.

"Great. Rob and Cora, go ahead."

Rob nodded and then leaned forward in his seat and smiled back at Cora. "As most of you know, we've been trying to have another baby after losing Kyle. Since it hasn't happened for us yet, we decided to get tested."

"Both of our tests showed that we were fine," Cora said with a shrug. "It's frustrating."

Sydney reached for Cora's hand and patted the top of it. "It is frustrating, especially when the professionals can't give you any answers. Jay and I experienced the same problem when we were trying again after losing Eric. Initially, we thought I had scar tissue or damage from the previous pregnancy, but that wasn't the case. It took us three years to have another baby. Don't give up."

"Don't make it a chore though either," a man added.

"Charlie." The woman sitting next to him glared, shaking her head.

"It's okay, Emma," Cora offered. "We know it's been hard for you guys from the beginning."

Emma pulled a handkerchief out of her purse and dabbed at her eyes. It was obvious that Charlie and Emma weren't as united as the rest of the couples around the circle. The tension between them was palpable.

"We've been thinking about getting a divorce," Charlie admitted gravely. "I can't do it again. All the doctor's visits and tests, the sex schedule that takes away the fun and spontaneity. We drained our savings to do the in vitro fertilization." He looked at Emma and continued. "You know, I don't regret a minute of it because it gave us Xander, but he's gone now and . . . I can't go through it all again. I love you, but I can't."

"I know," she cried, blowing her nose into her hanky.

Drake reached for my left hand and sandwiched it between both of his. He gazed at me with compassion swimming in his bright blue eyes, and I felt as if he was telepathically saying to me, *Thank God, that's not us.*

I agreed.

"Drake," Jay said, turning the group's attention on us. "Would you like to have the floor?"

Say no, I thought as he contemplated it. *Please say no.*

"Sure."

Crap.

He smiled weakly at me and then explained our story to the group. I couldn't look at any of them as he spoke. Even though he emphasized how young we'd been, I wasn't sure how they'd react when they found out I'd waited eleven years to tell him about Declan. They weren't supposed to judge, but that didn't stop them from mentally judging me. Hell, even I was guilty of it. I'd judged Jessie the second she mentioned wedding invitations without an actual wedding date.

When he finished, I gazed over at him and he kissed my hand. He appeared more relaxed after sharing, and any unease I felt toward the rest of the people in the room floated away. His feelings were the only ones that truly mattered.

The impact of Drake's words silenced the room for several minutes until Jessie pointed out the obvious.

"You were so young," she said in a shocked tone.

I nodded, unwilling to speak.

"It's hard to lose a child no matter how old we are," Sydney stated.

"And it doesn't matter that I found out eleven years later," Drake added, surprising me. "It feels like we lost him yesterday. Will that feeling ever go away?"

"Yes and no. I think it differs for everyone," Jay said, as the rest of them nodded in agreement. "It's a memory that's forever imprinted on our minds and on our hearts. We'll never forget the moment we found out our child died. We'll always be transported back to that day, and I think that's normal. I personally would rather relive that day over and over again than forget it altogether."

"Me too," Sydney said.

"Grief has no right or wrong. It does not judge. It does not hold back, but it can either free you or imprison you. How it affects you is your decision."

Jay ended the meeting on that note, and while most of the couples headed for the refreshments, the couple next to us stayed seated. They never offered to speak during the meeting, but as I grabbed my purse, the woman beside me touched my arm to stop me.

"We're sorry for your loss," she said in a soft voice. "I know you've probably heard that a lot, but we really mean it here, you know?"

"Thanks," I said, nodding.

"I'm Amber," she said with a smile. "This is my husband, J.T."

"It's nice to meet you," Drake said, shaking the man's hand. He pointed to the tags hanging around the man's neck. "Thanks for serving our country, man."

J.T. grabbed the chain around his neck and stared down at the tags wearily. "Three deployments, and we lost our son, Sean, during the last . . . about six months ago."

Amber reached for his hand and he dropped the tags. "He missed the birth and everything. It's been rough, but coming here helps, even if we don't speak at every meeting."

I nodded. "I'm sorry, too."

"Thank you," she said as she stood and slipped on her coat. "Will we see you next time?"

"Yeah," Drake answered, taking my hand. He helped me out of my seat and then placed his hand on the small of my back. "We'll be back."

"Good."

We followed J.T. and Amber out of the office and went our separate ways once we were back on the sidewalk. With his arm draped around me, Drake pulled me closer and asked, "Well, what'd you think?"

I sighed, smiling up at him. "It was heavy, but I didn't think it was bad."

"Me either," he said in an upbeat tone. "Thank you for coming with me."

"You're welcome."

We hailed a taxi to the gym and spent the next hour in the pool. With each lap I made, I thought about Amber and J.T. Just when I thought life couldn't get any crueler than losing a child, we meet them. He served our country. He kept our freedom intact, allowing us to rest easy at night. And he lost his son to SIDS. His son died with no explanation. That's what I hated most about SIDS—it had no cause. The physicians couldn't give an explanation or provide us any answers as to why our babies died. The longer I thought about it, the harder my body worked. I pumped my arms and kicked my legs as fast as they would go, suppressing the anger the best I could.

Life ruled unfairly; it could at least provide a reason for doing so.

I somersaulted and twisted my body to head to the other end, but Drake stopped me under the water by grabbing me around the waist. He pulled me up and I wrapped my legs around his waist.

"What's wrong?" he asked, removing my goggles. "You're crying."

I hadn't realized I was crying until he pointed it out. With labored breaths, I shook my head and grasped his shoulders. "It's just . . . it's not . . . it's not fair. They shouldn't lose their son while serving our country."

"I know," he said, pressing his lips to my temple. "Nobody should lose their child, but I know what you mean. Tonight was hard."

"Thank you for just wanting to play football," I said softly, leaning back to look at him. I pushed a fallen strand off of his forehead. "Maybe I shouldn't think that, but I'm glad you weren't overseas fighting in a war. I worried enough with you on the other side of the country playing football, and you still got hurt."

"I'm here now," he reassured, skimming his hands up my sides. He played with the band on my bikini top and smiled. "All that matters now is that I'm here with you."

Chapter Thirteen

Drake

Weeks later, the girls spent the weekend at a spa, which meant the guys were on babysitting duty. Before I arrived at Maverick and Harper's place today, I didn't believe it would take five men to watch one infant girl, but now that I'd been here for a couple of hours, I wholeheartedly accepted it.

It was fucking chaos.

Cash gagged whenever Seghen burped up milk. When he finally found the dried vomit stuck to him, he actually ran to the bathroom and threw up. Maverick had to teach Carter how to put a diaper on her, even though Elly was due in a week. Fletcher was the only one who could make Seghen laugh, and she preferred Justin's singing over the rest of ours. A bomb exploded in her diaper while I was holding her, and the diarrhetic debris ran out of her onesie onto my shirt.

By the time Maverick changed her into a new outfit, I'd put on the shirt he gave me, grabbed another beer, and joined the rest of the guys in the living room. It was three o'clock in the afternoon and we all were eager for a nap.

"Oh, come on, guys," Maverick teased, proudly carrying his daughter. "She hasn't been that bad."

"What do you feed her?" Justin asked with a cringe.

"She only gets Harper's milk."

"What's it laced with?" Fletcher quipped. "It smelled like a mixture of Thai food and raw eggs."

"Like I said," Maverick laughed, giving Seghen a kiss on the cheek, "Not bad. She's smelled worse."

"Not bad?" Cash retorted in disbelief. "I had dried vomit on me for hours, and none of you assholes cared to tell me!"

Carter pointed his beer at me and laughed. "She pooped on Drake."

"Yeah, man," I said, taking a swig of my beer. "Poop trumps vomit."

"Bullshit," Cash argued, glaring at me with his beer bottle near his mouth. "Did you change shirts? You did, didn't you? Mav, you gave him a shirt to wear after she shit on him?"

"It was diarrhea, Cash," Mav emphasized.

"So," he said, jumping up from his seat on the floor. He pulled his shirt off as he walked out of the living room still bitching. "Vomit is just as bad as poop! I'm borrowing a shirt, and I am never having children!"

We laughed at his ridiculous outburst and then turned our attention back to the game we were watching on TV.

"I can't wait until Cash has kids," Maverick stated mischievously. "I hope they all throw up on him."

"I hope he has twins," Justin mused with a smile. "Then there's the possibility of both of them throwing up on him at the same time."

"Milk vomit is nothing," Carter said with a shrug. "It looks just like milk when it comes back up. I'd hate to see how he reacts when he has a kid with the flu and they're blowing actual chunks."

"You couldn't put on a diaper," I said, downing the rest of my beer. "Your son will be shitting on you all the time."

Fletcher and Justin chuckled into their drinks as Cash returned to his spot on the floor, wearing a Jones Jym t-shirt that matched mine.

"Hey!" Carter retorted defensively. "Seghen wouldn't quit wiggling around."

"Elly's due in a week," Maverick pointed out. "You better figure out how to put a diaper on a moving baby."

"I know how to put a diaper on," he said confidently. "It's when they roll over that I have problems, and then you had to call Harper and tell her about it."

"She's never rolled over before!" he exclaimed, smiling brightly at Seghen who was chewing on her chubby hands. "Say, we had to call and tell Mommy about it."

Carter rolled his eyes, and I laughed as I stood from the couch and headed into the kitchen. The afternoon had been chaotic, but the beers were going down smoothly and the basketball game we were watching was actually getting interesting. Maverick and Harper's place was huge, which gave us enough space to comfortably hang out, but it also meant the place was littered with girly infant items. There were baby blankets, board books, and toys all over the floor. Baby bottles, along with our empty beer bottles, lined the kitchen countertops. Then there was Axel and his dog toys. The Great Dane took up his own corner of the living room with his massive dog bed.

It'd made for an exciting yet relaxing Saturday, especially when Axel found the dried vomit on Cash's shirt and started licking him.

Laughing, I grabbed another beer, leaned against one of the kitchen pillars, and smiled at the pictures of Maverick and Harper and their small family displayed on the fridge.

"You doing okay?" Maverick asked, walking into the kitchen with Seghen in tow.

I nodded. "Yeah, I'm fine."

He noticed what I'd been studying. "You know, it's okay if you're not. We're in the dad's club. I know we haven't known each other long, but you can talk to me."

I smiled and motioned to the pictures. "Were you ready to become a dad? Is it always this hectic?"

"Yes and no," he answered. "Harper and I hadn't been dating long when we found out she was pregnant. Hell, it'll be a year for us next month, so it all happened pretty fast." He grinned at his daughter and then blew on her belly. "Seghen wasn't planned, but I don't regret a single moment as her dad. Sure, I was terrified before she was born, because it was out of my hands. I constantly worried about her and Harper. Once she arrived, it was even more terrifying because I had no idea what I was doing. But I love my family, and we're figuring it out as we go. It's not always this hectic. I swear Seghen just likes to screw with the guys when Mom's off with her girlfriends. Some days are crazy, but even then, it's still fun. I've learned that you can't plan everything. Sometimes the best moments in life are the unexpected ones."

"I hadn't realized you guys hadn't been dating that long."

He patted me on the shoulder and smiled. "It doesn't matter if you've been with the girl for a month or fifteen years, when you're with the one, you know, right? Paige and you were just kids, but you knew then, didn't you?"

"Yeah," I replied with a nod. "I just wonder if she still wants a future with me. We used to talk about it all the time during high school, but we haven't talked about it at all lately. The support group has helped bring us closer, and it's nice to connect with other couples who've lost kids, but I'm curious about our future. I get we can't plan everything, but we can hope. I mean, is it weird that I hope for Saturdays like this with her that include exploding diapers and vomit-stained shirts, or a fridge covered in pictures of us?"

He laughed loudly, sporting a proud grin. "No, man, that's not weird at all, that's love. Did you notice how the only guy here today to freak out about anything was Cash? It's because he hasn't found that woman yet. Fletcher would do days like this with Bayler, Justin would do the same for Tessa, and Carter is about to have them with Elly. You didn't bitch when Seghen crapped on you, and that's why I offered you a new shirt. Cash deserved to wear her vomit for a while."

I laughed at his last comment. "Do you think he'll ever settle down?"

"It's going to take a badass chick to get that man to change his ways," he said, taking a swig of his beer. He gazed at me and tapped his beer bottle against mine. "I know you feel new to the dad's club, and that's understandable. You may have missed out on all of this with Declan, but you're still a good dad because you've forgiven his mom. You love and support her, that's what makes a great man an even better dad."

I playfully pinched Seghen's left cheek and smiled. "Thanks, Mav. I needed to hear that."

"Anytime," he said, wrapping his arm around my shoulders. "Come on. Let's see if KU can pull this win out of their asses."

***

Paige

"Am I supposed to feel like I'm floating?" Bayler asked curiously.

"Yes," Tessa replied, from her tub next to mine. "The mud will make you feel weightless."

The three of us were taking mud baths. It had been one of Tessa's bucket list items for Elly after her cancer scare two years ago. Since Elly was pregnant, she wasn't allowed to participate, and with Harper breastfeeding, she opted out of the adventure, too.

Lucky bitches.

For the last five minutes, Bayler, Tessa, and I had been submerged all the way up to our necks in warm, soft mud mixed with water. I wasn't sure of the exact temperature, but we were sweating our asses off. We each had a towel pillowed beneath our heads and a nearby attendant, who thankfully supplied us with water and dabbed our faces with a cool washcloth. It was supposed to be relaxing.

"How are you doing over there, Paige?" Tessa asked cheerfully.

"I don't understand how this is relaxing," I answered with a cringe. Despite growing up in the country, my idea of relaxation was not sitting naked in a tub full of mud. Bedford, New York was classy country—not down and dirty; relaxing meant sunbathing near an inground pool. "I feel like mud is getting into places it shouldn't be."

Bayler laughed from the tub on my left. "I like it. It's like a mud cocoon. My ass isn't even touching the bottom of the tub!"

"It's hot," I complained, taking a sip from my water cup. The lady wiped my forehead. "I can't remember the last time I sweat this much."

"It's cleansing our pores," Tessa explained. "It's sucking the stress out of us and removing the toxins from our bodies."

"No, it's not," I muttered, rolling my eyes as I laid my head back against the pillow and exhaled.

"You haven't been properly fucked if you can't remember a sweat fest like this," Bayler stated bluntly. "How long has it been for you?"

"You and Drake haven't done it again yet?" Tessa asked in a concerned tone.

"No," I answered harshly. "I mean, we've done other sexual things, but we haven't had sex."

"Why not?"

"I don't know." I knew why; I just didn't want to give the reason a voice. We'd rounded third several times since our reunion, and he almost slid into home the other night, but I stopped him, claiming I wasn't ready yet. I was long overdue for sex, but at the same time, I feared the possible consequences. What if I got pregnant again? What if my second child died, too? No matter how amazing Drake's hands and mouth felt on my body, those thoughts crossed my mind every time we were intimate. The past proved using protection was pointless. Declan was proof that Drake's sperm could defeat birth control pills and a Trojan Magnum.

Without warning, a glob of mud hit the left side of my face and stuck. I opened my eyes, turned my head toward Bayler and glared.

"Did you just throw mud at me?" I asked in an appalled voice. I attempted to reach up with my hand to remove it, but the thick mud made it difficult to move.

"Yes, I did," she stated proudly, making a face at me. "Your incessant bitching and negativity is ruining my mud bath."

By the time I got my hand out, I'd flung more mud at myself. I glanced up at my attendant and asked, "Are we almost done?"

She chuckled. "You have two minutes left."

"Okay," I said, relaxing back against my pillow.

It was the longest two minutes of my life.

Once we were finished, the attendants helped us out of our tubs and led us over to a shower area where we could wash off. They turned the water to cool, and we basked underneath the rush of relief. I'd never wanted a cold shower in my entire life until now. The cold water rejuvenated my hot, sweaty body. Then they provided us with soap, and I scrubbed my body so hard until I couldn't see a speck of brown on me.

After I stepped out of the shower and put my bikini back on, Bayler and Tessa were waiting on me. I tied the robe around my body and shrugged. "What?"

"Did you make sure to get squeaky clean?" Tessa teased.

Bayler laughed. "Drake won't get any mud in his mouth later, will he?"

"Enough," I said, shaking my head.

The main attendant smiled at us and then asked, "Would you ladies prefer to join your friends in the private pool or enjoy a session in the steam room?"

"Pool," I stated firmly, glaring at Tessa and Bayler. "I don't think I have any more sweat to perspire."

"That's not true," Tessa said. "But I agree, let's do the pool."

Bayler shrugged. "I'm game for whatever."

The attendant led us to the private pool. It was an indoor area with a large whirlpool in the center and a smoothie bar in the corner. Elly and Harper were already in the pool, looking carefree and relaxed, with a smoothie in their hands.

"Hey, guys!" Elly exclaimed. "How was it?"

"It was awful," I whined, untying my robe.

Bayler tossed her robe to the side with Tessa's and said, "Oh, don't believe her."

"It was amazing!" Tessa cheered, wading into the pool.

Harper took a sip of her smoothie and smiled. "Why didn't you like it, Paige?"

Stepping into the pool, I sighed contently at the feel of the cool water against my skin. I waded in farther and took a seat by her. "I felt like I was in a straightjacket of mud, sweating my ass off for a solid ten minutes."

Harper cringed. "That sounds awful."

"It wasn't," Bayler said, rolling her eyes. "She's making it sound bad. You float in warm, soft mud that's pretty thick, but it feels like you're floating on a cloud. It was awesome."

"And it was so relaxing," Tessa added happily.

"No," I said, downing a long gulp of strawberry-banana smoothie. "Next time, I'm doing this pool and smoothie thing."

Elly laughed, clinking her cup with Harper's. "It has been pretty nice in here. Although, I've had to get out quite a bit to pee."

"My boobs leaked a little bit of milk earlier," Harper said, wrinkling her nose.

"Please," Bayler said in a disgusted tone, shaking her head. "Do not talk about your leaky boobs."

"It happens to every mom," Harper stated nonchalantly as she took another drink of her smoothie. "Oh, and Mav called while you guys were getting your baths. Seghen rolled over for the first time! Can you believe that?"

We cheered and made a toast to her little girl's achievement.

"I hated missing it," Harper added, with a bummed smile. "But she'll do it again."

For the first time since telling them about Declan, the nag of jealousy never came. In fact, it had been absent since the day of Nana's funeral. I felt more like the mother hen in the group now. Earlier, I'd been the first one to notify the spa staff that we had an expecting mother and a nursing mother in our group, and they planned our day accordingly. On the drive up here, Elly had asked me questions about labor. So, when Harper reached over and grabbed my hand, I felt the support only another mother could provide emitting from her touch. Though I knew she was upset about missing a big step in Seghen's life, she was also aware that it reminded me of those achievements I missed with Declan.

"Seghen also pooped on Drake," Harper stated, attempting to hold back her laughter.

I choked on a gulp of smoothie. "You're kidding."

"I wish I was," she laughed, shaking her head. "Maverick said he handled it like a pro though."

"Better than Carter," Elly stated in an annoyed tone. "He couldn't even put a diaper on her today, and Cooper is coming in a week! Pray for me, girls, I'm gonna need it!"

***

After arriving back at Harper and Maverick's place, Justin grabbed Tessa and they left with Fletcher, Bayler and Cash, the five of them eager to spend their Saturday night at one of Fletcher's clubs. All that remained were the moms and dads of the gang.

Walking into the living room, Harper, Elly, and I found Drake with a sleeping Seghen in his arms, while Carter and Maverick whisper-yelled at the TV over a bad call the refs had made.

"Hey," I said softly, curling up on the couch beside him.

"Hey there, P.J.," he replied, his boyish smile perfectly intact. "How was your spa day?"

"It was all right." I shrugged and admired the sleeping beauty in his strong arms. I'd never seen him hold a baby before, and the sight of them together made my heart race as a need pooled deep in my belly. "I heard your day was filled with excitement."

"Oh, yeah," he said, laughing lightly. "I can mark off getting pooped on from my bucket list."

My smile widened. I loved his sense of humor. It was one of his many traits that made me fall for him so long ago. I kissed him and gazed down at Seghen in her adorable pink onesie that said, "I Run This Place." It pictured a cartoon of a mom and a dad falling on a treadmill with the baby leaning against the equipment like a personal trainer. One of Maverick's trainers at his gym must have gotten it for them.

"Declan pooped on me once," I stated nostalgically, running my finger along the top of Seghen's soft, chubby cheek. "I thought it was a fart at first, but then I noticed the brown liquid seeping out of his onesie. It was all over his back. It was so gross, but I blame myself for not having the diaper on tight enough."

When I realized everyone around us had stopped talking, I looked around, settling my gaze on Carter. "That's what happens when you don't get the diaper on right."

Elly smacked him in the chest. "Yeah, what she said."

"I know how to put a diaper on!" he exclaimed in a whisper. He eyed Elly and smiled at her lovingly. "You know, I know how to do it. I'm ready."

"I know you are," she said reassuringly, giving him a kiss. "I can't believe he's going to be here in a week!"

"I'm excited, too," he said, rubbing her big belly as he pulled at the hem of her jeans and checked her feet. "Your feet are swollen, babe. We should get you home. You need to lay down and rest."

"Yeah, yeah," she complained, allowing him to help lift her out of the chair.

"We'll see you guys later," Carter said.

"Bye!" Harper and I whispered as the guys nodded at them.

Drake grabbed my neck with his free hand and pulled me in for an unexpected kiss. His teeth nibbled on my bottom lip before his tongue swept out and begged me to open for him. He teased his way around my tongue and sucked hard, deepening the kiss further. It wasn't until I heard Seghen mewl that I remembered where we were and broke away from him, wearing a set of swollen lips and a smile.

"What was that for?" I asked in amazement.

"Because I love you." He caressed my cheek with his thumb and pressed his lips to mine again in a sweet manner. "For sharing that story about Declan."

My cheeks flushed under his heated gaze. "I love you, too."

"They're so cute together," Harper mused from where she sat, nestled in Maverick's lap on the recliner.

"So cute," Maverick mocked sarcastically, his eyes never leaving the TV. "Wasn't there something you wanted to talk to them about?"

"Oh, yes!" she exclaimed. "Thanks for reminding me, baby."

He nodded silently as he took a drink of his beer.

"So, have you guys heard the latest with Max?" she asked.

Maxton Waters was one of Harper's oldest friends. They met while working in the fashion industry together. He started modeling when he was a teenager, and they quickly became friends once Harper started designing clothes. He'd taken his career from modeling to acting, and now he was an A-list actor with a fan base full of women who thought the sun shined out of his ass. He'd recently starred in Marvel's latest big-screen hit, so he surely had comic book fans who thought he was the shit, too.

"No, what about him?" I asked curiously. "It wasn't another fan deal, was it?"

Last year, one of Max's deranged fans assaulted Harper because she believed—thanks to the media's ridiculous rumor mill—that Harper was Max's girlfriend, even though she was pregnant with Maverick's child at the time. Harper had been photographed with Max, and the media outlets falsified the picture into a love story.

"No," Harper said, rubbing Maverick's bicep. "I think he still feels bad about what happened to me. He's started drinking pretty heavily. I got a call about a month ago that he was in the hospital with a minor head injury. He ran his Lamborghini into a tree while on his way home from a party. He's okay, but he could've hurt somebody else or himself. I'm worried about him. After the media caught wind of the wreck, they were all over it. He fired his PR team."

"Shit," Drake said, shaking his head. "Has he had a drinking problem in the past?"

"No," Harper said adamantly. "Like I said, I think he's started drinking because he still feels bad. I was wondering if you could help him out, Paige. Maybe represent him?"

I glanced at Drake, even though I already knew his answer; the hard stare he sported begged me to say no. As one of the top publicists at S&E, I already had my hands full with A-list clients.

"You have enough clients," he stated. "There are other publicists at S&E who could take him."

I argued. "But he's Harper's friend."

He turned his attention to Harper. "I think it's great you want to help your friend, but have you talked to him about getting new representation?"

"Yes."

"And was he in favor or against it?"

Her hesitation told us everything we needed to know: Max didn't want new representation.

"Harper," I stated with a wince. "As much as I would like to—"

"Okay, so he's not on board yet," she interjected, "but he needs somebody like you, Paige. You're a badass with clients. You're not afraid to put them in their place, no matter who they are. He needs a publicist who is going to make him listen."

Drake exhaled a long, exasperated sigh. "I'm assuming he was charged with a DWI?"

"Yes," Harper answered. "It was his first DWI, but he's been charged with driving recklessly in the past. He was given six months of probation with three hundred hours of community service."

"Jesus Christ," Drake cursed in disbelief, dropping his head back against the couch.

"Isn't that a joke?" Maverick commented. "He should've at least had his license revoked like any other adult, but he's a movie star so he gets special treatment."

"I know," she said gravely. "So, do you think you can help?"

"Yes," I said, covering Drake's mouth with my hand. "He's going to have to listen to me and abide by his contract." Removing my hand from Drake's mouth, I smiled at him sweetly. "We can setup a short-term contract, and if it doesn't work out with him or he doesn't abide by it, we let him loose."

"Fine."

I kissed him chastely, basking in my victory. "Thank you."

"You'll need to decide which client you're passing off to somebody else."

"No," I scoffed. "I can handle it."

"Paige," he challenged. "If you want Max Waters, I will pass off a different client, or I'm giving Max to somebody else. That's what the senior account manager does."

"Ooh, burn!" Maverick teased, laughing under his breath. "Would you like some aloe vera, Paige?"

Drake laughed, giving him a high-five.

"You think you're cute?" I sneered. "Throwing your job back in my face?"

"No, I know I'm cute," he said, taking my chin in his hand. He pressed his lips to mine, and within seconds, his tongue eased the burn of aggravation into a warm pound of need. "I'm just reminding you who's the boss."

Chapter Fourteen

Drake

"Tonight, Jay and I would like to discuss the bond between you and your child," Sydney stated, gazing around the circle. "Some of you formed that bond, while others never had the opportunity. So, tonight, we'd like to take a moment to talk about it."

Paige and I were at our fourth support group meeting, and Sydney opened the meeting with a topic that made me uncomfortable. I was aware that I had missed the chance to form a bond with Declan, and it haunted me. When I thought about how much I'd missed, my chest ached. How was I supposed to talk about a bond I never made? A relationship that was stolen from me too soon?

"Who would like to go first?" Jay asked.

The room stayed silent for a second until J.T. offered. "I will."

"Thank you, J.T."

The brute man leaned forward in his chair, resting his elbows on his knees. His dog tags hung from his thick neck, and he ran his hands over them. "I should be proud of these. I should be proud to be a soldier and serve my country, but I'm not."

Amber rubbed his back, encouraging him to continue.

"We found out we were pregnant while I was home, between my second and third deployments," he said, smiling weakly. "But then a month later, I got the call and headed back out. I never worried about Amber and the baby. I knew they would be safe here at home. I was so excited when Amber called and told me we were having a boy."

I witnessed a tear fall from his eye and land on his boot, and I had to look away from him to keep my own composure.

"I was upset about missing his birth, but that's normal for guys in the military. I had friends out there who'd missed more than one of their kids' births. But when I got the call . . . the one that said he'd died . . . I fucking lost it."

Amber handed him a tissue, and I had to grab the back of Paige's chair to keep myself in my seat. I wanted to flee from listening to his story because he was the only other man in the room who'd missed what I missed.

"The first and last time I held Sean was the day we put him to rest," he stated, shaking his head. "I've been to a lot of funerals, watched a lot of my friends die, but those guys go into their job knowing they may die. Their families say good-bye knowing it might be the last time. When I kissed Amber and her baby bump good-bye, I never thought it would be the last time I'd kiss our son while he was alive. I've fought in a war, and I've killed people, but the hardest thing I have ever done was bury our son. They shouldn't make caskets that small."

Paige turned to my shoulder and quietly sobbed. I looked around the room to find the other women doing the same as their loved ones comforted them with tears in their eyes.

"After that, I quit my job because I'm not a soldier anymore. I'm a dad, and from now on, I will serve and protect my family. I will not miss the months of pregnancy, nor will I miss any more births. So, when I look at these dog tags, I don't feel proud of the work I've done. I'm not haunted by the things

I've seen. I just miss my son. I may not have had time to form a bond with him, but when I saw him for the first time in a picture Amber sent, I felt this overwhelming amount of joy rush through me. I felt him in my heart. He shared my eyes and the curve of his mother's lips." He grabbed Amber's hand for support and kissed her palm. "He was our boy, and forever ours he'll be."

"Forever ours he'll be," she repeated tenderly. She wrapped her arms around his neck and kissed him. J.T. dried his eyes, wiped the running mascara from his wife's, and then sat back in his seat stoically.

"Thank you for sharing, J.T.," Sydney said. "I know it may be hard for some of you to understand because you were there for those nine months and the birth of your child, but a bond can form with a simple photograph."

Her words eased the pain in my chest. The tension from J.T.'s story released through my shoulders. His courage gave me the strength to raise my hand. If the veteran could talk about the bond he never made, I owed it to him to talk about mine.

"Yes, Drake, go ahead," Jay said, nodding.

Paige smiled at me as I wiped my sweaty palms on my dress pants. "Most of you know that I recently found out about Declan. I saw a picture of him for the first time about a month ago. It wasn't until I had that picture in my hands that I felt a sense of fatherhood. I'm sure many of you guys experienced it when you felt your child kick for the first time or heard their heartbeat during a sonogram. All I had was a picture of Paige holding Declan, and even though I had no doubts that he was my son, I didn't know a love so big existed until I saw him. My love for him was instantaneous, greater than any affection I have ever felt for another human being."

"Love at first sight," Cora mused aloud, clenching her husband's hand.

"Exactly," I stated, excitedly. "It *was* love at first sight. I didn't get an opportunity to form a bond with him, but I don't blame Paige for that, we were just a couple of teenagers when we lost him. Whether we've formed bonds with our children or not, whether we lost them years ago or a few months ago, it hurts the same. I'm still a grieving father like the ones who have had that sense of fatherhood from conception. I still miss Declan as much as the dads here tonight miss their children."

Jay started clapping for me, and Sydney patted me on the back.

"That's why we talk about the bond," Jay said, pointing at me. "It's to make you guys realize that it doesn't matter how much time you had with your little one, it's how much you love them. Your memories will live on in the love you have for them. Good work, J.T. and Drake. Thank you for sharing."

Finally, I thought. I knew the support group wasn't a challenge—there were no winners or losers here—but I finally felt as if I was gaining something from coming here every week. The people around me helped alleviate the stress that came along with grief. The sleepless nights I lay beside Paige wondering how different our lives would've been if he were still here. I struggled with an inability to walk down the sidewalk without noticing a parent and their child, and not think about my own. Whenever I spent time around my friends and their children, I longed for those same interactions they shared. It didn't feel normal, but at the same time it did. I'd learned that it's normal for a grieving parent to miss their child and observe their surroundings in a way that always circled back to that child.

"Okay," Sydney stated excitedly, peeking down at her notebook. "Our next topic of discussion was brought to us by Amber and J.T. They asked the question after last week's session, how do you know when it's time to start trying for another baby? Who would like to start?"

I had no fucking clue. Paige and I never tried the first time, so I lacked expertise on timing.

"Okay," Jay said, eyeing Sydney. "We'll go first."

"We knew we were ready again when the topic of protection didn't come up anymore," Sydney stated positively. "You know that moment, when you're being intimate with your partner, and the topic of protection puts a halt to the action. Jay and I spent months taking precautions because we weren't ready for another baby, but over time, the topic became less and less significant. When it never came up, we started trying to get pregnant again. I think it differs for every couple."

Glancing over at Paige, I shared a smile with her. For weeks now, we'd been intimate together. Reconnecting with her after spending years apart rejuvenated our love. We'd make out like we were teenagers again, and we were saving plenty of water by showering together more often. We'd spent the night at each other's places on numerous occasions, but we had yet to actually have sex again. I wanted to badly—back in the day, my balls never sported the painful blues for this long with her—but if Paige wasn't ready, I respected her wishes. I definitely wanted more children with her someday, too. Every moment spent with our friends and their children confirmed how much I wanted the same in my own life. The memories from her pregnancy with Declan weren't enough to hold me over forever. I wanted a chance to truly experience it with her.

"I agree," Cora said, nodding. "It's different for each couple."

Rob smiled at her and looked around at the group. "We started trying again right away. We're nearing our forties, so time isn't in our favor."

Jessie cleared her throat. "Chris and I agreed that we would wait to start trying until after we got married."

"That's a good idea," Sydney said, in a reassuring tone. "Wedding planning can be very stressful, which could affect fertilization."

"I'm not sure if I'm ready for more kids," Charlie added, glancing over at Emma apprehensively.

Shit, I thought. These two worried me. While everyone else in the group projected positivity, Emma and Charlie sported a negative outlook, but grief cloaked everyone differently so who was I to judge.

She stopped filing her nails and corrected him. "No, what he means is, he doesn't want to have more children with me."

"You know that's not true," he argued, turning in his chair to face her. He grabbed her nail filer and threw it in her purse.

There you go, Charlie. Get her attention.

"I love you. I want to have more children with you. But I don't want to go through the hell we went through last time. Maybe next time it'll happen naturally."

"Or it won't happen at all," she retorted, tears welling in her eyes.

"You can't think that way," he begged, shaking his head. "Don't you miss the way we used to be? When we could spend the whole day in bed together?"

She stared down at her feet and nodded. "Yeah."

Lifting her chin, he smiled at her. "I want to keep sharing my life with you, Em, but I don't want our sex life to be a second job. If we can't have another child together, then we should be thankful for Xander and consider adopting."

A weak smile spread across her face as he caught her teardrop with his finger. "You're right."

"Yeah?" he asked incredulously.

She nodded quickly. "Yeah."

He grabbed her face and gave her a peck on the lips. "Did we just agree to not get a divorce?"

"I think so," she laughed, throwing her arms around his neck.

Thank God. I clapped along with the rest of the circle. Weeks ago they'd considered getting a divorce. They were in debt from the in vitro fertilization they'd used to have Xander. Charlie missed the spontaneity of their relationship while Emma wanted another child. Now, during one meeting, they'd reconciled on their stance for more children.

Their situation made me even more grateful for my own.

Grabbing Paige's hand, I threaded my fingers through hers and smiled.

"What about you guys?" Amber asked, turning the group's attention to us. "Do you want more kids?"

"Yes, definitely," I answered without hesitation.

All eyes landed on Paige as we awaited her answer. When her stare didn't move from the ground, my stomach plummeted. I held my breath. My hand, still interlinked with her sweaty palm, grew tense. I had expected an immediate repeat of my answer, but the longer she stayed quiet, the more I realized I was mistaken.

"Paige?" Sydney asked. "The group asked a question. We would like it if you participated."

She took a deep breath and slowly exhaled it. "After Declan died, I couldn't sleep because I needed answers, answers the doctors couldn't give to me. They diagnosed him with SIDS and sent me away, like it wasn't a big deal. So, I researched the syndrome and found a study on SIDS cases. I learned that in most cases, the deceased child was male, and they found a correlation between the mother's age and SIDS. Mothers under the age of twenty put their child at a higher risk for SIDS. I was eighteen when I—"

No. She can't believe that.

"Paige," I interjected softly, shaking my head in disbelief. I squatted down in front of her and took her other hand in mine. "You don't believe that, do you? It's a correlation, not a fact. You did not cause our son's death."

"I know," she whispered, staring at our linked hands with tears in her eyes. "But I needed answers. Was it me? Was it something I passed on to him in the womb? Was it you? Was it us? For a while, it helped believing it may not have been happenstance. We didn't try to get pregnant, it just happened, and just like that, he was gone. I'm scared of getting pregnant again because I still don't have an answer."

Her worries trembled through her words, igniting my own. Gripping her hands tighter, I pressed my lips to them and sighed. "An answer won't change anything. It won't bring him back. That's the scary thing about SIDS, there is no cause. You can't prevent bad things from happening."

Her eyes filled with unshed tears as they connected with mine. "That's exactly why I don't know if I want any more kids."

No. Don't do this, Paige.

Her words lit my blood on fire. Dropping her hands, my brows furrowed. "What do you mean, you don't know?"

"I-I just don't know, Drake. I don't want to lose another baby."

"Nobody here wants to lose another baby!" I stated harshly, motioning to the others. "That's not stopping them from wanting more kids."

"I'm just not sure!" she repeated.

I tilted my head and studied her, unsure of the woman sitting before me. How could we end up here? Like Charlie and Emma arguing over our future. I loved Paige, but I didn't like her right now. I understood she was scared. Hell, I was scared of losing another child, too. "What's our future look like to you?"

Exhaling a frustrated breath, she hung her head and whispered dejectedly, "I don't know."

"Okay," Jay announced. "I think this is a good stopping point for tonight. Thank you all for your participation this evening. We hope to see you next time."

***

I walked her to her door, but I'd decided before we walked into her building that I wasn't staying. I hadn't said a word to her since we left the meeting, so she knew I was pissed. We'd spent weeks attending the group meetings. I'd opened up to strangers about Declan and my feelings, while she sat closemouthed, refusing to contribute. Tonight was the one time she'd been put on the spot, and she'd said words I never thought I'd hear from her. She was scared of getting pregnant. She wasn't sure what our future holds.

The pain of losing Declan didn't change the way I felt about her; it didn't stop me from loving her. It didn't weaken the dreams I had for us; it solidified them. I imagined her in a white, fitted dress, holding on to Cal's left arm as he walked her down the aisle toward me in the church where we were confirmed. When I looked at pictures of her with Declan, I wanted her pregnant with our second child. I envisioned us taking family vacations and inviting our friends to come along. I fantasized about us sneaking away from the city to spend the weekend at the Massey Estate, which I'd bought before applying for the job at S&E.

Now, I wanted more than just words from her; I wanted her to stop thinking about herself. I wanted her to think about us, and how much easier life could be if we spent it together. I wanted the rest of her life.

Walking into her apartment, she stood, holding the door open for me. "Aren't you coming in?"

I shook my head and replied, "No. Not tonight."

"Drake," she stated ruefully, leaning against the doorjamb. "Look, I'm sorry about tonight. I just—"

"Don't know?" I retorted in a curt tone, repeating her words from earlier. "Do I matter to you?"

"Of course, you matter. You've always mattered."

"Well, tonight, you made me feel like I didn't."

Crossing her arms over her chest, she shook her head at me and scoffed. "Don't you get it? I can't plan for the future anymore. The last time I did that, it went to hell and I hurt everybody I loved. So, I don't know if I want more kids. I don't know if there's a future for us. Just thinking about it scares me."

"You know, we could have it much worse," I stated coolly, stepping toward her. "We aren't too old to have children. We don't need in vitro fertilization to get pregnant, and even if we did, we could afford it, we're not battling any debt. We haven't served our country, fought in any wars, or watched our friends die, because men and women and their families have made that sacrifice for us. We haven't missed our son's life because we were serving our country. We haven't had a wedding to plan, but I hope we never let the death of our son cripple us from celebrating our love." I took a deep breath and watched the empathy wash over her features. "I'm not saying that our loss isn't as significant as the others', but if there's one thing I've taken away from the support group, it's that we could have it a hell of a lot worse than we do."

I kissed her gently one last time and leaned my forehead against hers. "I'm scared, too, P.J. All I want is to ease the pain for us, but I'll never be able to do that. Not with a marriage proposal or another baby. Nothing will ever take the pain of losing Declan away. It is something we will live with forever, but I don't want his loss to hinder us from actually living. I want a life with you. I want to get down on one knee someday, knowing you're going to say yes. I want another child, who will know its older brother so well it's like he's still here with us. We'll probably experience more challenges as we go, but I believe we're strong enough to get through anything together.

"I don't want to dwell on the past or fear the future. Life is challenging, but it could be much worse. Don't make it harder than it already is. Have the courage to not give up on us, Paige. Allow yourself to be happy. We don't need to make plans. All I'm asking is for you to give me some hope. I think Declan would want that for us."

Taking a step back into the hall, the tears falling from her beautiful blue eyes, streaming down her angelic face, gutted me, but I restrained myself from comforting her. I wished she'd take her eyes off me so I could tell my legs to walk away. My heart wasn't going anywhere. She'd been the keeper of it for years, and despite all we'd been through and the anger she'd inflicted tonight, I hoped she never gave it back.

For years, she battled this grief alone. She shut out her family and friends. She stopped needing anyone a long time ago, and allowed her fears to run her life. If our love had any chance of surviving, she needed to take back control.

The tense ache in my chest continued throbbing, and I sent a silent prayer up to our boy, asking him to watch over her, to grant her the strength to give us a forever.

"Let me know when you decide to stop fearing a repeat of the past," I concluded dejectedly. "I'll be waiting."

Chapter Fifteen

Paige

Lying on my couch, I heard knocking on my apartment door. It was a Saturday afternoon, days after the support group meeting from hell, and I had no desire to get up and answer it. I preferred staying curled up in the comfort of my home, so I prayed the visitor went away. Even if it was Drake—though I highly doubted it—I didn't want him seeing me like this. My hair was a wavy mess around my face. I'd been sleeping on my couch because his pillow on my bed still smelled like him. My showers had been quick and much less satisfying without him. My body ached like it was missing a limb without him here.

The visitor slid a key into the lock outside my door, and I knew it was one of my friends. They were the only ones who had a key to my place.

"Paige?" Elly asked, peeking her head into the living room. She saw me on the couch and waddled her way in, closing the door behind her. "What happened? I haven't heard from or seen you in days."

"Aren't you supposed to be at home in bed?" She was five days overdue, and her doctor had officially put her on bed rest.

She rolled her eyes, placing a hand on top of her huge belly. "I can't lie in bed anymore! I read an article about activities that induce labor and bed rest is not one of them. Plus, Maverick texted me about Drake being in a piss-poor mood at basketball. I think he thought I'd just call you, but my advice is much more powerful when we're face-to-face."

Rolling my eyes, I sighed. "You should've just called. You could've seriously injured yourself and the baby on your way over here."

She was in a pair of black leggings and a striped tunic sweater. Her red hair was knotted on top of her head, and her swollen feet were stuffed into a pair of tennis shoes. She tossed her purse on the coffee table and attempted to sit down on the couch beside me, but her bump disabled her, so she settled her hands on the small of her back and looked around the room. The smile on her face widened as she eyed each picture frame. "You put up pictures. I don't think I've ever seen your living room decorated with pictures."

She was right. I hadn't put up any pictures of Declan, so I'd kept all of the others stored away, too. Since everyone knew about him now, I'd taken the time to find frames I liked and decorated my home with all the pictures I had. There were pictures of him in between pictures of me and my friends and Drake. I'd even asked Barrett and Zoey to send me a picture of their family. Now, you couldn't look around my place without seeing a memory.

"It was time," I said with a shrug.

"It looks nice," Elly agreed, nodding. "Now, what happened with you and Drake?"

Sitting up, I drew my knees up to my chest and ran a hand through my tangled hair. "It was that damn support group. We were talking about whether or not we wanted another baby, and of course, Drake immediately said yes."

"And you didn't," she stated understandingly.

"Elly, can you imagine me with another child?" I asked rhetorically. "I'd be a complete, paranoid mess. I can't shut off my mind from worrying about all the bad stuff that could happen."

She laughed lightly. "Every parent is paranoid. We're all worried something bad is going to happen to our children. You're not new to our club."

"Drake got so mad about it," I said, kneading my forehead with my fingers. "Then he asked where I saw our future going, and I didn't know. The last time I tried to plan our future, our son died."

She grabbed my hand from my forehead and clenched it in hers. "You love him, right?"

"Yes," I said without hesitation.

"Then what's more terrifying, spending the rest of your life alone, or spending it with your better half? I love you like a sister, so believe me when I tell you, Drake makes you better. You're not on your phone all the time or worried about work. You actually relax and have fun, and he makes you smile. I know you experienced a terrible tragedy, but you don't have to spend your life grieving alone or living in fear that it's going to happen again. You deserve to be happy, Paige. You have so many people to lean on for support now. Let us be here for you. Let him love you. I'm not going to let you push the love of your life away because you're scared. You wouldn't let me do that with Carter."

"I know," I said, nodding.

"Then don't do it with Drake," she said, covering our hands with her other. "It's okay to be scared, but you can't let those fears control your life."

Her cell started ringing from inside her purse, and she tried bending over to fetch it and failed. Grabbing her purse, I found her iPhone and handed it to her.

"Hello," she answered, clearly unsure of the caller. "What do you mean? Is he okay?"

Alerted, I sat up straight. Worry was evident in her tone.

"Okay, okay. I'm headed there now. Thank you for letting me know."

She ended the call and stared down at her phone. "That was my dad's building manager. I'm his emergency contact, and he said Dad was just taken to the hospital."

"Okay," I said urgently, slipping my feet into my Uggs. I rushed around my apartment in search of my necessities. "I'm coming with you to the hospital. Let me just grab my purse and keys and we'll go."

"Thanks," she offered, dropping her phone back into her bag.

With my things in hand, along with Elly's purse, I helped her out the door and locked it behind us. We hailed a cab to Langone, and I silently prayed that nothing serious had happened to him. Elly had lost her mom to cancer a long time ago. The last worry she needed now, being five days overdue, was whether or not her dad was okay.

***

When we arrived at the emergency room, Elly promptly told the staff who she was and why we were here. Most of them saw her baby bump and assumed she was in labor, but she corrected them, providing the information they needed from her so we could see her dad.

We walked into Keith Evans' room, and the first person I noticed was Charlotte Jones, Maverick's mother, sitting beside him on the bed.

Why is she here?

"Dad, what happened?" Elly asked in a concerned voice.

"Elly!" he stated, jolted by our appearance. "What are you guys doing here?"

Charlotte quickly moved away from the bed, and my eyes landed on the noticeable tent under Keith's hospital blanket. Oh. My. God. He tried concealing it by turning away from us, but moving must have caused him pain as he cringed.

"I'm listed as your emergency contact, and I got a call from your building that you'd been taken to the emergency room. What's wrong?" Elly repeated, eyeing him up and down. "Oh, dear God, that's your penis!"

Awkward! "I think I'll just give you guys some privacy."

Elly grabbed me with her superwoman pregnancy strength and glared. "Don't you dare leave me in here alone."

"Okay."

Turning back to her dad, she took a deep breath and exhaled. "I'm probably going to regret asking this, but what the hell is going on?"

He reached out his hand to Charlotte. "Come here, Char."

She slid her hand into his and sat down on the edge of his bed, smiling at him affectionately.

"Elly," he started, "Charlotte and I have been seeing each other for a while now. We've both been alone for so long, when we spent the weekend together in Texas for your wedding last year, it felt nice to be with someone. When we arrived back in New York, I asked her out, and we've been together since."

"Why didn't you say anything?" she asked.

"We didn't tell you or Maverick because we didn't want to get you guys involved yet," Charlotte explained.

"It's still new and different for us, but we make each other happy." Keith shared a knowing look with Char and smiled before continuing. "Anyway, the reason we're here is because I took a pill so we could—"

"Ohmigawd! I know!" Elly cringed. "You don't need to say it!"

Hunching over, she grabbed her belly with one hand and dug her nails into my arm with the other. "Paige."

Her voice made the hairs on my neck stand. "What's wrong?"

Timidly, she stated, "I think my water just broke."

"Holy shit," I muttered, eyeing the wetness seeping through the crotch of her leggings. Poking my head out into the hall, I yelled to the nurses standing around their station. "I need a wheelchair in here now!"

Within seconds, a woman rushed into the room with the chair, and we got Elly situated. I asked the nurse to notify the maternity staff that we were on our way.

"Okay," I said calmly. "I'm going to get Elly up to the delivery ward. Char, you call Carter and let him know."

"Calling!" she exclaimed, her phone already pressed to her ear.

Concern lined Keith's features. "I'm sorry I didn't tell you, Elly."

"I'm going to have a baby," she said in a shocked tone, her cringe turning upward into a glowing smile as she peered back at him. "As long as you're happy, I'm happy for you. But I don't ever want to see your erection again."

Laughing, he laid his head back against his pillow and nodded. "I don't want that either."

Taking her chair by the handles, I wheeled her out of the room and down the hall to the elevators. I tapped the up button and waited for the doors to open.

"Can you believe my dad is boning Maverick's mom?" Elly commented, clearly still in shock.

The doors opened, and I wheeled her in and pressed the delivery floor's button. "I can't wait to hear you tell your son this story someday."

Elly laughed and then moaned as the pain of a contraction swept through her.

"Have you been having contractions throughout the day?" I asked curiously.

"Yeah, and last night," she said, nodding. "They were pretty far apart though."

"How far apart?"

"Every hour maybe, and then it became every half hour."

The doors opened to the ward, and I wheeled her up to the nurses' station.

"We're the girls from the emergency room," I explained. "They were supposed to call and let you know we were coming."

"They did," a nurse said, nodding. "Ellyson Jennings, right this way. We've already contacted Dr. Kirby and notified her that you're here. She should be here shortly."

We followed the nurse into a private room. "We have a gown and everything ready for you. Have you started having any contractions?"

"Yes," I answered as Elly gripped the chair, battling through another one. "But they're becoming more frequent now that her water broke."

The nurse scribbled down the information. "Do you have any allergies?"

"No," I answered.

"Have you decided on whether or not you'd like an epidural?"

Elly gazed up at me, shaking her head. "She doesn't want it."

"Okay," she stated cheerfully. "If you'd like to get changed and situated, we'll be back in to check on you."

"Thanks," I said, grabbing Elly's hands. I lifted her out of the wheelchair and helped her sit on the edge of the bed.

"I don't have any of my stuff," Elly said, bewildered. "I don't have my iPod. I made a playlist to listen to during labor, you know, as a way to stay calm, and I don't have it. And Carter's not here. I thought I was ready for this, Paige, but I'm not."

"Hey," I said in a soothing voice as I pulled her sweater off. Taking her hands in mine, I smiled at her. "You *are* ready for this. I'm here, and I've given birth before. You're going to be okay. You don't need the music, and Carter is on his way. Okay?"

"You're right." Her grip tightened on my hands as another contraction took over, but I refrained from wincing. "You can't leave me. Even when he gets here, you can't leave. He's never done this before, and God knows whether or not he listened during Lamaze."

I nodded, reassuringly. "I won't leave. I'll be right here the entire time."

"Okay," she said, kicking off her shoes. She wiggled her butt out of her leggings and panties, and I peeled them the rest of the way off for her. She unhooked her bra and slipped her arms through the holes in the gown, and I tied it closed at the back of her neck and then helped her sit back in bed.

Her cheeks were already flushed and she hadn't even started pushing yet. Grasping my hand, she groaned as the contraction surged through her body.

"Should I be having them this close together?" she asked in a worried voice.

"Yeah, you've been in labor for hours," I said, nodding. "Are they getting stronger?"

"Mhmm," she hummed through gritted teeth.

The nurse walked back into the room. "Dr. Kirby just arrived, and she's asked me to check your dilation."

Elly nodded and sat back as the nurse lifted her blanket and used two fingers to check her. When the smile spread across the nurse's face, a wave of relief washed over me. The faster this went, the better. I wouldn't wish a long labor on any woman. Most first time moms experienced a lengthy labor, and since Elly had spent most of the day in labor, she deserved to have this part go quickly.

"You're close," she stated with a nod. "I'd say you're at an eight, but the way your contractions are going, you're probably going to be pushing soon."

She nodded again before the nurse left, and then turned toward me. "Where the fuck is Carter?"

"He's on his way." I took a washcloth and wet it down at the sink. After folding the damp material, I dabbed her forehead with it. "He'll be here."

"The doctor got here before him," she said in an irritated tone. "We're not that far from the gym, and I don't—"

The door burst open and Carter came running into the room. He cupped her face in his hands and kissed her, and then he pulled away and ran his eyes over her body. "I tried to get here as fast as I could. How are you doing, babe? What can I do?"

A contraction hit, and Elly clenched both of our hands this time, groaning loudly as the pain rolled through her and her nails penetrated my skin.

Jesus, she needs to clip her daggers.

It eventually subsided, and she went back to focusing on her breathing.

"Elly, talk to me," he begged, caressing her face.

"It hurts," she cried, leaning into the touch of the washcloth. "I'm already tired and I haven't started yet."

I looked across the bed at Carter and informed him, "She's at an eight."

"I don't have my music with me," she stressed again, shaking her head. She motioned to the wall across from her and stated, "And there's no focal point on that ugly wall. What the hell am I supposed to focus on when they do make me start pushing?"

Carter reached into his shorts and pulled out his wallet. He unfolded a sonogram picture and held it up to her. "You focus on this, the first picture of our Cooper. Okay?"

He sauntered over to the wall, making sure he was in her line of sight, and then he hung the picture up for her, sealing it to the wall with a piece of surgical tape.

"That doesn't help me with my mus—ahhh," she wailed, seizing my hand tightly. Carter came back to her other side and rubbed her back as the pain forced its way through. The contraction lasted longer than any of the previous ones, and when it ended, she shook her head. "I don't want to do this anymore. I can't do this."

"You can, babe," Carter encouraged, "Breathe, just like they taught us in class. You can do this."

"No, I can't," she argued, peering over at me with fear pooling in her brown eyes. "The pressure is too much. I can't."

"I'm trying to think of a song on your playlist," Carter stated, pressing a kiss to her temple. "Oh, I got it!"

He started rapping the first verse from Salt-N-Pepa's hit, "Push It," and Elly grimaced as more tears fell from her eyes. "No, you can't do that one. I'm not pushing yet! And you sound nothing like Salt-N-Pepa!"

Agreed.

"Okay, fine," he said, accepting the challenge. "What about Tom Petty? You love Tom Petty."

He began singing "I Won't Back Down," and he honestly didn't sound too bad. But then I felt Elly's hand nearly break mine, and I turned my attention back to her.

"You'd back down if you were in this much fucking pain!" she snapped as another contraction crashed through her.

"Okay, I think we can all agree that the singing isn't helping," I said, glaring over at Carter.

I'm sorry, he mouthed.

The door flew open again, and Dr. Kirby walked in wearing blue scrubs, her blonde hair tied back underneath a surgical cap.

"How are you doing, Elly?" she asked with a smile.

"I want him out," Elly replied bluntly, staring down the doctor. "Please tell me I can start pushing."

"Let's take a look." The doctor lifted the sheet, pulled the stirrups out and placed Elly's feet in them.

"It burns," Elly exclaimed in a soft whisper, glancing up at me. "Is that normal?"

"Yes," I said quietly, nodding.

"We're crowning!" the doctor announced. "We're going to start pushing, Elly. You need to focus and listen to me, okay?"

"Oh, God," she objected, lying back against the pillow. Her breathing became more labored the more she worried. "I don't know."

"I love you," Carter said, kissing her. He wiped a droplet of sweat from her forehead and smiled. "I know you can do this, babe. If you can beat cancer, you can have our baby."

"He's right," I said, my eyes filling with tears. "The moment you hear him cry for the first time will sound better than any music you could've put on a playlist, and when they place him in your arms, it'll make all this pain worth it, I promise."

"O-okay," she said, nodding. "Let's do this."

Dr. Kirby rubbed her glove-clad hands together and smiled. "Elly, when I tell you to push, I want good, hard pushes, okay? If you can give me that every time I ask, I'll be able to give you your son as quickly as possible."

"Got it."

Carter took her hand and pressed another kiss to her temple. I blinked away the moisture from my eyes and grasped her other hand tightly.

"When you're not pushing," I started, dabbing her forehead with a wet cloth, "don't forget to breathe."

She nodded silently, and then the doctor told her to push. She squeezed our hands, curling her forearms into her shoulders, and projected all the strength she could muster into the push. Keeping her eyes trained on the sonogram picture, more sweat broke out across her hairline as she trembled from the intensity, gritting her teeth. When the doctor offered her a moment to relax, she took it, and Carter helped her focus on her breathing while I cooled her with the cloth.

"Just like that, girl," I said proudly.

"We've got a head," the doctor declared. "A few more pushes like that and you're done, Elly."

After two more strong pushes and a few curse words thrown in, we heard the loud wail from a tiny set of lungs, and the room rejoiced.

"Is he okay?" Elly asked with tears streaming down her face. "Is he all right?"

Carter cupped her face and covered her lips with his. "He's perfect."

"Would Dad like to cut the cord?" Dr. Kirby asked.

Carter quickly moved to the end of the bed and took the scissors. While they kept him busy and fixed Elly up, I kept her focus on me. Her face glistened from her sweat and tears mixing together, but I knew more than anything that she was happy. I knew exactly how quickly the exhaustion took over but the elation still quivered through her bones. Now, I'd been on the other side, coaching my best friend through it all, and I couldn't have been more proud of her.

Now, I knew how my mom felt when she coached me through this with Declan.

"Congratulations," I said, smiling down at her as I wiped her face one more time with the cloth. "You did great."

"I don't know how you did this at eighteen," she said, shaking her head. "Thank you for helping me through it. I wanted to strangle Carter when he started singing."

"Yeah," I laughed lightly. "He should stick to teaching."

"Agreed." She nodded.

Carter slowly walked back over to us, carrying their son, and then placed him in Elly's arms.

"Oh, look at him," she awed as the waterworks started up again. Carter leaned his head against hers, and they admired their boy together. "He's beautiful."

"He is," Carter said, brushing his lips against her temple. "Thank you, babe. Thank you so much for him."

"I couldn't have done it without you."

The two of them shared another kiss, and then the nurse interrupted.

"Do you guys have a name picked out?"

They nodded, and then Elly stated proudly, "Cooper Keith Jennings."

"Congratulations," she offered before leaving the room.

They deserved their privacy, even though I could've stayed and basked in their joy forever, eagerly wishing I had the same in my own life. "I think I'll let you guys have a moment alone with him."

"Please don't," Elly said, never taking her eyes off of him. "I want you to be the first to hold him."

Peering down at the cute bundle of joy, I expected the anxiety of holding someone else's baby to wash over me, or the memory of Declan to deter me away but neither did. Instead, a longing that I'd never felt before crept through me. I hadn't held another child since holding my own, but now my hands itched for the new boy swaddled in blue. The sight of Carter and Elly with Cooper affected me the most. The unity they shared, as they spoke softly to their son, made my heart swell.

I missed this with Drake and Declan.

"Okay," I said, nodding.

Leaning over, I held my arms out and Elly slowly transferred Cooper to me. The smile on my face grew the second his weight filled my arms. His brown hair wasn't sticking out from beneath his stocking cap, but he still reminded me of Declan. With his lips pursed together and his small, chubby hands making their way out of the swaddle, he slept peacefully in my arms.

"Oh my gosh," I cooed, shaking my head. "He's adorable."

"Why are you crying?" Elly asked therapeutically as a tear slid down my cheek.

I wiped my face on my shoulder, unable to take my eyes off the tiny human snuggling in my arms. "He's so tiny. I love the feel of him. I've missed this."

"You look good with a baby," Elly stated.

I laughed lightly as Cooper clenched my pinkie, causing more tears to flow as the realization hit me. "I can't believe I was scared about wanting another baby. How could I not want this with Drake? How could I not want to spend the rest of my life with him?"

"I don't know," Elly said, leaning her head on Carter's shoulder. "It's amazing, isn't it, when you finally realize how much you love someone?"

"Yeah," I said, nodding.

"It's scary, but it's worth it."

"Definitely."

After a few more minutes, I heard Carter whisper to Elly, "Is she ever going to give him back?"

The question ignited laughter throughout the room, so I moved back over to the bed and placed Cooper in his mother's arms.

"Thank you," I said, smiling down at my best friend and her new family. "I needed that."

"I know," Elly said wisely.

"Should I go tell the gang that our newest member has arrived?" I asked.

"Yes!" Elly exclaimed. "Send them all back!"

"Okay."

I started toward the door, but before I made it out to the hall, Carter caught me around the arm, stopping me in my tracks.

"I just wanted to let you know that he's out there," Carter said, referring to Drake. "He was playing basketball with us when I got the call. He didn't want to come with us at first, but we told him you'd need him here. Don't make us look like a bunch of wrong assholes when you go out there, okay? He really cares about you, and he's getting pretty good at basketball. We need him around."

"Thanks, June," I laughed, wrapping my arms around his shoulders. "Congratulations, again."

"Thank you for being here for us. I was worthless in there. Can we keep the singing between the three of us?"

"No way," I teased, shaking my head. "Just be glad I didn't get it on video."

He pushed me out the door, and I headed out to the waiting room. Our friends sat in a group, anxiously waiting for news, but I had my eyes set on the guy leaning against the wall. When Tessa saw me, she jumped up from her seat and squealed.

"Is he here?" she asked excitedly.

"Yes," I laughed, nodding. "Momma and Cooper are doing well. You're all welcome to go back and meet him."

They sprang from their chairs and rushed to the hall toward Elly's room, leaving me alone in the waiting room with Drake. He looked delicious in his black gym shorts that showed off the lean cut of his calves and a black t-shirt that molded to his biceps. He was my past, my present, and my future wrapped up in a six-foot-something, two-hundred-pound package that I couldn't wait to open.

He uncrossed his arms and pushed off the wall. "How are you doing?"

With determined steps, I walked up to him, grabbed his shirt, and covered his mouth with mine. It'd been days since I'd felt his lips, and a second more without them was a second too long. At first, they were soft and sweet, a tender hello after a short good-bye, but they quickly turned greedy as he tilted my head and dove in at a better angle, devouring me like he'd missed me as much as I'd missed him.

"I'm sorry about the other night," I said against his lips. "Watching them admire their son together, all I could think about was how I wanted the same with you."

Taking a breath, he caressed my cheek and kissed the other. "It's okay."

The grin spread across my face. "I wish I had a great speech prepared for you, but I don't. All I have is me, and all I want is you. It's that simple. Marry me tomorrow. Get me pregnant the day after. I don't care. When I think about our future, I want it all with you, Drake. I know some days are going to be harder than others, but I'm up for the challenges life throws our way as long as you're with me. The rest of my days are yours."

Wrapping his arms around my waist, he smiled. "That was a pretty damn good speech."

"Thanks," I said with a shrug. "What do you say?"

He chuckled against my mouth. "I'm up for them, too."

***

We arrived back at my place, and he led us down the hall to my bedroom, his lips never leaving my neck as his hands trailed over my body. When he tore my shirt off, a wave of adrenaline rushed through my body, which was eager to have the rest of my clothes ripped off.

I hadn't felt this liberated since the night we conceived Declan in the bed of Old Blue.

Lying back on my bed, I kicked my boots off as Drake went to work on my jeans. He flicked open the button, unzipped, and slid his hands under the waistband, taking my panties down with the denim. He pulled them off, along with my socks, and I lay before him in only my bra, without an ounce of insecurity lingering in my mind.

"You're wearing too many clothes," I complained, crooking a finger at him.

He smiled as he hovered over me, stealing a kiss as I leaned forward and slid my hands under his shirt. I trailed my fingers up along the ridge of his abs, taking the cotton material with me. He lifted his arms as I approached his shoulders and then shrugged out of it completely. His boxers peeked out from the band of his shorts, begging my hands to remove them.

He toed off his tennis shoes and socks, and then crawled on top of the bed with me. He scooted us up to the mountain of pillows and unhooked my bra, tossing it on the floor with the rest of my clothes. Beneath him, I was naked, and I evened the score as I worked my hands into his boxer briefs and pulled them down, freeing his rigid cock from its imprisonment.

Drake kicked them all the way off, and then he settled over me and trailed kisses along my neck. He skimmed his hands up my sides and under my shoulders. My body ached for his touch everywhere. He sucked and caressed, causing the need to build to relentless proportions. I appreciated his tenderness now, but it'd been so long, I needed him bad.

"Drake," I sighed, capturing his mouth with mine as I wrapped my legs around his waist and ran my hands through his dark chest hair. "Make love to me."

Breaking away, he rested his head against mine, breathing heavily. "Are you sure?"

"More sure than I've ever been," I answered, reassuring him with a kiss.

His cock throbbed against me, so I reached between us and stroked the thick, taut muscle. He rocked into my hand and groaned, the softness of my hand eliciting a wanton desire much like my own. I'd never felt as powerful as I did when I heard the shiver-inducing sound of Drake's moans. I could stroke him all day long and never tire of hearing his arousal.

"I have a condom in my wallet," he stated gruffly.

"We don't need it," I said, arching up to kiss him. "Unless you think we do."

"Are you serious?" he asked incredulously. "Are you saying you want to try?"

"Yes, but only if you want to." My lips curled up into a grin, and I used my feet to urge him into me. "After holding Cooper, I realized how much I want another baby. *Your* baby."

"Sweet, Jesus," he gritted, rocketing his hips forward. His cock surged into me hard and fast, and I moaned in relief as he filled me. He allowed a moment for our bodies to reunite, and kissed me hard on the mouth. "Say it again. Tell me what you want."

"I want your baby, Drake," I stated breathlessly as he pulled back slightly.

"I want that, too," he said, pounding back into me. He skated his lips down my neck and along my collarbone. His hands skimmed their way back down to my waist, where they grasped me tightly. He tilted my hips up and pushed back in more swiftly than before, hitting a depth I didn't even know existed.

"Oh, fuck," I said, rolling my hips against him. "Yes. Right. There."

"God, you feel so good, P.J."

The veins in his neck and arms protruded as he sped up, and my body trembled with each of his thrusts. We were like two bombs ignited, chasing down that pleasurable explosion. Grasping his shoulders, I tightened my legs around his waist as my insides clenched his length.

"You're close, aren't you," he questioned in a teasing voice. He sucked his way up my chest, torturing me more as he wrapped his lips around a nipple and sucked hard.

"Drake," I cried, arching into him, begging for more. Sliding my hand down his arm, I removed his from my waist and positioned his fingers against my clit. "Touch me."

He brushed his knuckles along the hood of my clit, his cock never relenting in his own pursuit of pleasure. I whimpered at the sensational feel of his fingers stimulating me. He glided up and over and around my clit in a figure eight motion that made me see stars. The pound of his cock projected me into an orgasmic orbit, where I felt weightless and free, allowing the ripples of pleasure to wash over me as my insides squeezed around his length and released years of tension.

I came back to the sight of Drake seconds away from erupting. His body tensed, hips thrusting hard, fully displaying his muscles. He groaned loudly, making my toes curl, and then he finally let the pleasure take over as he powered through his release before collapsing on top of me.

"P.J.," he said, gasping for air. "That was . . . phenomenal."

His cock jerked inside of me as it slowly softened and I sighed, basking in the feel of him. "You feel so good."

His arms wrapped around my waist as he rested his head on my chest. With my legs still curled around his hips, I ran my fingers along the planes of his back and up to his hair. We were sweaty and the bedding was all screwed up, but I didn't want to move.

His eyes were an intense shade of blue as he gazed back at me wearing a mischievous smile. "Tell me again what you want."

"I want to have your baby."

His cock twitched again and he moaned, pressing a hard kiss to my lips. "Say that enough, and I'll get hard again. Do you know what hearing that does to me?"

"It turns you on?"

"It does," he chuckled, "But it also reminds me of when you were pregnant with Declan and how you glowed. I don't care how long it takes us, I'm putting another baby in you."

Chapter Sixteen

When I walked into my office on Monday and found Mercedes and Trish already seated at my desk, I knew my time at Sabre & Edelmen was coming to an end. Skye had texted me earlier in the morning saying that the Banger Sisters were demanding to see me, so their presence didn't shock me. Instead, I took a seat on the other side and smiled at them.

"I'd say it's nice to see you, but it isn't," I said with a sneer. "What do you two want?"

Trish looked at Mercedes and nodded.

Mercedes pulled a manila envelope out of her bag and removed its contents. Pictures of Drake and me leaving the office together scattered across my desk. There were some with us holding hands. In one picture, he was pressing a kiss to the back of my head as I led us out of the building.

"Would you like to explain your little rendezvous with Mr. Wilkins?" Trish asked.

Before I answered, I studied them from across the oak desk. Mercedes admired her manicure while Trish glared back at me. I didn't owe them an explanation. In fact, I owed them nothing. I ran this goddamn ship they owned, while they paraded around the city, blowing their daddies' money. My relationship with Drake was none of their business.

"No," I stated surely, shaking my head. "I would like to keep it between Mr. Wilkins and myself."

Trish scoffed, rolling her eyes. "You know this kind of behavior calls for termination of employment, right?"

I leaned forward and smiled. "Go ahead. Fire me."

The words felt as liberating as the sex Drake and I had had several times over the weekend. The chains of my past were painful, but I'd finally freed myself from them. I deserved to live a happy life—one that wasn't shackled down by the past or entitled individuals who had no business running a company. I deserved to wake up every morning and enjoy going to work. I deserved to love whom I wanted to love.

"You do realize you can't take your clients with you?" Mercedes added.

"Yes, I know," I said curtly.

They looked at one another shocked, obviously expecting more of an outburst from me, but I was done fighting with them. What they didn't realize was that their company's contract lacked a special clause that I referred to as the assignment clause. The contract needed a clause about another publicist being assigned to the client. When a company lacked this clause, it gave the client an easy way to get out of their contract, especially if they weren't notified of the assignment change. I'd used the assignment clause to get some of my current clients out of their previous PR contracts. Trish and Mercedes had no idea I'd use it again to take my clients with me.

"Okay," Trish said, standing from her seat. "Then I suggest you pack up your office and leave as soon as possible because as of now, you are no longer employed by Sabre & Edelmen."

Mercedes quickly gathered up the photos, but I put my finger over the one with Drake kissing me.

"You mind if I keep this one?" I asked, pushing away from my desk. "I'd like to put it in a frame."

"No," she scowled. "We're just going to toss them anyway."

"Thanks."

I admired the photograph as the two of them left my office for the last time, the click of their heels loud and crisp against the marble flooring. The photo was a still from the security cameras, but I didn't care. It was a clear picture of a man and a woman in love, and it represented what we were willing to do for that love.

"Did they fire you?" Skye asked nervously.

I slid the picture into my bag and nodded. "Yeah, I'm supposed to pack up my office and leave. Should be easy since I only have a stress ball and a few personal items in my drawer."

"You can't leave," she whined, leaning against the wall. "I don't want to be an assistant for someone else, especially if they hire someone new. I'll probably hate them."

I laughed. "If you do me a favor, I promise you can be an assistant for me the rest of your life, and you can date whoever the hell you want to date and dye your hair purple."

"Seriously?" she asked, perking up. "Name it."

On a Post-it, I scribbled down an email address and handed it to her. "Scan a copy of all my clients' contracts, and email it to this address. You won't be able to do it from here. You'll have to take them home and scan them or else they'll sue you for sharing the information."

"You're going to take them with you, aren't you?" she mused, a deviant grin lingering on her lips.

"You bet your ass I'm going to," I said, tossing the stress ball into my bag.

"This is why I like working with you," Skye said proudly. "So, what'd they fire you for?"

I emptied the remainder of my desk and walked toward her. "Let's just say, I let Mr. Wilkins visit my South Pole, and they found out about it."

"You did not!" she exclaimed incredulously. "Here in the office? Did they catch you? Details, Paige! Come on."

"You don't need details," I said, shaking my head. I reached into my bag and saw no missed calls or texts, so I turned it off. I wanted to spend the rest of the day unplugged.

"What are you going to do with the rest of your day?"

Tossing my phone back into my purse, I smiled at my favorite assistant. "I'm going somewhere I haven't been in a long time."

***

Drake

"What do you mean, she was fired?" I asked harshly, glaring at Mercedes and Trish.

An hour before lunch, the two of them called me into Trish's office. When they showed me the pictures of Paige and me, I knew right away why Paige wasn't answering any of my texts.

"It's in the employee handbook that no fraternization is to take place between co-workers," Trish stated.

I shook my head and asked, "So, are you firing me, too?"

"We thought about it," Mercedes answered.

Trish smiled. "But—"

"You know what," I said, standing from my seat. "No, don't even answer that because I quit. The fact that you guys have a no fraternization policy is ridiculous. There are employees here who hide their sexuality because of that policy, and that's discrimination. It's also discriminatory that you don't allow any of the staff to express themselves. You formally requested Skye dye her hair back to a more normal color just because you didn't like it. Who are you to dictate what's normal?"

"It's a reflection back on the firm," Trish stated defensively. "How is anyone supposed to take her seriously with her purple hair?"

"If it doesn't affect her work ethic, it shouldn't matter," I argued, running a hand over the back of my neck. "If anything, it would show the firm's diversity, but God forbid there be any diversity around here."

Turning my back on them, I exited the office and headed straight for Paige's. I took my phone out of my pocket and tried calling her, but it went straight to voicemail again.

Goddammit.

I rounded the corner and felt relieved when I found Skye sitting at her desk. "Do you know where Paige went?"

She shrugged, shaking her head. "She said she was going somewhere she hadn't been in a while, but I have no idea what she meant by that."

Tapping my fingers against the doorjamb, I gazed into Paige's office and found it completely empty. *Somewhere she hasn't been in a while.* We'd just been to Declan's grave about a month ago when we were back for Jane's funeral, so I didn't think she'd go there.

"Did they fire you, too?" Skye asked curiously.

"No," I said with a sigh. "But I quit."

"Well, I'm sorry I couldn't be of more help," she said, staring back at her computer screen. "Maybe try calling one of her friends. They might know."

"Thanks."

I hurried out of the building and hailed a cab to Jones Jym. She enjoyed working out when she was stressed, and she always turned her phone off while she was there. When we pulled up to the curb of Maverick's gym, I asked the cabbie to wait at least fifteen minutes for me. Then I ran into the gym and up the stairs to Maverick's office, where I found him sitting at his desk.

"Have you seen Paige here this morning?" I asked, breathing heavy.

"No," he said in worried tone as he rose from his desk. "She should be at work, and she's not?"

Shaking my head, I winced. "She was fired, and now she's not answering my texts and my phone calls are going straight to voicemail. She told her assistant she was going somewhere she hadn't been in a while. I have no idea what the hell that means. Is there somewhere here in the city that she goes that I don't know about?"

"No, just stop and think for a minute, man." He rounded his desk and leaned against it, crossing his arms over his chest. "Is there any place back home that she used to visit a lot? Before her grandma's funeral, she hadn't been back to Bedford in a while."

"I thought about Declan's grave, but we went there while we were back for Jane's funeral," I said, pacing the width of his office.

"Is there someplace else that's significant to her besides the cemetery?"

Holy shit.
"Yes."
The Massey Estate.
A smile lit up his face. "Go there."

"Thanks, Mav!" I shouted as I jogged out of his office. I hopped back into the cab and asked the driver to take me back to my place.

I needed Old Blue for this trip.

***

Paige

After leaving work, I went home and changed out of my navy pantsuit, opting for a more comfortable outfit. I pulled on skinny jeans and riding boots and threw one of Drake's flannel button-ups over my white camisole. I did a load of laundry, cleaned my apartment, and headed out to rent a car. Just an hour shy of lunch, I was on my way to Bedford. I hadn't been to the Massey Estate in years. I wasn't even sure who owned it now, but I wanted to see the place I'd always dreamed of calling home.

Pulling up to the broken gates, I turned the car into the driveway. In shock, I slammed on the brakes. The yard was littered with landscapers and construction vehicles. I recognized Barrett Gallagher's construction team hard at work on their current project.

"What the hell?" I said, stepping on the gas. I powered the car all the way up the drive and parked behind a Gallagher Construction truck. Turning the car off, I jumped out and sauntered toward the open front door, determined for answers. A few of the construction guys whistled at me as I walked by. "Don't you dare whistle at me. Where is Barrett Gallagher? I need to speak with him."

"In here!" a female voice called.

Slowly, I walked over the threshold into the home and I winced as tears came rushing into my eyes. The interior had been gutted. The sound of destruction buzzed around me. I could see through the house into the backyard, where more workers labored over the inground pool. The place had been abandoned for at least twenty years, so it needed the work. It'd been passed on to the Massey's relatives, but none of them had the heart to do any upkeep on it. On a spread of forty acres, they allowed this beautiful home to rot, but they'd obviously sold it to someone else now, and that person was turning the place into their dream home.

Wiping away a tear, I sighed, running my hand over the bones of the wall. It was too late for me.

Zoey stepped into the foyer with her girls trailing behind her, holding hands.

"Paige," she said in a surprised voice. "What are you doing here?"

I smiled at them and shrugged. "I wasn't working today, so I thought I'd come by and see the place. I didn't realize someone had bought it."

"Girls," Zoey said to her little ones, "Why don't you go find Daddy and see if there's anything you can help him with?"

"Okay!" they cheered, taking off toward the backyard.

I laughed lightly as the older one helped the youngest down the broken steps. "They're adorable."

"They love stopping by when Barrett has big projects like this."

I nodded, stuffing my hands in my pocket. "Do you know who bought it? I'm just curious. The Masseys had it for years and never did anything with it, you know. They never once put it up for sale."

"It never did go on the market," she stated, nodding toward the backyard. I followed her gaze to the mass of beautiful greenery before me. "I think they were charmed into selling it."

"By who?" I asked, glancing over at her. "Come on, you have to tell me, Zoey. You know how I feel about this place. I thought I was going to throw up when I pulled in and saw all these construction workers."

She laughed just as giggling erupted from the pool area. We turned to see the girls smiling and laughing.

"Uncle Quack!" Ziggy screamed, running toward a suited-up Drake. She clutched onto his leg and smiled up at him. "There's a lady in your house talking to Mommy."

Your house? No . . .

"Yeah," Quinn said, pointing to Zoey and me. "The one with the dead nana."

Ryce crossed her arms and glared at him. "When is your pool going to have water in it? I want to come over and swim."

"Ooh!" Quinn cheered, grabbing Drake's hand. "Can you please get some ponies for the barn? You have to have animals if you have a barn!"

Zoey nudged me forward, laughing, so I rushed down the steps toward the new owner. My heart was pounding with each step and I never took my eyes off him. When I neared, he knelt down to the girls and held their attention.

"I will give you a pool with water and you a barn full of animals if you let me talk to this lady for a minute," he promised, giving them each a kiss on the head.

"What do I get?" Ziggy asked, crossing her arms over her chest.

Drake chuckled. "What would you like, sweetheart?"

She pursed her lips together as she eyed the backyard and mulled it over. Her eyes landed on the big oak tree, and a smile broke out across her face. "I want a tree house in that tree."

"You got it," Drake said, giving her a high-five.

"Thanks, Uncle Quack!" she shouted, running off toward her sisters.

Drake glanced at me and shrugged. "Hey."

"You bought the Massey Estate!" I exclaimed, holding back laughter. I put my hands on my hips and shook my head at him. "When?"

He laughed, wrapping his arm around my shoulders as he led us over to the bed of Old Blue. He lowered the tailgate, and we sat down and watched the men hard at work. "I talked them into selling it when I came back from California. I hadn't applied to S&E yet, and I knew I'd need something to keep me busy. I planned on helping Barrett and his crew with the remodel."

"So, before you started working with me," I mused, glancing over at him.

"Yes," he stated, taking my hand in his. "Even then I still wanted it. It's part of our history. The first time I kissed you was against that oak tree, and the first time we had sex was right here in the back of this truck parked somewhere in this yard."

I laughed, nodding.

"This is our dream home, P.J.," he continued. "Do you remember when we'd come out here on a Saturday afternoon and talk about all the things we wanted to do to this place? The parties we'd host for our friends and families, and the nights and weekends we'd spend relaxing near our pool or having dinner on the massive deck I wanted to add that overlooked all our acres."

Tears sprung in my eyes again. "Of course I do."

"Well, now it's ours," he said, cupping my chin. He pressed a chaste kiss to my lips and smiled. "We can make it our own. Right now, they're just gutting the place, and I've had some landscapers come out to build the yard back up. Beyond that, nothing else has been planned yet." He eyed Barrett carrying all three of his girls and laughed—Ziggy was in one arm, Quinn in the other, and Ryce was piggybacking. "Except, I do owe Ryce a pool with water and Quinn some animals and a tree house for Zigs."

I laughed, leaning my head against his shoulder. "I think we can manage that."

"Yeah?" he asked incredulously, grasping my thigh.

"Yes," I said with certainty, threading my arm through his. "I've always dreamed of growing old with you here. I know we'll have to work in the city, but this place will be our home—our getaway, just like it was when we were young."

"Speaking of work," he grunted.

"They fired me," I said apathetically.

"I know," he sighed, linking his fingers with mine. "And I quit."

"They didn't fire you, too?" I asked, irritated. "That's a bunch of sexist bullshit."

"Agreed."

Crossing my legs, I smiled and watched as more rotten wood was carried out of our home. "You know what I was thinking about on my drive up here?"

"What's that?"

I glanced up at him and stated my idea, "Why don't we start our own PR firm? Skye's already agreed to be an assistant. I'm sure we could get Owen to quit S&E and join us. I know the only client we'd have right now is Maxton Waters, but I can easily get all my clients out of their S&E contracts."

The smile on his face widened as his brows furrowed. "Are you feeling okay?"

"I feel fine, why?"

He checked my forehead with his hand, dramatically feeling around for a temperature, and then he laughed. "We're trying for a baby. We're fixing up our dream home. Now, you want to add starting our own business to the list. Did you hit your head on something when you walked through the house?"

"No." I nudged him playfully and laughed. "I know it's a lot, and it's happening pretty quick, but—"

He shut me up with an urgent kiss and then said, with his lips hovering over mine, "I'm in, P.J. As long as it involves you, I'm always in."

"Really?" I asked incredulously. "You don't think we'll want to kill each other by running a company together?"

"Nah," he said, shaking his head. "We'll have separate offices where we can bitch to our assistants about one another."

I drew his lips down to mine and kissed him deeply. "I love you."

"I love you, too."

The noise of a shop vac broke us apart, and we turned our attention back to the construction. Barrett's girls followed him, wearing thick work gloves and duct masks that covered their faces as they helped him by carrying small pieces of debris out to the bin.

"What are we going to call our new firm?" I asked excitedly.

"What about Abram and Wilkins, Inc.?" he offered.

Shaking my head, I wrinkled my nose. "It's too much like Sabre & Edelmen. Plus, I don't plan on staying an Abram forever."

"Really? You don't want to keep your maiden name?" he asked jokingly. "You know, for someone who was scared of making plans, we've made a lot in a short period of time. How do you feel about that?"

"I feel free," I answered honestly. "Sure, I'm still scared, those fears are never going to go away, but I've stopped letting them control my life. I'm in control now, and it feels good to take on everything I've ever wanted, especially with you. And I'm positive I have a notebook somewhere in my parents' house that has 'Paige Wilkins' doodled all over the pages with the I's topped with hearts instead of dots."

"Good," he laughed, kissing me again. "What about Wilkins & Company? It's not just about us, but our clients, and the company we keep."

"Wilkins & Company," I stated, trying the name out. I relished in the smooth way it rolled off my tongue, and I loved the way he described it. "I think it's perfect."

"We have a lot of work to do," he said, pulling me closer.

"I know." I tossed my legs over his lap as I leaned into him and placed my hand over his heart. "But for now, let's spend the day talking about all the things we want to do to our house. Like old times."

Chapter Seventeen

One Month Later

Drake

It was a Saturday night, and all of us were over at Justin and Tessa's place. They'd found the home they wanted a while back, put in an offer, and closed on it earlier this week. To celebrate, they invited everyone over for one last hurrah in this apartment before they started packing it all up. I hadn't been around this group for long, but they'd made me feel like we'd been friends for years. I wasn't sure if it was because of Paige or because I was actually getting pretty decent at basketball and they needed me. Whatever the case, I was happy her friends had welcomed me into their group so willingly.

With Paige nestled into my side, cradling a sleeping Cooper Jennings in her arms, I took a swig of my beer and smiled at her. The women were crazy about the babies, always passing them around like they were footballs. It'd been a month since Paige and I started trying to have a baby, and nothing had happened yet except for a lot of great sex. We weren't worried though. We had a lot going on right now with the remodel of our new home, and we were still trying to get Wilkins & Company underway. We needed an office, because I was tired of working out of our apartments. So, we were content just being around our friends' babies instead of trying to raise our own. It would happen when it was supposed to happen; that was our philosophy.

"My turn," Harper said, taking Cooper from Paige.

Tessa handed Seghen over to Elly and offered to grab everyone another round of drinks.

"With the exception of Cash, because he's Cash, everyone is progressing," Fletcher said, wrapping his arms around Bayler's waist. "Aren't siblings supposed to have rivalries? Carter and Harper are one up on us in the child department. Don't you want to win?"

Bayler rolled her eyes. "If you love my vagina at all, you will settle for losing that competition."

He groaned and the rest of us laughed at his relentlessness. "Now, you don't want kids?"

"I want kids," she stated surely. "But in time, babe. Can't we keep being the cool aunt and uncle right now? I was hoping we'd have kids a few years later, when Harper and Carter's kids were old enough to watch them for free."

"This is why I love you," Fletcher said before kissing her.

Carter and Harper shared a look of annoyance.

"What about you and Justin, Tessa?" Elly asked excitedly. "Have you guys talked about making babies?"

Tessa sat down on Justin's lap and smiled at him as she played with the rock on her left hand. "There may have been some discussion of baby-making during our honeymoon."

"Ooh," Paige cheered. "Only a few months away. Have you decided where you're going after the wedding?"

Justin nodded. "We're visiting Mauritius. It's an island off the eastern coast of Madagascar."

"They have huts in the water like the ones in Bora Bora!" Tessa explained. "We've booked a honeymoon hut."

"Why not just go to Bora Bora?" Cash asked in confusion.

"Yeah," Fletcher said with a nod. "I've never even heard of Mauritius."

"Do you know where Bora Bora is?" Justin asked before taking a swig of his beer. "It's in the middle of nowhere, in between Hawaii and New Zealand. I refuse to fly over that much water."

"Yeah," Tessa said, nodding. "It is a lot of water."

"Shit." Cash tapped around on his phone and brought up a map. "I wouldn't go there either." He leaned over to show Fletcher.

"Fuck, if the plane crashes, you're shark bait."

"Exactly," Justin deadpanned.

Carter pointed his beer at Paige and me. "What about you two? Any wedding bells or babies on the way?"

"No," Paige said contently, patting my thigh. "We're busy enough with the house and the business."

We'd agreed to not tell anyone we were trying for a baby. We didn't want the pressure that came along with others knowing. They knew about our house in Bedford though. We'd invited them out with us last weekend to show them what we had planned. Most of them were surprised at how much ground forty acres offered, but then again, most of them were from the city where you couldn't see for miles in any direction.

"But you want to marry her, right?" Fletcher asked, downing his beer. "I can't be the only bastard who wants my girl to live with me and have my last name and give birth to our beautiful children."

The group laughed and I nodded as Bayler gulped down the rest of her drink like it was a shot.

Maverick handed Fletcher another beer. "You're not alone, Fletch, but every couple is different."

"Yeah," Harper said, smiling up at Maverick. "We've already agreed that we'll probably get married after we're done having kids."

"Are you pregnant?" Bayler asked bluntly, staring at her sister. "You cannot have another one yet. Fletcher will whisk me off to Vegas and some fake Elvis guy will tell us when to say 'I do,' meaning you'll never get to be my maid of honor."

"Just move in with him, you practically live there already!" Harper exclaimed. "And no, I am not pregnant! If one more person asks me that, I'm going to kick their ass."

***

Instead of taking a cab home after the party, I directed the driver to take us to an address Paige wouldn't recognize. Working out of our own homes was growing more difficult by the week, so I'd taken it upon myself to find an office for us to lease. The main issue we had with working from home was that we didn't have to leave. She could wake up, throw on one of my shirts, and parade around the apartment as she talked on the phone wearing nothing but a pair of panties and my button-up. She didn't realize how hot she was, half-naked and making demands. She made it impossible for me to get any shit done when I was sporting a hard-on.

God, thinking about her like that is making me hot, I thought, undoing the top button of my shirt.

This was why we had to find an office, so she had to leave the apartment wearing clothes that covered every inch of her.

Glancing over at me, she smiled. "Where are we going?"

"It's a surprise," I said, leaning in to kiss her neck.

"A surprise?" she mused, her eyes dancing with excitement. "What kind of surprise?"

"There are different kinds of surprises?" I asked, entertaining the notion. "Do tell."

"Well, there are the surprises that I like," she started, giggling as I brushed my stubble against her cheek. "And then there are the surprises that are more shocking than uplifting that I freak out over. Which one is this going to be?"

I laughed. "Well, I hope it's one you like."

The cab pulled over to the curb, and I tipped the driver extra to wait for us. I helped Paige out of the backseat and led her up the steps. My palms started to sweat the closer we got to the door. I wanted her to like it. There were lots of offices in the city that were crap, but I didn't want to remodel an office on top of remodeling a home. The building in front of us was the best I could find in our budget that required no work.

I pushed open the door and held it for her, and then I led us over to a bank of elevators and tapped the up button. Even though it was a Saturday night, the building still had a few weekend workers hanging around trying to get more accomplished. Once we were in the elevator, I pressed the third floor button and reached for her hand.

"You seem nervous," she said, peering up at me. "Why are you nervous?"

We arrived at our designated floor before I had a chance to answer, so I pulled her out of the elevator and into the empty reception area of the office.

"What do you think?" I asked, smiling as I stretched my arms out from my side. "The whole third floor could be Wilkins & Company if we want to lease it."

"Are you serious?" she stated excitedly, turning around in a circle.

The office, enveloped by windows, was set up around a square hallway. It held a large conference room, and several decent-sized offices lined the hall. Two big offices sat on the north corners while the conference room was on the south side. Even though it was only on the third floor, it still offered a great view of the city. Anything was better than ground level.

"How did you find this place?" she asked in amazement. "It's beautiful. I love the floor-to-ceiling windows and all the glass in the interior."

"Keith Evans helped me," I said with a shrug. "That guy knows a lot of people."

"Yeah, he does," she laughed, smiling back at me. "What do you think? Do you like it?"

I sauntered over to her and ran my fingers through her short blond hair before cupping her face in my palms. "I think we need somewhere to work. I can't take working with you from home anymore. It's like a constant hard-on."

"I know what you mean," she giggled softly, pressing her lips to mine. "We can't have a bed or a couch or a kitchen table in the vicinity of work."

I laughed. "I need you to actually put on clothes to go to work."

"Me?" she exclaimed incredulously. "Have you seen what you wear to work at home? No shirt and just your boxer briefs. That's less than what I wear."

"You don't wear a bra!" I challenged.

"Do you know how restrictive bras are?" she argued.

"Then you should be glad I wear my underwear because briefs are just as restrictive as bras."

Silently, we stood staring at one another, waiting for the next jab to be thrown, but then her lips slowly curled up into a sexy smirk and we started laughing until we couldn't breathe.

"I think it's safe to say we need an office," she laughed, settling her hands on my waist.

"Yeah, we do," I said, nodding. "So, what do you think?"

"I love it," she stated honestly, gazing at our surroundings. "I think it's perfect."

"Me too." I covered her lips with mine and sank into her. Her tongue twisted around mine, and I sucked, long and hard, reveling in her touch. She tasted so sweet from the wine she'd had earlier, I felt like I could get drunk on her. Kissing Paige would never grow old. The familiar give and take of our kisses was something I'd treasured since I was a teen, when I wasn't even sure if I was kissing her right. Now that I had her back in my arms, my world was once again filled with sunshine even on the cloudiest of days. It may have taken us years. We may have experienced a loss so great others found it unimaginable, but we lived through it. Some days were harder than others, but not a day went by without us talking about Declan. Our boy would be forever in our hearts and minds. We had a lot to be thankful for already, but I hoped life gave us so much more.

Smiling, I broke away and then proudly stated against her pink, swollen lips, "Welcome to Wilkins & Company."

Acknowledgements

This book was an actual challenge for me to write, fitting given its title. If you ugly cried while reading it, just know I did too while writing it. I'd like to extend a huge thanks to Beth Suit and April Faulkner for bringing out the best in my writing. You're an editing duo I truly love working with, though the editing/copyediting process never really feels like work with you girls. Brenda Wright, thank you for always taking the time to perfect my book's formatting. Your willingness to ensure my readers' happiness and my own is a blessing. Michelle Preast, I had to have this photo as the cover and you made it work! I cannot thank you enough for creating such a beautiful brand for the Love in the City series. To my Nuss Navy crew, I love our group so much! Thank you for your endless support and encouragement. I love having a place to go and talk about my love of books with others who love them just as much as I do. Southern Belle Promotions, thank you for organizing my release day blitz and blog tour. You girls make releasing a book less stressful! To all the book bloggers, thank you for your continuous support of the writing community. So many of us wouldn't be able to do what we love without you sharing, liking, reposting, tagging, commenting, reviewing, creating teasers and blog posts, so much more! To you, the reader, thank you for taking a chance on Paige's story. I know I made fans wait longer than expected for her story, and I thank you for your patience. I love writing the Love in the City gang more and more with each book. I hope you're enjoying their stories as much as I am and ask that you please consider leaving a review on your sales platform of choice. Thank you.

About the Author

Steph Nuss was born and raised in rural Kansas, where she currently resides with her black Labrador son named Gunner. She grew up with a passion for reading and writing. When she's not immersed into the land of fiction, she enjoys listening to music that came before her time, watching movies and reruns of her favorite shows, and hanging out with her family and friends. She also has a bachelor's degree in psychology that she'll never use…unless she's profiling her characters of course.

For more information about the Love in the City series and Steph's upcoming books, please subscribe to www.stephnuss.com.

Made in the USA
Middletown, DE
03 April 2017